The Great Matter Monologues

Katherine, Henry, Anne

The Great Matter Monologues

Katherine, Henry, Anne

Thomas Crockett

TOP HAT
BOOKS

Winchester, UK
Washington, USA

JOHN HUNT PUBLISHING

First published by Top Hat Books, 2019
Top Hat Books is an imprint of John Hunt Publishing Ltd., No. 3 East St., Alresford,
Hampshire SO24 9EE, UK
office@jhpbooks.com
www.johnhuntpublishing.com
www.tophat-books.com

For distributor details and how to order please visit the 'Ordering' section on our website.

Text copyright: Thomas Crockett 2018

ISBN: 978 1 78904 249 8
978 1 78904 250 4 (ebook)
Library of Congress Control Number: 2018961981

A CIP catalogue record for this book is available from the British Library.

Design: Stuart Davies

Printed and bound by CPI Group (UK) Ltd, Croydon, CR0 4YY

We operate a distinctive and ethical publishing philosophy in
all areas of our business, from our global network of authors to
production and worldwide distribution.

Contents

Preface   1

The Great Matter Monologues   3

Acknowledgements   330

About the Author   331

Author's Note   332

Also by Thomas Crockett

Thorns in a Realm of Roses
ISBN 9781789040340

The Florentine Trinity
ISBN 9780692815014

The Hitchhiking Journals
ISBN 9780692744949

Hope Beyond All Hope: New York Stories
ISBN 9780692506257

Teaching Drama: Fundamentals and Beyond
ISBN 9780692254035

Courage is not simply
one of the virtues but the form of
every virtue at the testing point.
C.S. Lewis

Preface

The idea of this book and its resulting style have their source in theater, particularly in the work of the late Irish playwright Brian Friel, whose plays *Faith Healer* and *Molly Sweeney* are divided by the monologues of three characters, all of whom experience the same story from their unique angles, lending a natural complexity and irony to the overall story, giving it many layers of interpretation and understanding. As a drama teacher, I employed the guidelines of Friel's plays in exercises and assignments with students, witnessing the potency of storytelling in the absence of a fourth wall to divide the actor and his audience, resulting in a communication that is more direct and unfiltered, and in most cases more emotive.

Several years ago, I joined this theatrical style with prose in writing *The Florentine Trinity*, told as three intertwining autobiographies from the points of view of Lorenzo de Medici, Girolamo Savonarola and Niccolo Machiavelli. I wanted the writing of *The Great Matter Monologues* to be similar, desiring that each of the characters—Katherine, Henry and Anne—speak as if they were standing in front of an audience, though I didn't want to write a play. I wanted to write a novel, aware that though this subject has been much written about and shown in films there was still much insight that could be gained by adding flesh to the historical characters' mythic bones, by having them reveal themselves personally to their readers, placing the emphasis not on what happens but on how the "what" affects each of them in their relationships to each other and in their pursuits of power, control and survival.

Though I experimented with style, I did not change history. The story of this complex, triangular affair remains remarkable. I merely offer a fresh perspective, making the history appear as if it is happening now and for the first time.

T. Crockett

1

1

Katherine

I stand near the open window and look out on the Greenwich landscape, where nary a bird flies in the cloudless sky, and leaves hang motionless on the trees. The breeze is still, as the earth itself for all I know. I recall my earliest memory, four years old, feeling the soft grip of my mother's hand, as we stood on a veranda, facing the country of my birth; the warmth of the Spanish sun, under which dogs ran in the fields and hawks soared in the sky and the branches of trees shook with life, waking the sleeping bees and the scent of honey. Caterina, my mother said, you shall be Queen of England. I asked, what is a queen? A queen, she said, is the most beautiful woman in her realm. I asked, are you a queen, mother, for you are the most beautiful woman I know? Yes, she said, I am Queen of Castile, Aragon, and all of Spain. I replied, if you are queen, then I desire to be queen, to be as beautiful as you. It is already done, she reassured me. You will wed the future King of England, eldest son of Henry Tudor. I knew nothing of England, though I did, in time, learn to spell and say my future husband's name, Arthur, in his native language. I learned, as well, he was a boy, younger than me by nine months. Sometime later, several years, in fact, his mother, Elizabeth of York, wrote me a letter, saying I needed to speak French and learn to drink wine, for the English did not drink water.

I hold to this memory, for I have always been Queen of England, either in betrothal or marriage, and as such I will die. What happened earlier, though it fills me with shame, only strengthens my resolve. When Henry entered my room, I wanted to believe he had come to renew our love. I reached for him, my body and soul eager. He brushed past me, turning his eyes from mine, saying he wished to separate from me, calling the titles I held as wife and queen illegitimate, that our union as husband and wife needed to be nullified, that he desired to marry again to have another chance at fathering male heirs. He rushed out of the room, leaving a void, as if air had escaped from my lungs. I fell to the floor and prayed.

Please, God, show my husband his way back to me. Do not allow him to nullify our marriage and in disgrace, against Your laws and the laws of man, marry his mistress, my former lady-in-wait. Show him his way back to You, for he is a man of deep faith, evident in his requesting we attend mass several times a day; evident in his writing *Defence of the Seven Sacraments* against Martin Luther, stating, We will set forth the pope's authority to the uttermost; wherein, the pope called him the Defender of the Faith.

He still possesses that faith, God. Just as he still loves me. I hold the proof in my hand, reading the words he wrote during our betrothal, hoping the landscape before my eyes will hear my voice and awake the heartbeat of my former life.

I desire you, Katherine, above all women. I love only you and long to wed you.

I hold to his words. I hold to his faith. I hold to the marriage vows we exchanged before God. I hold to the day England anointed me its queen, when bells rang at St. Paul's and Westminster Abbey and the banners of Spain and England conjoined and the people on the streets called my name, Queen Katherine, daughter of Isabella and Ferdinand, King and Queen of Aragon, Castile and Spain. Bless you. Bless us. Bless God and our newly appointed King Henry, son of Elizabeth and Henry Tudor, younger brother of Arthur, my first husband, who died at fifteen years of age. I hold to having lived for eighteen years in the realm of heaven, in the movement of dreams, rich and regal. I hold to these truths, for I have nothing else to hold to, alone as I am, fearful of what lies ahead.

2

Henry

I tried to talk sensibly, Kate, though you persisted in senselessness instead of sense to everything I said. You can't dispute the Book of Leviticus, its words come from God.

If a man shall take his brother's wife, it is an unclean thing; he hath uncovered his brother's nakedness; they shall be childless.

Don't tell me it has no relevance to us because your marriage to my brother was never consummated. It's not to be believed, Kate, being as it is beyond the bounds of natural laws between a man and woman, who lay together. You wish to say it was only six months. How should I respond other than laugh, knowing well what a man can do in six months' time, though he be occasionally sick? Arthur was a hot-blooded Tudor male, like me. Don't make me conjure up images I don't wish to see, the two of you in bed together. We already committed incest for eighteen years. I'm done with that. It's time to move on, for both our sakes, spiritually speaking, because we're not going to live forever, Kate, and when the time comes to stand before God, He's going to condemn you for having been negligent, for having been steadfast in your sin, for not having put a stop to it sooner, for not having acted responsibly as the elder one in the marriage, six years my senior. I'm not saying I'm going to receive a pass, but at least I can say to Him I tried to end it.

It wasn't my idea to get a special dispensation from the pope, allowing us to marry when canon law strictly forbade a man to marry his brother's widow. What did I know? I was ten years old. My brother had just died. I was named heir, at which time my life became a prison, kept in a room that had no entrance or exit except through my father's chamber, for six years, until, on his deathbed, he made me promise him I would marry you to produce heirs and secure the dynasty. Even at seventeen, I couldn't have known I was committing incest and damning my soul, bringing a curse upon myself that would last until now.

The pope had no right to do what he did. I'm just trying to correct the wrongs of the past before it's too late. If you fight me on this, you will lose, for I have on my side the only truth that matters: You and your pomegranate device with its symbol of fertility have failed me. Where are the sons you promised me? Dead, that's where. The first, my namesake, having lived only nine weeks, the second dead in your womb. What have you given me, other than a healthy girl? A king needs sons. You know that, and if you can't give them to me, and given your age you will never do so, I must get them from another. Don't be selfish, Kate. If you really love me, as you plead you do, you will do what's right by me and the realm, for the future of the Tudor reign, and submit to my will and desire, allowing our marriage to be nullified.

I don't wish to hurt you, Kate. Quite the contrary. I wish to see you live well, with your daughter. Yes, my daughter, too, continuing to receive every comfort for which you are accustomed, wherein I shall call you ever more my sister.

3

Anne

Here in England, men and women whisper a popular refrain: It is God's will, with Henry's influence. What better way to explain my circumstance, being courted by the king when it was not what I desired? When I returned from France, I ate the forbidden fruit of love, despite the many warnings from my father. Beware this wayward force which recklessly disorders the wits and drives the lover to madness, sabotaging arrangements for matrimony. Ward off this disease by religious devotion. Love of God, not love of flesh. He wished me to move to Ireland, to marry James Butler, who stood to become Earl of Ormond, saying marriage was not an institution of the heart but of the properties. Land married land and fortune married fortune. I understood and still do; yet what he failed to say was how the heart works independent of the brain. Blame it on the French influence and culture, of which he immersed me for eight years. The women there act audaciously, not shrinking in the face of danger. To not pursue love, when it is in their best interest to do so, is a sin against self. A woman is nothing if not coy, if she does not learn erotic flirtation. I learned well. I practiced, for it is what the French do, unlike here in England where the women do nothing and know nothing about the art of attraction. I learned to use my eyes, to make them shine and glean or pierce and penetrate. Little magnetic glances I call them, tilting my head in a hundred thousand ways, half-smiling, lips opened and closed, hinting, teasing, varying my voice and laugh. I learned how to make my neck beautiful with creams and oils, my hands inviting with jewels and rings, applying lotions and perfumes to my skin and face, to heighten and disguise, to make my locks long and lavish under a French hood, which shows, not hides, the hair. I practiced gestures of the hand, a wave, an inch up or down, fluttering, inviting, grasping light and loose, and moving my feet as if they touched not ground nor made a sound. Call me the glass of fashion, the rival of Venus. Others, beggars at the altar of promise, have.

One such man was Henry Percy. I shall spare the details. He prayed for my love, and I answered, falling irresistibly into his arms. We loved eagerly, openly and vowed to marry. Until it became God's will, with Henry's influence, that Cardinal Wolsey interfered, tearing my young lover down. You must give this girl up. She is beneath you in birth. You stand to become the Earl of Northumberland. You are, in fact, betrothed to Lady Mary Talbot, the daughter of the Earl of Shrewsbury. This affair must end at once. Already you have forfeited the high estimation that others have held of you, and your reputation. What's that, you say? It's too late. You exchanged vows and agreed to marry? I should know, you say, that it is binding in the eyes of the church. You are wrong, young man. Nothing is binding if it is not in the best interests of the king, as this affair is clearly not. You shall move north, marry Lady Mary Talbot, and respect your father and your king, both of whom you have offended, and you shall never again see that Boleyn woman. She is a witless, defiant, foolish girl, lightheaded and loose in morals.

That disappointment and shame will never go away, nor will my hard feelings for the cardinal. Was I surprised by the turn of events? No, I expected them, for the king had already come at me wet with sweat, with hunger and greed, with pulsing energy and dripping blue eyes.

Good thing my sister had been his mistress. Through her, I knew I didn't want to be a man's whore, though that man wore a crown, to be used and discarded, yesterday's flower, bygone, forgotten, no more.

4

Katherine

It's not to be believed, Kate, he said to me, *being as it is beyond the bounds of natural laws between a man and woman.* I should like to respond: Who should decide what is natural or not? Surely not one who wasn't present. God knows the truth, as does Arthur, yet neither can speak on my behalf. I must speak alone, though I wish not to bring further shame, speaking what should be kept private. What should I say? Should I tell about the bishops and prelates who recited Latin, sprinkling holy water on the marriage bed, while the crowd looked on, whispering their good wishes, curious to see the young heirs to the throne, descendants of kings and queens, consummate and fulfill their duty to their families, their countries and their realms by delivering to all a healthy boy and in doing so solidify the succession and prevent disputes over rightful heirs and tie a permanent knot between Spain and England? You shall bear fruit, my mother had told me early and often; plentiful fruit, as the fruit that grew in abundance under the Spanish sun, in the multitudes of orchards and gardens of Granada and the Alhambra: oranges, lemons, apples, pears, figs, cherries and pomegranate. Especially pomegranate, the symbol of fertility, which I took as my personal device. You shall be as a tree, bearing fruit seasonally, fruit large and ripe, healthy in form, shape and texture. I waited all my life to be that tree, the bearer of fruit. All I had to do was take the future King of England's seed. My womb would do the rest. My mother knew. Five times she had borne the fruit of which she spoke.

She prepared me for my wedding night. Lay back, relax, in a state of surrender, and hold your pomegranate device in your right hand. Wait for his advance. If necessary, close your eyes. In the morning, I should notice spots of blood on the sheets. It would mean I had fulfilled my duty. I did as she said, except I kept my eyes open. We lay under a canopy of gold cloth, covered on all sides in satins and silks. What the onlookers did not know, what my mother did not know, what only I could ever know, was the sight and essence of the boy next to me, my husband, barely fifteen years old, nine months younger than me; the invisible crown on his head bearing down on him; the burning candles blinding his eyes, the incense filling his nose, the Latin incantations and the prayers to the Virgin Mary and the duty to his father and his country sounding in his ears, the threat of wars and the weighty affairs of state occupying his mind. I alone saw him; his clenched jaw, his eyes white with fear, rolling backwards, the sweat on his brow. I alone heard his breath, quick and heavy. I alone felt his long, shivering limbs, shaking beneath the sheets. I alone knew the truth. He, exhausted and overwrought, wished not to advance. What should I do? I thought. My mother hadn't presented me an alternative scenario, wherein instead of advancing he shivered and shook, gasping for breath, sliding further from me, saying nary a word.

I did not shiver or shake as him. I shared his silence, for I did not speak his language, nor he mine. I waited, for it was my job to wait; my job to produce, and, while shutting my eyes, I prayed to the Virgin Mary that he would soon advance, for I wanted nothing more than a chance to become the tree I had always dreamed of becoming, to be able to write my mother and tell her that fruit had begun to grow on it. I remembered his final letter to me, written in Latin, our shared language, before I departed from Spain. I recited the words, for they filled me with hope.

Let your coming to me be hastened, that instead of being absent we may be present with each other, and the love conceived between us and the wished-for joys may reap their proper fruit.

An hour passed, wherein I wondered: Do I not attract him? Am I not scented? Does he repulse me? Finally, I opened my eyes and saw that his were closed. His lips had parted; his breathing had slowed, becoming quiet and still; his shivering and shaking had stopped. He appeared at peace, in sleep, where he didn't have to be heir to the throne. He could be a boy, weak-kneed, awkward, happy in retreat.

I did not sleep. I lay awake, believing God was punishing me, for He knew my marriage had been made in blood. My father would not send me to England as long as Henry Tudor's position as dynastic ruler remained in doubt. The Earl of Warwick, nephew of Edward IV and Richard III, possessed ancestral rights to the throne, which Henry usurped, and Perkin Warbeck claimed to be one of the missing princes in the Tower. To appease my father, Henry Tudor beheaded both men to show Spain that no challengers to Arthur's title existed. That same year, in the fall of 1501, at the age of fifteen, I left Spain, never to see my mother and father and the country of my birth again, to become the future Queen of England, to bear sons to Arthur, to be called the Savior of the English world.

But in the morning after my wedding night, I faced uncertainty, for there was no blood on the sheets. The only blood was that on my conscience, and as I now know, many years later, that is a blood much harder to remove.

5

Henry

Shouldn't I, a king, know better than to embroil myself in a great folly? Not the folly of my discourse with Kate. The folly of love, of which I did not ask to be struck by its penetrating dart. Blame Cupid, the insidious god. It was he who placed this slender, graceful woman in my court, sweeping in and out of my presence; her abundant black hair and even blacker, captivating eyes, the silky cream of her skin, the music of her French; offering me an elixir of hope, wherein I am drunk with desire, believing myself reborn, looking past my sad view of the world, where no man can be trusted, least of all Kate's nephew Charles, the emperor, once my friend, now my foe, forcing me into the arms of King Francis, whom I hate cordially. All the more reason to view this love as a benediction.

If only she felt the same. Despite my efforts, imploring her to be my mistress, she holds me at bay, perhaps believing I will discontinue my pursuit. She will learn I am a tireless hunter. Ask the fleeing deer on its delicate hinds, seeking invisible hedgerows. She can answer that my arrow is long and straight, always hitting its mark. Anne, though, is more practiced than any in the chase, often leaving me panting breathlessly behind, inducing in me a proper question: Is this love or witchery, wherein I am given to madness, bereft of my faculty of reason, immersed in fits of blabbering, loose-tongued, giddy-eyed, exhorting all kinds of unnatural behaviors, crying and laughing in the same moment, that seem not human?

I am not alone in my feeling. Others have suffered for her charms. Henry Percy first. He and Anne, by all reports, had made quite a scene at court. Silly boy. Did he really think I would allow him to take her from me? Wolsey took care of the issue, bringing the boy's father, the Earl of Northumberland, to court to threaten his son with a loss of inheritance if he married someone beneath him. Turns out the young man was conveniently betrothed to a Lady Talbot. Last I heard they were married, living in the north, and not very happy, though he should be glad his property and title are intact. My friend Thomas Wyatt followed in Percy's path, weaving a poetic net around Anne, famously saying to me, in reference to his pursuit of Anne: Fainting I follow. Now, thanks to that information, he's in Italy on a diplomatic mission with no intended purpose other than his brushing up on the Italian language. Suffice it to say, I need no rivals for her affection. She's hard enough to snare.

6

Anne

I can play cards as well as anyone, having learned in France never to show my hand. I haven't yet, after two years and am prepared to wait longer, though I often ask myself: What is it I wait for? I have told him I must have everything before he receives anything. Thus, he has promised me everything. How, then, should it happen? I have said. You have a wife. The pope will never allow you to leave her to marry another, and she is a proud woman, aunt to the emperor, who, upon her persuasion, will force your surrender. Wait and see, he says. It shall be done, and you shall be mine. Would you like that? To sit on the throne, bejeweled, loved as a treasure come from the bottom of the sea, referred to by the people of England as the mother of the heir? What woman wouldn't want that? I do not answer him. I keep that card hidden. My father and uncle wish to educate me on how best to proceed, but I do not need them to tell me how to be coy, to lead the king about like a sniffing dog, foaming, yelping, walking on his hind legs, doing tricks. It is a woman's deceit I possess. They wouldn't understand.

So, I wait for him to move the unmovable, to attain the unattainable, to shake the ground under which he walks, to rid himself of a woman who, if truth be told, has made of the throne a grave, in possession of dead babies and promises unfulfilled. I can do better, if I so desire, and that is the daunting dilemma, causing me to respond with trepidation, for I do not love the king, surely not as I loved Henry Percy. He senses that. He beseeches me with poetry and letters, with compositions, with gifts and money, with dreams he has painted clearly for me. Can you see yourself superbly gowned and regal, attended by maidens and pages who carry your train, walking in the royal chapel, scented with incense and lit with bright torches, the walls covered with colorful hangings and the floor ankle-deep in sweet-smelling herbs and rushes, while nobles admire respectfully the next Queen of England?

Imagine that. I, Anna de Boullans, as the French called me, dark as a gypsy, not in possession of my sister's golden beauty, nor fair-skinned and fresh as the auburn-haired women of nobility, seated beside the boyishly handsome king, his red-blond hair, his beard, his massive height, as the most powerful woman in the land. At times, I allow this dream to supplant my better sense and ask: Why shouldn't it happen? Though I am not descended from kings and queens, I am no backwater provincial servant woman. My father is the king's leading diplomat. My mother is a Howard. I received the finest education in France. I am adept at music and dance and have brought new fashion to England. I speak fluent French and have friends across the channel and in the scholarly halls of Cambridge.

Hold on to that card, I tell myself. A time may come when I will use it.

7

Katherine

Please, God, only You can abate his madness, which clouds his judgment. Let him keep Anne Boleyn as his mistress, let him be satisfied with that, as he was with her sister, Mary. That I can bear. I refuse to become my sister Juana, mad with jealousy over her husband's affairs, roaring with rage like an African lioness on a veranda in Alhambra. I have always prided myself in being self-composed, whatever the trial or tribulations You have sent me, and there have been many. You know the humiliations I have suffered, such as seeing Elizabeth Blount bear a son for him, a torment much worse than Henry having a mistress. To hear him call this illegitimate boy by the name Henry; to see, in fanfare and ceremony, him receive titles upon reaching his sixth birthday: Knight of the Garter, Earl of Nottingham, Duke of Richmond, Duke of Somerset and Lord Admiral of England; to become one of the highest ranking, wealthiest people in the land, supplanting our daughter Mary, the legitimate heir to the throne.

Worse, I am reminded each time I see his face and hear his voice of the son I bore the king on New Year's Day, 1511, producing a joy I had never experienced up till then or since, remembering well the celebrations that followed: canons roaring from the Tower, bonfires blazing, wine flowing in the streets, and each day jousting tournaments, banquets and masques, and singing and dancing from morning to night, and always my husband standing center court, shouting to the world: I have a son. His name is Henry, and he shall be heir to the throne. The Tudor reign is now secure. Henry set off on a pilgrimage of thanksgiving to the Shrine of Our Lady at Walsingham. I went to church, where I knelt and prayed, thanking You for seeing me safely through childbirth, knowing my sister Isabel and Henry's mother Elizabeth died in the act. I thanked You for the gift of life, for planting my tree firmly in the earth, from which I could produce more fruit with each passing year. I had never smiled so much, never felt such joy.

You allowed that joy for nine weeks. Then You took him. Why, God? To make amends for Your own son, who died in sacrifice for our sins? I did not question Your will, nor would I ever. If it was Your will to take our son and give the king a son with another woman, I have borne that as best I could. I have endured your trials, God, you know I have, but this trial, this separation from my husband, his wanting to leave me for another woman, to make her queen, to supplant my daughter with other children he wishes to have, making her a bastard, this I cannot bear. Take pity on my suffering heart. I ask only this.

8

Henry

How quickly the tide rushes in and washes away the castles of sand upon which we make our dreams, I wish to say to you, Kate. Your nephew has betrayed me. First, by backing out of the marriage with our daughter. That I might excuse, given his age and hers. But reneging on his promise to help me achieve my Great Enterprise, winning back our ancestral right in France is a betrayal I cannot forgive. We shall henceforth make a treaty with France instead.

Yes, the dream is over, both mine and yours. What we had hoped to achieve in our union has not, nor will it ever be, achieved. Spain is lost to us; there is no heir as we thought to join our countries. We look to France now. Mary shall have to wed the son of Francis or Francis himself. I know how that must repulse you. It matters not. We make decisions based on what's best for the realm, not to appease our feelings. The same is true for us. You want to speak of love for eighteen years, but it has never been about love, only promise and property, power and position, and after eighteen years the promise has been unfulfilled, the property has not been possessed, our power is less than it should be, and our position is fragile without an heir.

Thus, do not speak to me of love. I am a king. I shouldn't have to remind you. My father didn't marry my mother for love. She had more legal right to the throne, being the daughter of a Yorkist king, though he secretly despised her for that, even as she bore him eight children, four of whom survived, most importantly two boys. I use that as an example, for a royal marriage is always about providing sons and securing a dynasty. You failed to do that. So, we must build new castles in the sand, hoping this time they are secure enough to withstand the next tide.

9

Anne

I have tried to tell you: Your wife, Katherine, spies for the emperor. Do you not see it? You may not be aligned with Spain, but she is, and always will be. Could you not then have her tried for treason? Wouldn't that be an easier way to get rid of her than trying to procure a divorce? You need Pope Clement for that, and he will never grant it. You know he won't, for he owes his election to Katherine's nephew. You are sometimes naïve, dearest Henry. Open your eyes, see what is before you. Listen with your ears, hear what is being said. All those servants she keeps, including her doctors and chaplains, they speak Spanish, for they are Spanish. Do you not worry what they say under their breaths in a language foreign to you? I can assure you they are not speaking of satins and silks for their newest gowns; nor are they reciting scripture or planning charity for the poor. They are plotting, using Ambassador Mendoza as their purveyor, sending messages to the emperor, your enemy, informing him about your plans to dispatch her, hoping he will respond with action against you. The situation is much more dangerous than you know. It is the reason I am here at Hever instead of at court with you, and I shall stay as long as necessary until the issue is resolved. Do what's right. Have Cardinal Wolsey do what he does best. Spy on her. Watch her. Listen to her conversations. I know what I say. My father informs me, as does Uncle Norfolk and your favorite duke, Suffolk. Everyone knows, yet you seem to turn a blind eye and a deaf ear. If you say you love me as you profess, if you say you cannot live without me, if you say, as you do in your many letters, that I am the only one you desire and wish to move mountains on my behalf, then you will heed what I say. Spend less time writing and more time paying attention to the actions of your wife. She is proud and willful. She is Spanish.

Need I say more. I know you, rather I respond to your letters with equal emotion and outpouring of love sentiment, but we live in a world of intrigue and mistrust. It is everywhere, especially in your own household. Take my words for what they are, for they are written with the uttermost concern for your health and welfare, as well as for the security of our future union.

10

Katherine

Forty days now the rain has fallen, flooding the fields, ruining the crops, washing away bridges, making mud of the roads, leaving the poor starving. I recall Ludlow Castle, where I accompanied my husband Arthur after our wedding, he bearing the title Prince of Wales. We encountered nothing but cold and rain in that bleak, isolated place, far from the sun and warmth and lemon-scented blossoms of Alhambra, where peaches fell from the trees in mouth-watering abundance. Arthur became sick from the start, with fevers and coughs. I suspected the worst, the sweating sickness. He recovered enough to visit my bed numerous times, though he never touched me. He shivered and shook, clearing his throat, until in a mad sweat he slipped mercifully into sleep. I, not wanting to offend him, remained still on each occurrence, though inside my blood ran rapid. I cried my first tears in England in that damp room. My only solace was knowing that in the morning I could visit the nearby chapel dedicated to Saint Mary Magdalene.

The day Arthur died the rains fell so heavily that the cart carrying his body became immobilized in mud. The rain fell in loud bursts, amid a wind that swirled and whistled, cracking the branches of trees. The men shouted commands. They pushed against the cart in vain, finally carrying the box, his body, on their shoulders, slipping and falling with it in the mud all the way to Worcester, the burial site. Amid the chaos, Arthur alone knew peace, inside the box, where his shivering and shaking came to a stop, his body at rest ready for God, who cares not whether one is a prince or a commoner, whether he wears silks and satins or jewels on his fingers, or whether he succeeds in consummating his marriage.

From the earliest age, I learned I would have two husbands:

Christ and Arthur. When I returned to London, I had only Christ. I hadn't yet been informed that I would marry Arthur's ten-year-old brother. Truth is, I wanted to go home to my mother and father, to Alhambra, to the sun and warmth, to the fruit and vegetables, to the dogs and donkeys, to the shining, golden hills, to the chirping birds and the music of the Spanish tongue. Never was my longing greater than when I received the wrath of Arthur's father, who, in his unabashed grieving, blamed me for his son's death, saying that my lasciviousness had sapped Arthur's strength, that my wickedness and evil had allowed him to die.

I was to blame and always have been, starting with the execution of two men I had never seen or met, long before I arrived in England; for Arthur's death; for my father's refusal to give Henry Tudor the dowry he owed; for the death of my son Henry at nine weeks old; for having borne a healthy girl instead of a healthy boy; for my nephew's betrayal of my husband; for being a proud Spaniard who chooses to disobey her husband, not wishing to concede her title and her marriage to another woman.

The rains shall never end. The island of England will wash away, and there shall be no Noah or his ark to save anyone. It is God's will, his wrath, upon the head of this realm, my husband, Henry, until he atones for his sin and returns to me, his lawful wife, his queen, whom he promised eighteen years ago to live with till death do us part.

11

Henry

I await word from Cardinal Wolsey. He meets with churchmen and experts in canon law at his Westminster palace to discuss the validity of my marriage to the queen. What is there to discuss? I said to him earlier. Get me out of it. That is all. I want to hear nothing of discussion. Can you do that? Yes, of course, he answered. I don't like the way he said it, though. I don't like that I had to ask him the question in the first place. I just want him to tell me it's done. Come to me with that news, I demanded. That is all. Yes, he said. It shall be a private legatine court. You shall be summoned. Evidence will be brought against you and sentence passed. What type of sentence? I asked. Am I to be sent to the Tower? To Newgate? Am I to be put on the rack and made to confess to crimes I did not commit? He smiled that devious clerical smile of his, a smile that could hoodwink a hundred thousand angels into walking through the doors of hell, believing they led to heaven. To think, I trusted that smile with my life. Nothing of the sort, Your Majesty, he said. If it is shown that you have transgressed divine law by living with your brother's widow and sharing her bed, you will be made to answer the charge and renounce your sin. Renounce? How so? Again, that smile of his. Remove the cause and thus the effect, he said. Speak clearly, cardinal, I yelled. You wish to remove your wife, do you not? He asked. I wish to relieve my conscience. Wipe that smile from your face, cardinal, unless you want me to wipe it away for you. He bowed. Yes, of course. And stop saying, yes, of course. It sounds disingenuous. For a reason, Your Majesty, he said. Yes, of course, I said, deliberately, to make my point. He straightened his lips. You will be placed in a defensive, rather than offensive, position, as a defendant on trial. You must do what the court says. I am a victim, then? I asked. Yes ... He stopped himself.

We shared a smile. You are the accused instead of the accuser. You will be found guilty of living in sin and ordered to leave the woman you had erroneously believed to be your wife. And that is all? I will be free? Again, that phony smile of his. Yes, that is all, you will be free, once we receive papal confirmation of the findings at the trial. Good, I said, but keep it secret. I don't want it made public. Her supporters will shout her cause from every rooftop in London. We can't have that. Yes, of course, he added. I sighed and told him to leave my sight, to get to his business and not tarry a moment longer. So, here I am, waiting, tapping my fingers, realizing time has never been and will never be my ally.

.

12

Anne

Papal confirmation of the findings at the trial? How ridiculous that sounds now after the recent events, of which you, by now, have heard. I have just today received my father's letter informing me that Rome has been sacked by Charles' mercenary soldiers. My initial reaction to the news: It is God's will to put an end to clerical corruption, to see the destruction of so many holy objects. Though to learn of the pope's imprisonment brings much consternation to me, as I'm sure it does to you, for it means he will not be passing judgment on your case anytime soon.

Meanwhile, I grow impatient. You say time is not your ally. What of me? What of my womb? Do you not know what I have sacrificed these past two years? I could be married well, already a mother. I have waited, and now my patience wanes. Have you considered that the cardinal, your supposed friend, does not wish to see your divorce if it results in your marriage to me? Don't be naïve when I say this. You know he dislikes me. You know he despises my father for his growing closeness to you. You know what I say is true. He prefers to see you married to a foreign princess, to make a French alliance. That was made clear before your marriage interest in me. He wishes to have his feet in a thousand shoes, wanting to be the beginning, middle and end, to dominate affairs, to be the only voice you hear and the only ear that hears yours.

For that, he should not be trusted. What, after all, has he done for you in the past two years to make our union more possible? You know the answer to that question. I need not tell you he has done nothing. The reason should be clear. He wishes to delay, hoping you will tire of me, as you tired of my sister. Perhaps I will go away, as well, as easily as her and marry beneath me, as she did. Do not dismiss these feelings of mine. If you want my love, you must heed them and accept them for what they are, true feelings, the result of this long anguish I suffer at the hands of a promise not fulfilled. Why should I believe it will ever be fulfilled? Give me cause, if you can. This latest setback weighs heavily on my heart. Your letters and gifts do not appease these feelings. I want action only. Either make the cardinal do what you demand or get someone else to do your bidding.

13

Katherine

I do not wish to think of her, yet today it could not be helped. Out riding with my Spanish ladies, I stopped to see a falcon overhead and watched it dive at an alarming speed to kill a rabbit, using its tooth on the side of its beak. I now know why she wears a falcon on her badge. She is a bird of prey, flying on thin, tapered wings at high speed, changing directions as it suits her. She may as well have a tooth on the side of her beak with which to peck and devour.

She professes to be holy. I know not by which definition of holy she lives. It is not mine, that I know. I suspect her talk of holiness is nothing more than a mask; that she is no different than her sister, who has been called names no woman should ever be called. It is to be expected, though, when one lived for so many years in the house of that horrid King Francis, who, it is said of him, drinks the waters of many fountains.

I should have never allowed her in my household as a maid of honor, for I should have suspected she was interested in something greater, evident from the first in how she danced and sang and turned heads, wearing a French hood, her hair loose, her neck long like a swan's, her dark eyes hungry to seek and learn, her manner and movements choreographed, her voice rehearsed, her scent as she passed more powdered than the women here or back home in Spain. Haughty, I thought, for one so low of birth. Dangerously cordial and artfully flirtatious, making the young men of court wag their tails, like beasts in the fields. They came to my rooms sinful in their thoughts, come to have the newest of my maids. Henry Percy first, making a scene, as if he were Adam fawning over Eve in the garden until, like the first man of God, he was banished. Thomas Wyatt followed, forming flowers with his mouth and lips, such was the beauty of his words, though to no avail, since my husband wanted the girl for himself. I should need to look away, I told myself, as I had trained myself to do. She made it not easy to do. Once while playing cards with me and my ladies, she kept turning up a king. I said to her: My Lady Anne, you have good fortune to stop at a king, but you are not like others. You will have all or nothing. She did not respond. She turned her cards, her expression still and measured. She heard me, though. She knew what I said was true, and it remains true, even more so now that secret courts convene to make her what I have always been, Queen of England.

Cardinal Wolsey is now in France, meeting with clerics there, hoping to convince them he should act as pope during the pope's confinement. How should I know this? Spanish ladies spy well. Yes, I can play the game of subterfuge as well, though I may not be as adept as the cardinal. Though he is gone, his spies are ever present, watching and listening. I know what they report. She meets with Ambassador Mendoza; they speak Spanish, they plot treasonous acts, smuggling notes to her nephew, the emperor. None of which is true. I do not want war. I want justice only. I want all secret trials dismissed. I want the pope to remain steadfast and not allow himself to be supplanted by one with corrupt objectives. I want him to pass proper judgment. Have the trial, if there is to be one, held in Rome. Let the pope, God's vessel, decide on this case. I do not trust Wolsey. I do not trust the French, our enemy always. I do not trust Anne. I do not trust Henry, my husband, for he is no longer himself, listening as he does to the cardinal, who I am convinced is behind the divorce proceedings. He courts the French and always has, his hatred of Spain and my nephew and me evident in the lies he whispers to the king to fulfill his evil intentions. He believes himself my better now that he holds the king's ear. I wish to say to him that which I would say as well to Lady Anne, both of whom have risen: Though fortune extends its grace upon you, do not trust so much its fickle favor. You will learn this truth for yourselves, as I have had to learn, as we all must.

14

Henry

I understand her emotions. She is a woman, after all. She wishes, as do I, that this affair is settled and done with, so we can proceed with our plans to marry and bring further issue into the realm, for the sake of our dynasty. I will not, however, under any circumstance, dismiss Cardinal Wolsey or allow her detrimental views of him to influence my decision making. He has served me well for many years, long before she ever arrived and made of my life a folly, if not a madness. I will hear no such talk about his treasonous intentions. Though he hasn't yet procured the divorce I seek, I shall continue for the present to put my faith in him, though I must admit his failures have been upsetting to me as well.

It is the pope who is my greater enemy in this affair. Why should it be so hard for him to sign a document? Have I not always been his faithful servant, lavishing him with numerous benefits? Have I not defended the faith against Luther and his heresies? Should I not be granted favors for having done so? He is a heartless priest, I say, who considers neither the exigencies of my honor or the peace of my conscience or the prosperity of my kingdom. He is a hypocrite, covering himself in a cloak of friendship towards me, flattering me with his crafty practices, though by refusing me my request telling me, in effect, that it matters little if I and my kingdom perish. He wishes to be represented as a harmless dove, though in truth he is more like a serpent, biting me with his malice. Be a man, I wish to say to him. Appear from under the coattails of the emperor and the skirts of Margaret of Austria, another of Katherine's relatives. Do what is right by me and allow Cardinal Wolsey, here in England, to hear the case. Let him decide, if you cannot or will not.

He tells me I must retain my wife and frequent her bed, and I have said, more than once, I am utterly resolved and determined never to use her body again. He must be made to realize that if he continues to thwart me, England might turn its back on the papacy, wherein Luther's heresy will spread further. How should you like that? I wish to ask him.

15

Anne

His letters come with greater frequency. Today, he writes: My mistress and friend, I and my heart put ourselves in your hands, begging you to have them suitors for your good favor, and that your affection for them should not grow less through absence. For it would be a great pity to increase their sorrow since absence does it sufficiently, and more than ever I could have thought possible reminding us of a point in astronomy, which is, that the longer the days are the farther off is the sun, and yet more fierce. So it is with our love, for by absence we are parted yet nevertheless it keeps its fervor, at least on my side, and I hope on yours also: assuring you that on my side the ennui of absence is already too much for me and when I think of the increase of what I must suffer it would be unbearable for me were it not for the firm hope I have and as I cannot be with you in person, I am sending you the nearest possible thing to that, namely, my picture set in a bracelet, with the whole device which you already know. Wishing myself in their place when it shall please you. This by the hand of your loyal servant and friend, H. R.

He expects in return words assuring him of my affection. I have no such words. I will send instead a gift: a lonely damsel in a storm-tossed ship, for the feelings I possess now remind me of those I felt when I was twelve years old, journeying to France as part of Mary Tudor's household, subjected as I was to the blackening clouds, the fog and blistering cold, the wind and unremitting rain, the wretched rocking and swaying, the creaks and groans, the churning waves and the belief that my death was imminent. Too numb to move or speak, too sick to eat, I shielded myself under a blanket and prayed to the Virgin Mary, promising her that if she saw me safely through the passage, I would be her servant for life.

I pray again. Henry's reckless love is a force of nature as great as the sea during a storm. I am again on the boat. Only this time Henry is the helmsman. I ask: Is he, as well, my protector? Or do I embark unprotected on these waters that can drown one's dreams in a lightning flash? I have only myself to steer the course, to come safely into the harbor, to avoid being dashed against the rocks. Heavenly Mother, help me.

16

Katherine

Ambassador Mendoza has informed me that Pope Clement is sending Cardinal Campeggio to England to hear the case. He and Cardinal Wolsey will preside over the trial and pass sentence, acting as papal legates in the pope's place. It is what Henry, Anne and Wolsey want. I have never felt more alone, for if this trial proceeds here, rather than in Rome, where it rightfully, belongs, I stand not a chance, for Henry will ensure that every theologian, scholar and lawyer present, all men he owns, will not rule against him. He will be presented as the victim, having unknowingly married his brother's widow, not understanding it was against God's law. He will beg to be released from his sin, saying that he loved me, his queen, but for the sake of his conscience, he needs to divorce me to make amends with God. He will speak in a high-pitched voice, appearing as an innocent boy; he may even cry. I will be expected to testify and make public my private affairs with Arthur. I will not do it. I will not shame myself or the memory of my former husband. I will not be believed, anyway. I am a woman, the daughter of Eve. Therefore, I am already condemned in the eyes of men. I shall look to God, as I always have, for He knows the truth, and that suffices for me.

It does not surprise me to hear, at the same time, of His wrath. He sees and hears what we do. Henry's actions have displeased him. The sweating sickness he has sent to the streets of London is the latest example. Ambassador Mendoza reports that people have boarded up their houses, shut their shops, and have fled along the roads. To no avail, though, for already thousands have died, and the sight and smell of death are everywhere, evident in the ceaseless tolling of church bells, ringing for the dead, the carts rolling through the streets piled high with corpses, thick as flies, while fires burn to purge the fetid air that hangs over the city. It is only a matter of time before it reaches us here in Greenwich, from the foul stenches of the contaminated Thames, sweeping through the royal establishment like a fire, consuming first the kitchen servants, the masons, the grooms and the apothecaries, until it possesses the court nobles who see themselves as above God's commandments.

17

Henry

I dread disease and death more than anything. Maybe it's my brother's early death or my mother's sudden death in childbirth, or the relentless headaches I suffer or the frequent bouts of fever and dry throat and spitting and coughing that I endure or the recent jousting accident which has caused pain and bleeding in my leg. I can't say for sure where my fear manifests. I just know that when I see disease and feel the specter of death around me, I flee from it, which is the reason I am here at Waltham, far from London, because during such a time as this when the sweating sickness is rampant it is important to breathe only wholesome air and keep to oneself except for a few servants and companions, such as my secretary, apothecary and doctor, who are absolutely free of infection. To survive the sweating sickness requires knowledge. Only through the application of study can one acquire this knowledge. I have made it my business to learn, for I wish to live, not die, like so many who are ignorant of preventives. Perhaps I shall write a treatise and share my knowledge with others, or, at the very least, record my routine and habits. Here is what I've been doing in Waltham: I walk in the garden, alone, in the mornings and practice shooting with a crossbow between dinner and supper, though I eat and drink sparingly, choosing to take mostly medicinal compounds, the which I have studied carefully, knowing my life depends on the intake of their properties. I mix saffron, mustard seed and ginger with white wine. I drink it twice a day, along with treacle and medicinal waters, for as many days as necessary. I make an herbal plaster, usually rosemary, fennel, mandrake and hemlock and apply it for an hour to my skin to draw out venom. I live in rooms where my servants keep braziers of live coals burning and where each wall and floor is washed in vinegar. The smells are unpleasant, though I don't complain, for given that I am alive and recording this information, it appears my strategy has been successful.

18

Anne

I am twelve years old, again on the boat to France. Only now I am dead. Not in the boat, but in the waves, where I am now, under the water, lying lifeless at the bottom. I see and hear nothing. My voice cannot be heard. Such is the way it is when one is dead, as I am dead, as the maid who came to my room is dead, as I saw her fall to the floor, her face red, spotted with black marks, overcome with sweat, screaming, holding her stomach, ripping at her clothes. Or was that me, not the maid, holding my stomach and screaming, turning red and sweating, burning with fire, ripping the clothes from my body, before I fell in the waves, before I died and became ... What is it that I became? Who or what am I, now that I am lying at the bottom of the waves, a blanket over me? Why is the blanket dry, though I am wet? Why should I be carried? Who lives at the bottom of the sea other than those, like me, who are dead? Still, a fire rages inside me. The waves have done nothing to relieve it. Nothing can relieve it, not even death. How should that be, unless this death has brought me to that most unimaginable of places. I shall not say its name. I shall not acknowledge it. I wish to tell those who carry me not to say it, but I have no voice. I hear only a voice inside me. It says Heavenly Mother. I knew a Heavenly Mother once. She was the helmsman of the boat. She steered us into a storm. I called to her. She didn't hear me. Why is she not also at the bottom of the sea, lying dead alongside me? Now I say the word Henry. Why should I say that word? It is a name, I am certain. But who is it? Is he the boy I was supposed to marry? Yes, but at twelve years old we were too young to marry. We would have to wait. I recall voices saying that. I shall have to tell him I can no longer wait, for I am dead. He shall have to marry without me. If I had eyes to see and a voice to speak, I should tell him the storm has taken me. That ship should have never pushed off. I shouldn't have gotten on it. I should have never trusted the helmsman, the Heavenly Mother. Look where it has brought me, carried as I am, swaddled in blankets, dripping with the sea, being taken I know not where. It does not matter, I wish to say, if I had a voice, if I could be heard, if I could see. Do with me what you will, for I am dead and shall never sail again. I am not sorry for that.

19

Henry

I can think of nothing more grievous than the news of Anne's sickness and delirium, which came to me suddenly at night. Will these curses upon my head, come from my forebears, never end? Hasn't our family already made restitution? Henry V lost his reign and his life quickly after murdering Richard II. His son, Henry VI, lost that which his father gained, that being France, and soon after lost his throne, dying insane. My father paid dearly for having killed my uncle Richard III, for having taken the crown without ancestral right, losing his son, my brother, heir to his throne, and soon after his wife, my mother, in childbirth. I lost my son Henry, nine weeks old. What more, God? I wish to shout. What repentance more? I have acknowledged my sin, marrying my brother's widow. I have done everything a man can do to repent. I have heard mass and made confession, twice daily, if not more. I have confessed my sin in a secret court. I will confess again in the upcoming trial headed by Cardinal Campeggio and Cardinal Wolsey. I ask only to be resolved of any wrongdoing and allowed to marry Anne, whom I love dearly. I am thirty-seven years of age. I have no male heir. Allow her to live. Allow her to bear me sons. I am the inheritor of this curse, not its creator.

I write these words with a trembling hand: My uneasy qualms regarding your health have much troubled and alarmed me, and I shall have no ease without the certainty of your recovery and good health. Keep faith, dearest love, whom I esteem more than all the world and whose health I desire as my own. Know that I would willingly bear half of your illness to have you cured. I am sending to you Dr. Butts, the only one of my doctors left, praying to God that soon he can put you in health again, prescribing medicines which I myself take, in which event I shall love him more than ever. I pray that you be governed by his advice regarding your illness, and in doing so I hope soon to see you again, which will remedy me more than all the precious stones of the world, for this absence from you is my greatest enemy.

Cardinal Campeggio comes soon to London to preside over the trial, wherein you and I will soon be married legally in the eyes of Rome and God. Allow that news to invigorate your heart and soul, in addition to the medicines and treatments that will heal your body. It should comfort you to know it is true as they say, that few women or none have this malady, and moreover none of our court, and that few elsewhere have died of it. Therefore, I beg of you, my wholly beloved, to have no fear nor to be uneasy at our absence, for wherever I may be, I am yours, although we must sometimes submit to fortune, for who wishes to struggle against fortune is usually very often the farther from his desire. Therefore, comfort yourself and be brave, and avoid the evil as much as you can, and I hope shortly to make you sing for joy of your return. I wish myself in your arms, my sweetheart, whose pretty duckies I trust shortly to kiss. This by the hand of your loyal servant and friend, H. R.

20

Anne

Those serving me said I spoke of feverish musings, a confusion of fearsome images, until the chaplain came to administer last rites, at which time I recovered, released from the stranglehold of blind panic, during his ritual standing over me, touching my forehead, more a specter than real, speaking Latin, which I do not understand. I asked: What is the meaning of your presence? Can you not see this is a lady's chamber? The startled chaplain fell back, mumbling: You speak. I speak? I asked. Why shouldn't I speak? Those near my bed wept, saying: You are well; you have survived. Survived what? I demanded to know. Do you not remember, my lady, falling ill, screaming in pain, turning red and full of sweat, burning with fever? No, I said. I remember ... I stopped short of saying I remembered dying at twelve years old, aboard the ship to France, lying at the bottom of the ocean, being washed by the waves.

Upon further inquiry, I learned the maid who served me in Greenwich fell ill and died suddenly from the sweating sickness. I became infected, at which time my father's entourage had me carried to Hever, wrapped in blankets, kept warm by their touch and protected by their whispered prayers. A man who calls himself Dr. Butts stands where the chaplain stood. His smile stretches the length of the room. He was sent by the king, he tells me. He administered to me while I lay in a state of delirium for days, forced to stay awake in what he calls a dream of shadows, which, according to him, is better than living entirely in shadows, without dreams. I thanked him, wishing to know what he did to save me. He made clear that he did not save me. God did. Yes, I acknowledge, though as God's good doctor you played a part, I respond. Did you not, good doctor? His smile widens. I treated you the way the king explicitly directed me to treat you, for he is a master of medicines, a scholar when it comes to preventives. I used his very own herbal potions, making sure you sipped them, though you were not aware; applying as well poultices to your skin day and night, and bleeding you from your shoulders to your feet, while keeping coal burning in your room, to fight the extreme fever with extreme heat. He shall be pleased to know you are well. He is well then, I say. Oh, yes, the broad man laughs. Nothing ill can touch him, for he is divinely appointed.

21

Katherine

I had been anxious to meet Cardinal Campeggio, hoping that as the pope's colleague he would prove my ally; though within minutes of his arrival, I learned he had come to do Wolsey's bidding. Why else would he say to me what he did, only days before the trial is to begin? Your husband, the king, has confessed to me that he hasn't slept in your bed for three years. Yield to his displeasure. You have nothing to gain and everything to lose by bringing this affair to trial and submitting your cause to the hazard of sentence. Consider your reputation. Consider your dower, which will be forfeited, leaving you with nothing other than the king's mercy. Why risk that, along with the scandal that will ensue? If you comply, you will retain your dower, the guardianship of the Princess Mary, your rank and whatever else you choose to demand. You would neither offend God nor your conscience. Therefore, relent, for you must know after three years of marital abandonment you will never recover his love. Take a vow of perpetual chastity, become a nun and move into a convent. It is what is best for you, for the king and for all of Christendom, which shouldn't be put on trial as well, suffering humiliation and disrespecting the names and honor of the Lord and his son, Jesus Christ.

Cardinal Wolsey stood silently in the room, nodding his head in approval of the words spoken by the cardinal from Rome; words that had the stink and stain of Wolsey all over them. I demanded that I should be allowed to speak with Cardinal Campeggio alone. Cardinal Wolsey winced at the idea, saying he and Cardinal Campeggio, as decreed by Pope Clement, shared equal jurisdiction in this affair, and thereby whatever I desired to say to the cardinal from Rome he, Cardinal Wolsey, by law, was required to hear. No, I shouted, looking at Cardinal

Campeggio. I will not speak in this man's presence. He is against me and has been for many years and would like nothing better than to see me deposed. Your Grace, Wolsey said, I harbor no ill will toward you. I am the king's advisor, and if he wishes to divorce from you it is my job to assist him in any way I can. I am his loyal servant. You must understand that. You serve yourself above all others, Cardinal Wolsey, I said. You look to profit from my fall. Know this, though (and here I looked at both men), I will never comply with your request to enter a convent. I intend to live and die in the state of matrimony to which God has called me and as decreed and executed lawfully in the year 1509, according to the brief issued by the pope, clearing Henry to marry me, his brother's widow, though very much intact and uncorrupted as the day I left my mother's womb, as God is my witness. That brief is the entirety of my right to remain queen. I shall always hold this opinion and nothing you do can change that. You can tear me limb from limb and I will remain firm, and if I were brought back to life again, I would prefer to die over again rather than change. I wish to remain clear and resolute that my conscience, sincere as ever, is not for sale. I am resolved to die in the Faith and in the obedience to God and his Holy Church, the which neither of you seem to have much association.

They began to leave. I shouted after them. Can you not see, Cardinal Campeggio, that I am a lone woman and a stranger here in England, without friend or advisor? The old cardinal stopped and turned to me, saying: Seek advice from God, for unless you give up your cause, this trial will cause you much shame and suffering. I need not tell you how. You know the question that will be asked: How does a woman marry for six months and not consummate her marriage? The world will want to know. I hope you have a good answer. He left with Cardinal Wolsey, without a word more, leaving me to rehearse my answer. How should I tell the cardinal or others that when Arthur came to my bed, all of seven times, he did so for company, nothing else? They will say that is too unnatural to believe. What is natural? I shall say. In the human dilemma, everything is natural. Who knows what lurks in the mind and body of any one person? Only that person himself knows. They are convinced they know the ways of Arthur better than me, though I was the one married to him. I was the one who felt his trembling limbs and heard his coughs and saw his eyes flutter even when closed. I saw his thin bones, his frail demeanor. I heard his labored breath. And yet they are experts in his behavior and so sure what he did in bed with me and how often. Men make this world with bricks of lies. What can I, a lone woman, do to unmake them?

22

Henry

It is her way to make things hard for herself and everyone else. I offered her an easy way out. She will not take it. As if her defiance isn't bad enough, she smiles. Not to me, of course. To the people, out among them, in the courts and in the streets of London. I do not like that smile, for there behind it lies an arrogance, a confidence, a belief she is infallible, for she has her nephew, who owns the pope, who may as well be a doll sitting atop the emperor's lap, for he cannot move or speak without the emperor's direction. She sneaks out notes to him, asking for his assistance, telling him he must not allow this divorce for the sake of Christendom and the alliance between Spain and England that our fathers and mothers forged in blood. That blood must be honored, and only he could do that by doing what he could to ensure she remain Queen of England.

I told her, Kate, do not smile. You are dissimulating, pretending, putting on a face. She said, it is my job as queen to present myself in a manner suitable to my position. It is what my supporters want. Supporters? Oh, I see how it is. You are smiling at them to gain their support. Support for what? For an uprising, a rebellion, preparing them for the day your nephew comes riding into town with his Imperialist army, prepared to sack London as he sacked Rome? I am their queen, she said, I have been their queen for nearly twenty years. Do not make it sound like I just arrived yesterday. I have longevity. They respect that, unlike others. Others? Don't be so arrogant, Kate. I know who you mean by others. Just say my name and get it over with. I have news for you. I am King of England, and as such I forbid you to smile. Do you hear me? Smile to yourself if you wish to, but do not smile to my courtiers or to the common people of London or to anyone for that matter. Cry, look pensive, as I look, for I am not smiling. No, of course not, she said. Why should you smile? You know you sin against me and God and the pope and all Christendom, creating scandal here in England, wanting to dispose of me and marry a woman beneath both you and me in birth, someone not worthy to sit on the throne as I am. You have wronged me. You have wronged everything that is decent and fair. You have wronged God. That is why you don't smile. You're wrong, Kate, I snapped. I don't smile because you have made of my life a misery these past two years, defying me with your pride and stubbornness. When this trial is over and the court, headed by Cardinal Campeggio, he of your blessed Rome, sent by the pope, rules in my favor, then I will smile. I will, in fact, do more than smile. I will howl and leap and flutter about, as a wolf, a deer, or a newborn bird flying from its nest; happy to not have to see you smile anymore because you will have no further need to dissimulate or pretend or put on a face because you won't be queen. You will be Lady Katherine, my sister, if it pleases me, and if it doesn't, just Lady Katherine. You will have no need to smile for your supporters, for you will have none. I shall continue to act as queen consort, she said, for that is what I am and will forever be. Your threats or actions cannot change that. With that, she left my presence. If nothing else, I succeeded in wiping the smile from her face. As for not being able to change her mind, we shall see, for I haven't yet used my trump card to break her will. I can take away her dower and her many residences. I can take away her allowance, her servants, her grooms, her ladies of the house, and I can take away that which she most treasures and adores, her daughter. I can leave her with nothing except the illusion of a title, an empty shell, a hollow reminder of what she will no longer possess.

23

Anne

Recovering from the sickness has been transformative, to the point where I no longer look warily on Henry's advances, thinking of his love as a great storm I must weather. It is not his letters and gifts and songs of love that have brought about my change, nor a growing affection I feel. Rather the vision of what I can achieve for my faith, wherein I see a greater divorce than Henry's from Katherine: the divorce of England from Rome. Dr. Butts did more than cure me of the sweat. He has become one of my chief contacts with those who desire religious reform, both here and abroad. I now have two men in Antwerp—I shall not name them for fear of someone learning their identities— who supply me with books, smuggled into London, past the spying eyes of Wolsey's men. I shall have Henry read these books, hoping when he does that he will alter his thinking, which he greatly needs, for he is held back by old superstitions, believing a threat of excommunication from the pope damages his immortal soul, believing he must appease God's wrath by good work and pilgrimages and by hearing mass every day. His primitive fears are in conflict with his intellect, and it is my job, as chosen by God, as I now believe, to enlighten him, to change his view, to make him understand that salvation cannot be bought; that it is a matter of faith. Read the books, I will say to him. Read William Tyndale's *The Obedience of a Christian Man*. Read Simon Fish's *Supplication for Beggars*. Read the words of these men, patriots both, who live in exile, for fear that Wolsey's men will imprison them, burn their books and in subsequence their flesh. Read their words to understand it is only through emancipation from the pope, from his lies, his pomp, his pride, that this country of ours can achieve greatness. Read their words to understand we have arrived at a new dawn of worship for

God. Read their words, and say, along with me and many others: Away with false mythology, evident in the rituals of the church as a means to salvation. Just put out your hands to receive God's gift. Away with crucifying Christ time and again, as if his one sacrifice was not enough for our sins. Away with the worship of images, forbidden in God's Ten Commandments. Away with the selling of indulgences and the singing of mass and the lingering existence of Purgatory, when it is nowhere proved. Above all, let us allow our priests to marry, for God never intended the nature of man to be lived unnaturally. Let the authority of the New Testament speak for itself. Church traditions and human intervention stand between God and the people, but we shall see an end to that.

I feel now as if my life has been nothing but a preparation for this new beginning, wherein I have been called by God to act as Queen Esther, chosen from all other women by a great king, to deliver his subjects from the Egyptian darkness and Babylonian bonds that the pope had brought him and his subjects under, to free them from the shackles of ignorance and the slavery of Rome, to bring them the new religion, far from the persecution of the old favored by fanatics, who condemn men for learning God's holy word in the vernacular language. If that's my reward for marrying Henry, I am willing to pay whatever price I must pay in return, for though I dream of being revered by the English people as their savior, I am not a foolish woman, given to illusion. I know, having lived in Queen Claude's French court, that the greatest gains often come with the greatest losses.

24

Katherine

I have received in writing from the king's councilors a letter, reprimanding me for acting selfishly toward the king, who, the author reminds me, is revered by all. Is it not then to be expected his own wife would honor and revere him? If I honored and loved him, as I so often profess, why then wouldn't I show it? What follows are accusations against my conduct and behavior, attacks on my character, chastising me in a manner hardly befitting for one who has been for twenty years Queen of England. The list is long, and I am smart enough to know the words do not belong to my husband. They are Cardinal Wolsey's, who wishes to portray me as a woman diseased in body and mind.

I am accused of sedition, treason, plotting to murder the king, to take for myself the crown or give it to my daughter. I have hired conspirators and ill-disposed personages to carry out my plan. I have always lusted after the crown. It began when I was Regent. I loved war. I wanted to send the body of a dead man to Henry. I am mad. I pretended pregnancy. I deceived the king. I had too many illnesses before I married the king. These illnesses caused me to lose my babies. I was never stable. I have always been unfit. I have failed in my wifely duties, having denied the king access to my bed. Is it any wonder he has no male heirs when I have allowed him few opportunities? The king is pensive, yet I am cheerful. It is apparent in my countenance, in my apparel, and in all my actions. I encourage ladies and gentlemen of the court to dance and pass time in merriment. I should instead encourage them to pray. I smile too much in public, purposely inciting the people of England to be on my side, against the king, evident in the remarks of malice he hears towards him and the cheers and encouragement they show for me, proving that I wish to start a rebellion and proceed with my evil intent to usurp the king.

The king, therefore, feels it best, justifiably so, that he should stay away from me and my Spanish servants, who cannot be trusted, for they know the secrets of poison herbs, learned in a backward country. Our continued separation is the only way to assure his safety from one who outwardly, as well as inwardly, hates him. Given the reckless, uncaring nature of my behavior, it is also best that Princess Mary be kept from my presence, despite how evidently grievous such an action will be to me. If I wish to prove my allegiance to the king and, at the same time, disprove my traitorous intents, and once again live in the company of my daughter, I must hand over the brief, said to be in my possession, written by Pope Julius to my mother on her deathbed, consisting of my right to marry, assuring my dying mother that my future had been settled legally in the eyes of the pope and God, that no one could argue against its legitimacy. Until then, my acts will continue to show that I am behind the delay of the trial, for I have secret correspondence with lawyers from Spain and Flanders. I should understand that I will not be allowed these lawyers, and even if they were to come to England, they would not be safe. I, in fact, will meet my utter undoing and destruction if I act to make my subversive plans a reality.

I am now more than ever made to feel like an unwelcomed stranger in a foreign land, an outcast, a Spaniard from across the sea, the enemy. All because I refuse to go to a convent and become a nun; because I refuse to accept the title, king's sister; because I have said to Henry: How can the pope condemn me without a hearing? I know very well that if the judges are impartial, and I am granted a hearing, my cause shall be gained, for no judge will be found unjust enough to condemn me.

25

Henry

Wolsey said, Drop the part about her having had conjugal relations with your brother. It's not important, and she remains obstinate in her stance. Let us concentrate instead on her having been married, whether she had relations or not. It is enough. No, it's not enough, I responded. We must prove before the court that she had relations. It is the reason I am bothered in conscience and have nary a son with her. I have rested my case on Leviticus, and I shall continue to do so, for if her consummation can be proved then the people of England shall come around and side with me and understand I am doing what I must do in divorcing the queen. Find me proof that she had relations, even if it means you speak with God, whom she says is the only witness.

The following day, he brought to me an old man, who bowed before me and was quick to say, mumbling as he did: My name is Sir William Thomas, Your Majesty. As you can see, I am now long in the tooth, aged fifty-nine. I served in your brother's household when he married the queen, who, as you are aware, I shouldn't have to tell you, was not the queen then, just the queen in waiting, as your brother was the king in waiting. You wouldn't have remembered me, Your Majesty. You were a lad of ten then, if my memory serves correctly. Your brother was a lad of fifteen, the same age as me when I first experienced the mystery of womanhood and the glory that comes from unmasking it. A man, looking back, doesn't forget something like that. It stays with you, I can tell you, just as what your brother told me, now going on twenty-eight years, if my calculations are correct, has stayed with me all these years, and if my telling you what he told me helps your cause and the cause of the English people, I am more than happy to tell my side of it, for I am nothing if not a loyal servant, Your Majesty. I thanked the man for his loyalty and made clear I wished for him to skip any further preface to the reason for his being there. The proof, man. Give us the proof.

Yes, yes, he mumbled. That very morning, after his wedding night, your brother appeared from his marriage chamber, with sweat upon his brow, asking for water. He said he had been in Spain all night and was very dry. Dutifully, without delay, I brought him a tall goblet of water and watched him drink it lustily, sighing with satisfaction as he did. Wiping his lips, he said he had traveled far south to a region he had never before known, that he wished to visit it again later that night, for it was the most beautiful country imaginable; that he wished to be king of this country as well as king of England, for it was a fair-weathered place, warm and most suitable to a young man such as himself. He finished the water and handed the goblet to me, saying, I am a man, sir. I am a man. With that, he took his smiling face and his satisfaction to the next chamber to get dressed, though that was not the end of it. The following morning, he repeated the routine, coming to me with sweat on his brow, asking for water and afterwards drinking it, saying that while the water clenched his thirst it did little to whet his desirous appetite. He called himself the luckiest man in the world to visit a country, such as Spain, of which he had heard so much. To experience it for himself was so much greater than the youthful dreams he had long harbored and suffered in the turbulence of his body. I asked, who else can corroborate your story? More than a dozen men, Your Majesty, he replied, for your brother loosened his mouth wherever he traveled in his chambers, pronouncing to the happy ears of all who served him: I am a man. I am the great conqueror of Spain.

After the old man left my room, Cardinal Wolsey, beaming, told me he had already contacted the other men, all of whom were prepared to appear in court and give their individual testimony, proving the queen had consummated her marriage to my brother. Did that please me? He wanted to know. I told him it was, at the same time, the best and worst news, for it meant that during all our years of marriage, she had lied to me. Could there be any doubt left now that I should divorce her and in doing so be vindicated from any wrongdoing?

26

Anne

I cannot, at present, read the books you have given me, for I must prepare for the imminent trial. Once it is over and the case settled in my favor, I will read the books, marry you and be forever free of Katherine, the pope and Rome. That should please you, should it not?

Fine, I responded, but I should not wait around. Already, I feel like a shadow, though living here at Greenwich, in my own household, waiting for you to follow through on your promise to no longer spend time with her. You say one thing but do another. You appear with her in public because, as you say, the two of you are obliged to behave as if nothing were strange, at least until you are granted the divorce from the pope. You attend mass with her every day, saying your confessions. What do you confess? Has she convinced you to return to her, to save Christendom, though you say that will never happen? Did I not tell you that whenever you dispute with her, she is sure to have the upper hand? I see that some fine morning you will succumb to her reasoning, and that you will cast me off. I have been waiting long, and might in the meantime have contracted some advantageous marriage, out of which I might have had issue, which is the greatest consolation in this world; but alas! Farewell to my time and youth spent to no purpose at all.

I have said to you, and have thought many times to myself: What if you are not granted a divorce? You are naïve believing the machinations of the pope and her nephew Charles, and even Cardinal Wolsey, he the son of a provincial butcher, whom you trust too easily. I don't. I believe this trial is little more than a show. Do you not question why it has been eight months now since Cardinal Campeggio arrived and still the trial hasn't started? The pope, it is clear to me, has instructed the cardinal to buy time, hoping you will weaken, succumb to Katherine's pleas and the growing possibility of an invasion, which you fear more than anything, enough perhaps to back out of your promise to me and choose to live in misery with the queen, if it means peace for England and security for your crown.

I do not believe the pope will bend his will and act against Katherine and in doing so anger the emperor, and even if he were to, where does that leave us? You yourself have said the pope needs to grant us a special dispensation for us to marry, for we are related by affinity, being as you were my sister's paramour. I know you have not forgotten that, though you have forgotten my sister. I'm sure you have heard news that her husband, William Carey, succumbed to the sweat. She lives destitute, with two children, always asking me to ask you for assistance. I have not done so, for I know you wish not to support her, though her children bear your resemblance. I shall not further distress you with this matter, since you are already distressed by the upcoming trial, which appears to be anything but upcoming. It appears more of a hoax, if my opinion matters. Know that I am returning to Hever until this affair ends, for I cannot go out in the streets for fear of my safety. The people jeer me and make threats. I wish not to be mistreated. I am already mistreated by this wait, this hollow-headed promise which seems never to show its face. Inform me when you have good news to deliver to me. Until then, know that I am not pleased and wish to sequester myself in the countryside, reading my books, which you, to my dismay, feel not the pertinence to read at this time, though if you read them you would understand their pertinence, more now than ever. How disappointing that is to me.

27

Katherine

Henry sat under his gold canopy, master of the room, not once looking at me. He spoke. I listened, pained, anguished, feeling small, of no consequence, wanting to believe his words, though understanding the performance and intent behind them, as he looked not once in my direction. I assure you she is a woman of most gentleness, humility and buxomness, he began, addressing the lawyers, bishops and theologians with whom he had shown favors in return for their loyalty. She is without comparison. So, that if I were to marry again, I would choose her above all women. I am sorrowful to leave such a good lady and loving companion, but it is because we have lived in adultery to God's great displeasure and these be the sores that vex my mind, these be the pangs that trouble my conscience.

His conscience should be troubled, but not for the reason he stated. He had brought to that room witness after witness, men too old to remember their names yet astute in imagination, for that is the only way to describe their testimonies in regard to my maidenhood and the purity of the boy, fifteen years of age, I had married and saw die without him ever laying touch to me. How could my husband of twenty years allow these men to speak with false words, putting words in his brother's mouth, words that were never spoken? God knows they weren't and Arthur, his soul resting in peace, knows as well. Shame on those men. Shame on Wolsey, who brought them there. Shame on the lawyers, bishops and theologians, men forced by the favors of Henry to show loyalty to a case that is unjust.

Only Bishop Fisher stood among them as an honest man. Only he had the courage to stand and defend me, saying a king did not have the right to do whatever he pleased. Everyone, king or not, should submit themselves to the decrees of the Church.

He referred to the New Testament book of Matthew, as I had with Henry many times: A marriage made and joined by God to a good intent, as was mine and Henry's, could not be broken or loosed by the power of man. He declared he would lay down his life for my cause, as did John the Baptist when he lost his head, challenging King Herod's decision to change wives.

Henry shouted at the bishop, I am not King Herod! How do you, a bishop, profess to know the truth? I know that God is truth itself, Bishop Fisher answered. Henry fumed. His lawyers and other bishops demanded that Bishop Fisher take his seat and keep his treasonous views to himself. I thought, if he should die a martyr, God will bless the bishop's soul, for the courageous act as Christ, though they meet his fate and carry the cross to their own crucifixion. We all must die anyway, in the end. Let us die intact, in virtue, honesty and especially with courage, which is the highest of all virtues that informs all others.

Henry made another plea. Conscience should take moral priority over the laws of Rome. Katherine and I should have never received a dispensation from Pope Julius. Even popes can be wrong. God, however, knows the truth. He has not given me a son, and isn't that proof enough that in marrying as I did, without the knowledge I was committing incest, I defiled God's laws? I cannot redo what has already been done. I ask only for restitution, for the chance to redeem my life's sins and be given the opportunity to marry again, to father sons, as any king should, for without sons the threat of civil war hangs above our heads as the clouds do in the sky.

I stood and walked over to the king and knelt where he sat, forcing him to do what he had avoided, with great effort, to do, look me in my eyes. I spoke words that were not practiced or rehearsed for the truth needs no practice. It is natural. Unlike those witnesses, who fabricated wild tales in an attempt to prove I consummated my marriage, men with no backbone, men bought and sold cheaply like corn at a market. I do not barter the truth. I honor it.

Sir, I said, I beseech you for all the love that has been between us and for the love of God, let me have justice and right. Take of me some pity and compassion, for I am a poor woman and a stranger, born out of your dominion. I have here no assured friends, and much less indifferent council. I flee to you as to the head of justice within this realm. Alas, sir, wherein have I offended you, or what occasion of displeasure have I deserved against your will or pleasure? Intending, as I perceive, to put me from you, I take God and all the world to witness that I have been to you a true, humble, and obedient wife, ever conforming to your will and pleasure, that never said or did anything to the contrary thereof. For twenty years, I have lived your life, loving your friends and hating your enemies, content to shape my will entirely to yours, without once complaining or showing discontent, and I have borne your children, a number of them, and though only one of them has survived it is not my fault, but God's will, and when you had me at the first (I take God to be my judge) I was a true maid without touch of man, and whether it be true or not, I put it to your conscience. If there be any just cause by the law that he can allege against me, either of dishonesty or any other impediment, to banish and put me from you, I am well content to depart to my great shame and dishonor, and if there be none, then here I must lowly beseech you let me remain in my former estate and to receive justice at your princely hands. Therefore, I most humbly require you in the way of charity and for the love of God, who is the just judge, to spare the extremity of this new court, for it is, as you know, a new invention invented against me, manifestly unfair since I am unable to defend myself, having no lawyers of my own. I ask, then, one last thing. Would you give your permission, as my husband and master, for me to write directly to the pope to defend my honor and conscience and advertise what way and order my friends in Spain will advise me to take? If you will not extend to me so much indifferent favor, your pleasure then be fulfilled, I then to God commit my case.

His blue eyes warmed, becoming recognizable as eyes I had once known. Yes, he said, reaching for my hands, raising me to my feet. You have my permission. I made a curtsy and thanked him and walked out the hall, hearing as I did the calls of the court crier demanding my return. On, on, I said. It makes no matter, for it is no impartial court for me, therefore I will not tarry. Go on.

28

Henry

I am at times soft to a fault. She knows and used it against me, kneeling near me, making me look in her eyes. I should have looked away and closed my ears to her impassioned speech, refusing her request to appeal to the pope. How foolish of me to give my permission. I won't let it happen again. That is the last of her beseeching to which I will succumb. I heard that when she left, the crowd outside cheered for her, calling her name: Queen Katherine, keep the fight, you shall win, you are our queen and will always be our queen. She probably smiled at them; that smile I despise. After hearing from the many witnesses who verified that she and my brother consummated their marriage, she should have left the court crying, not smiling. She shouldn't have used her tricks of dissembling at a time like that. I did not hear cheers when I left. I heard jeers. A voice, a woman's, yelled from a throng of faceless people: Your conscience to the dogs, it is not to be believed. Many echoed her. I did not engage them. I did not wish to incite them further. They are Katherine's people, not mine, and I thought it best to leave quickly for there's no telling what an agitated mob can do.

It matters not whether they believe my conscience. It matters only that the lawyers, bishops and presiding cardinals believe it. I care only for their sentence, nullifying my marriage once and for all. I care only for the result of that action, wherein I shall marry Anne and make heirs to the throne. When that happens, the people of London will become silent and respectful, bowing to me and their new queen, as they should, appreciative that the realm of England is secure for years to come.

If she thinks that by leaving the court and avoiding it she can make both it and the business of divorce disappear, she is mistaken. I shall not quit. I will keep hounding her. I will send the cardinals to her again. She won't like that. They won't, in fact, like that. I don't care. I want her submission. It would save everyone a great deal of time. Even the pope wants her submission, if not her death, for my ambassadors have reported to me what he was heard saying: I would, for the wealth of Christendom, the queen were in her grave. Perhaps I should tell her that when next I see her, which, if I am fortunate, shall not be for some time.

29

Katherine

I met them in my presence chamber, attended by my ladies, purposely keeping the skein of white thread around my neck to inform the cardinals I was at that very moment sewing one of Henry's shirts. It is, after all, what wives do for their husbands, and until the pope, who is God on earth, tells me otherwise he shall continue to be my husband. Neither man looked well. Cardinal Wolsey appeared with sweat upon his brow, his eyes small and colorless, his hands clasped tightly at his waist. Cardinal Campeggio had already taken a seat, wherein he rubbed his knee and groaned, mumbling that his gout had worsened in the English weather.

Cardinal Wolsey asked if they could talk with me in my privy chamber. I refused, saying, whatever it is you have to say, say it in front of my ladies, for I should want all to hear and see what it is you allege against me. Cardinal Wolsey spoke to me in Latin. I interrupted him and said, speak English. He bowed. Madam, he said, if it please Your Grace, we come both to know your mind, how you are disposed in this matter between the king and you and to declare secretly our opinions and our counsel unto you.

I responded sharply to the cardinal's weary face. I am surprised, Cardinal Wolsey, that you speak to me of council when there is none. I am a simple woman, destitute and barren of friendship and counsel here in a foreign region. Those in whom I do intend to put my trust are not here. They are in Spain, in my native country.

There you are wrong, Madam, he said, for we, though the king's subjects, are impartial to your cause. Impartial? My voice rose, as I intended, looking in the cardinal's eyes, barely open, looking faraway. I know who has given the king the advice he is following; it is you. I have not ministered to your pride. I have blamed your conduct. I have complained of your tyranny, and my nephew the emperor has not made you Pope. Hence all my misfortunes. To revenge yourself you have kindled a war in Europe and have stirred up against me this most wicked matter. God will be my judge, and yours. Now, as you can see, I am set among my maidens at work. I must excuse myself. Tell the king his shirt shall be ready before the night has fallen.

30

Anne

I am dismayed by the news you sent me, though not surprised. I warned you, did I not? I told you I trusted neither Cardinal Campeggio, Cardinal Wolsey or your wife. I told you she was deceitful, which should have been clear to you from the beginning of your marriage, when she first lied about being a maid and then later claiming to be pregnant, making you believe she carried your heir, only to learn her womb was empty. What kind of woman lies like that to her husband, a man she professes to love?

And now this, the latest, having asked for your permission for something she had already done, having asked, before the trial began, for the case to be tried in Rome. In light of that news it comes as no surprise that Cardinal Campeggio suspended passing a sentence, adjourning the trial to later in the year, giving as an excuse that in Rome the reaping and harvesting holidays had begun, wherein the courts did not sit. Clearly, he never intended to rule in your favor. He had come to get your wife's submission and barring that, meant to stall for as long as possible until he managed to concoct his fanciful excuse to suspend passing sentence.

As for Cardinal Wolsey, this latest failure of his should leave no doubt in your mind, as it doesn't in mine, that he cannot be trusted with this affair any longer. He knew, as Campeggio knew and Pope Clement knew and Katherine herself knew what you, apparently the only one, didn't know: The trial was a hoax from the start. You have been hoodwinked, Henry. How do you plan to answer their deceit?

31

Henry

Can news get any worse? First the adjournment without a sentence and now this: Katherine winning her appeal and the pope calling me to Rome to have the case heard there. I know now Pope Clement wants what Katherine wants and what the emperor wants. They, all three, want me to go to Rome. They want to feed me to the lions, but I have news for them. I am not a Christian martyr. I am King of England. I shall send your father, my best diplomat, to persuade the pope to reconsider his decision. It is not wise of him, for he should have learned from the actions in Germany, where papal authority is a thing of the past, that if he wants our continued love, he must give us his.

For you see, dearest Anne, I did read one of the books you gave me. It is truly a book for all kings to read, and for me particularly. My only regret is not having read it before the trial, as you had implored me to do, wherein I, through no fault but my own, believing the trial took precedence over its wisdom, failed to heed your persuasion. You will, in fact, be happy to know that as I write to you the book sits beside me, the page you thumb-nailed within my sight. If you want further proof, here they are, the words in my own handwriting, from my pen to the paper and deep inside my brain, where they shall plant a new beginning for us if the pope continues to fail us. As you read these words – and I understand you know them well – I hope you can hear my voice speaking them as I write from Tyndale's book, *The Obedience of a Christian Man*.

The King is in the room of God in this world. He that resists the king, resists God; he that judges the king, judges God. He is the minister of God to defend thee. Let kings, if they had rather be Christians in deed than so to be called, give themselves altogether to the well-being of their realms after the example of Jesus Christ, remembering that the people are God's, and not theirs; yea, are Christ's inheritance, bought with his blood. The most despised person in his realm (if he is a Christian) is equal with him in the kingdom of God and of Christ. Let the king put off all pride, and become a brother to the poorest of his subjects.

Can you hear my voice ringing loud, dearest Anne, saying, we shall marry, regardless, for I am in the room of God, and no man on earth can prevent the dominance of my will?

32

Anne

My father, having returned from Rome, has conveyed to me a story that has buoyed my spirits. He brought with him to Rome a spaniel to give to the pope as a gift, hoping the gesture might help change the pope's mind about having Henry's case heard there. When my father entered the papal chamber, holding the spaniel, flanked by Emperor Charles and a bevy of cardinals, he refused to kiss the pope's foot, as was the custom for men who followed the God-fearing faith of Rome and all of Europe, excepting Luther's Germany. The pope raised his foot and demanded that my father show his proper respect; at which time the spaniel ran from my father's grasp and bit the pope in the very foot where he had preferred to be kissed. The pope cried out: This dog is a heretic. I do not want it. I shall keep him for myself, my father replied, for his act teaches us that a pope's foot is more likely to be bitten by dogs than kissed by Christian men.

The meeting did not go well after that, as might be imagined. While the pope's servants cared for his wounded foot, the pope dismissed Henry's case for a divorce, for it had no precedent in Christendom. My father offered an ultimatum. If denied a chance for a new marriage and a legitimate heir, England would declare its independence from Rome and the Catholic Church, and when King Henry married me, his daughter, its example would not fail to be imitated by other kingdoms in Christendom. The pope looked at Charles. The emperor looked away, seeing, my father believed, his kingdom engaged in a war with the infidels in Islam; the matter of his aunt's divorce a secondary concern. Pope Clement spoke one last time, saying his conscience condemned a union contrary to the laws of God. My father spoke for his king when he said: You, Pope Clement, are evidently ignorant of the laws of God.

He took his dog and left. When he returned to London, to continue his work as the vanguard of the secret church of God, developing and organizing a secret network of Lutherans, all of whom lived in the shadows, one step ahead of Thomas More and Cardinal Wolsey and the other fanatics of the old faith, he said to his friends: The little spaniel knew its mind when it bit the pope, understanding that living as a heretic in England is much preferred to living with the stink of the pope and all of Rome.

33

Henry

I believe more than ever I am in the room of God. Such evidence came to me as a miracle in the shape of man. When I returned to Greenwich from my recent progress, Stephen Gardiner and Edward Fox came eagerly to my privy chamber, telling me about a Cambridge colleague of theirs, who they made clear had a solution to my continued frustration to procure a divorce and marry Anne legally. You must meet this man, Your Majesty, they said. He is a cleric, a doctor of theology. His name is Thomas Cranmer. Listen to him, for if you do you are sure to say, he has the sow by the right ear.

He came, a sober-faced man, timid and soft spoken. Yet his words were anything but underwhelming as his appearance. I listened, on the edge of my seat, following the flight of his eyes and the music of his voice and the vision he painted in bright colors, wherein I commanded my own fate and that of England's. Do not look to Roman canon law, he said. Win the support of the theologians at the great universities. What right had the pope to command a divinely appointed king? The king is under God's authority, not that of Rome. So, am I to understand, I asked, that the pope's intervention is unnecessary? He answered as I had hoped. If the divines in the universities, men trained for such a task, give it as their opinion, based on correct interpretation of Scripture, that Your Majesty's marriage is invalid, then invalid it must be, and all that is required is an official pronouncement by the Archbishop of Canterbury to that effect, leaving Your Majesty free to marry.

I ordered him to set all other business aside and take pains to see my cause furthered according to his devices. He should begin by writing a treatise expounding his views and then writing an appeal to the appropriate academics in Europe. Produce for me arguments for the annulment, I implored him, and I shall grant you favors the likes of which you could have never imagined. As for lodging, he need not concern himself. I will send him to live and write in comfort in Thomas Boleyn's house at Durham Place.

He called himself my servant, my loyal subject, and quickly set off to do my bidding. As he left, I thought: There is something about this man. He is a man of God and an embodiment of Christ. As for the latter, I do not believe I am wrong, for he shall be my savior in my great matter. I have never had a stronger inclination in my life.

34

Katherine

It is the Feast of St. Andrew. He comes to me, finally, after a long absence, obliging me with his presence at dinner. I feel like a dog that has been thrown a bone. I tell him I live in purgatory because he shuns me. He does not go to mass with me anymore. He does not ride and hunt with me. He does not visit my apartments. Why should I? He says. I am not your legitimate husband. You have betrayed me, seeking your nephew's help, getting the case moved to Rome, where I will never go. You must understand that. He says he has men working on his case here and in Rome and Europe, finding evidence in support of his annulment, scouring the great universities and gathering opinions from the most learned scholars on the continent, including the illustrious theologians in Paris, all of whom are on his side.

You have paid these men to take your side, I respond. He says, I expect as much from you, for in your desperation you wish to diminish my cause, though know this, Kate: It will only gain strength because of comments such as those you say to me. I plan to present these latest esteemed opinions to the pope, and if Clement does not declare our marriage null and void I will denounce him as a heretic and then marry whomever I like. For I can sever England from Rome; I can win the divines here; I can do what I want.

At the risk of your immortal soul, I say. He stands, pushes his chair aside and responds, raising his voice: I am no longer intimidated by threats made to my immortal soul, either from you or the pope. Men more learned in divine law than him have told me my immortal soul is under the jurisdiction of God, not that of the pope or any other mortal man or woman.

I ask him to admit that he knew I was a maid on our wedding night. He says, Enough of that! It has already been proved that you were not. Proved by whom? I ask. By liars? By men who knew my brother intimately, he says. More than a dozen men. Are you saying they are all liars? Yes, I say, they are all liars, for someone, either you or Cardinal Wolsey, paid them to lie.

If you are so certain, why, then, won't you sign a sworn statement before God about not believing me when I said I was a maid? Enough! He says. Did I not say enough? It makes no difference now. What matters is that you and I were never married legally. According to whom? I ask. According to those who are expert in the field of theology and law, he answers.

I am beside myself with fury. I care not a straw, I stammer. I have studied the nuances of canon and divine laws just as you have and I can challenge you in a court of law if it were done fairly. If you give me permission to procure counsel's opinion in this matter, I do not hesitate to say that for each doctor or lawyer who might decide in your favor and against me, I shall find one thousand to declare that the marriage is good and indissoluble. He begins to walk away. It is a mistake to have dinner with you, he says. It shouldn't happen again. Go to your mistress, then, I say, though I understand she will never be queen, not as I am queen, not beloved as I am. She will always be known as the other woman, and you will never have peace, Henry, my husband, for the good people of England will rally for my restoration and she will be banished to France, where she and her haughty manners belong. Do you hear me?

By then, he is already gone, and I am left to rebuild my composure and the foundation of my married life, brick by brick. I shall never quit. Regardless of these disputes, my plea is not against him, but against the abettors and inventors of this divorce case. If only I could wrestle him away from Anne for a few weeks or two uninterrupted months, I could win him back for good, for I have faith in the natural goodness and virtues he possesses. Give me time with him, just the two of us, as it used to be, and I alone would be enough to make him forget what has happened. His counselors know this, especially Cardinal Wolsey. It is the reason they do not let me be with him. I would make him remember why he married me from the first, our royal bloodlines, our Christian faith, our discussions of medicine, theology and especially war, which I know above all other subjects he favors. What can his mistress discuss with him of this matter? She knows nothing. How could she, for she was just a babe, when I ruled as Regent in Henry's absence when he went to France to win back land, backed by armies sent by my father, when Spain and England were conjoined, not as now.

The people of this good country have not forgotten how I, their queen and leader, set out northward to join the war against the Scots, who on the persuasion of money sent to them by their French allies, decided to attack England, with the hope that in doing so Henry would cease his attack in France to return home. Not necessary, said I, for I possessed the heart and lineage to manage the war on the home front, as my mother once did, in full armor, going off to fight the Moors without my father. Why should I not do the same against the Scots? I sent money and provisions to the northern borders, along with artillery, gunners and a fleet of eight ships. Soon after, I sat atop a white horse, wearing a rounded, broad-rimmed shaped helmet and bearing banners with the arms of England and Spain, as well as those bearing the cross of St. George and the image of the Virgin Mary. Surrounded by trumpeters and the cheers of the English people, I left Greenwich as the designated captain and commander of the third line of defense. All along the roads of England people called my name, Queen Katherine, Regent Katherine, a stronger, more fearless woman there never was in England, our Joan of Arc.

The Earl of Surrey's army, the first line of defense at the border, routed the Scots near the Northumberland village of Branxton at Flodden Field. Among the Scottish dead, the king himself, James IV, husband to Henry's sister Margaret. I received from Surrey as a trophy James's coat of armor, which I quickly sent to Henry to inform him we remained strong at home, even in his absence. I wanted to send the dead king's body as well, though the Earl of Surrey refused me this request, believing the dead, even enemies deserve respect. I conceded, choosing instead to send my husband my proud words. To me, I wrote, it is the greatest honor that ever a prince had for his subjects in his absence not only to have victory but also to slay the king and many of his noblemen. This matter is so marvelous that it seems to be of God's doing alone. I trust you shall remember to thank him for it. He did thank God, as did I, when he returned and we visited the shrine at Walshingham, the abode of saints, where our Lady stands in the dark at the right side of the altar shining on all sides with gems, gold and silver.

I should take him there again, if I could, walking barefoot, the both of us, to the Lady's shrine, to remind him who we were, king and queen, conquerors of France and Scotland, humble servants of God above all else. He would like that. I know he would, there in the presence of the Lady, standing in the dark, though emitting light, wherein we both bask in the promise of our future.

35

Anne

The letters Henry wrote me, kept in my Greenwich apartments, are missing. I suspect Cardinal Wolsey took them. He works alongside Cardinal Campeggio and spies for the pope. Is not the debacle of the Blackfriars not proof enough? He has done everything to block my advancement and my growing religious influence on the king, and I can only imagine that what he hopes to find in those letters is evidence that I have been the king's mistress for years, proving, I suppose, that I am unfit to be his wife, that he will have to forfeit his plans with me, that he will have to take back his wife. Yes, if he and the pope can only prove that I am a whore of significant ill-repute, their justification to block the divorce and subsequent marriage would be that much greater. They will be dismayed to know that the letters reveal no such thing. Just the opposite, in fact. For they will find little but poems and songs of longing and unrequited love and excerpts of medical treatises and preventives. They will find that I have kept the king at bay, keeping my virtue intact, making clear that only in marriage will I give myself to him. Yes, they will learn everything about me they don't want to know, and they will have stolen without reward.

I have heard the cardinal calls me the night crow, a slight, I assume, on my dark complexion, or a backhanded compliment perhaps on my ability to fly at night, wherein he calls me as well the enemy that never sleeps. This I cannot dispute, for I shall not rest until I see his large shadow, long fallen across my path, laid at my altar, made small as any supplicant's. His demise is certain now that he walks on his heels, having failed the king yet again. Wait till Henry learns what my father has learned and what the Dukes of Norfolk and Suffolk, and other men at court, know as well, that Cardinal Wolsey has betrayed his country. First with oppressive taxes and disastrous wars, leading us into France when the emperor had already made a treaty with the French, placing England at serious risk. Then failing to win the king's divorce, hoodwinking Henry every step of the way, making clear that his only intention was to conspire with Rome, evident in his secret messages, wishing Katherine to remain as queen. The details of his conspiratorial acts are now being fleshed out and made to be reported, at which time he will not have an opportunity to call me further names. Is it any surprise then, desperate as he is, that he steals my letters, hoping to win the pope's praise and lay in the lap of his support and protection, far from the king's wrath when he learns of the cardinal's sinister practices?

36

Henry

He had to be sacrificed to the cause, hers, not mine, for I knew she wasn't the cardinal's friend, apparent in the persuasiveness of her words, which came increasingly to my ears, sharp and high-strung, stinging in their rebuke. Sir, she asked, is it not a marvelous thing to consider what debt and danger the cardinal has brought you in with all your subjects? How so? I replied. Do not be negligent of your senses, she said. Think about all the things he has done to slander and dishonor you and your realm. If any nobleman had done half so much, he would be worthy to lose his head. Yes, true, I said, yet still, should I just forget what he has done for me? Done for you? She snapped her teeth, as if to bite my ears. You sound like a child, speaking of his wet nurse, having nurtured him with life. Here's what he has done for you: He has allowed a foreign power to challenge English law. He has betrayed the very seat of power upon which you sit.

No, I replied. He has denied his involvement with Rome. He has sworn by God that there was nothing he desired more than nullifying my marriage to Katherine and advancing the cause of our marriage. She laughed derisively. Should the hen believe the fox as well when he says the day is bright and beautiful, come from your cage and have a look? No, sir, she should not, unless she wished to be eaten. Are you as gullible as to believe a man who dissembled the truth for a living? If he dissembled the truth, I said, it was to further his love for me and my reign. She unleased a storm of tears. Do you wish to choose, sir? For on one side sits the cardinal and on the other me. Make your choice. You shall not lie in bed with both of us. He must be arrested and brought to trial, made to face the many allegations against him.

So, it is done. I stripped him of his title, forcing him to surrender his Chancellor seal, taking from him his properties and possessions: York Place and Hampton Palace, his tapestries, beds and chests, tables and art treasures, vestments studded with gems and gilded candelabras, chalices and his heavy gold processional cross, which I melted into a fortune. I gave everything to Anne, hoping to appease her dissatisfaction with recent events that stall our plans to marry.

I sent the cardinal away, to live in Esher. He has written to me, pleading his innocence against all charges, asking: Did not Thomas Becket, an archbishop like me, stain the altar with his blood? I shall respond by sending him a cartload of furnishings to warm himself against the winter weather. I will not tell Anne, for I know what she will say. Let him freeze to death.

37

Katherine

Cardinal Wolsey is gone. Anne has taken his place in the performance of spying. She watches me, eyes dark, tongue poisonous. The serpentine enemy, the cardinal called her. We agreed on that, if nothing else. She does not like that the king has sent me some cloth to be made into shirts for him. She wishes to punish the gentleman of the bedchamber who brought me the material. I have sent a message to Henry: Did not this man do only what you yourself ordered him to do? I wait for his reply. Meanwhile, I cut the cloth and I sew, making shirts for my husband as I have always done and always hope to do. She is upset that he doesn't ask her to do the same. Why should he? I wish to say to her, though we do not speak. You are a plaything, a new womb, a promise that may never amount to anything more. I have borne the king children five times. It is not easy. Sometimes they die. You may learn that as well, and when you do, he will realize it is not me who is to blame for their deaths. It is God's will. He decides, not you, and not Henry.

She orders the king, though she is not queen. She tells him which of my ladies should stay and which should go. She replaces some with others. Her spies, I call them. For they watch and listen, though their teeth are not as sharp as hers and their eyes more hollow than deep. I can only imagine what they say when reporting back to her. The queen fasts and prays in the morning and at night, hearing mass in the afternoon. She cuts cloth and sews most of the day, except for brief interludes when she and her ladies summon musicians to play for them, wherein they dance and sometimes sing, both in Latin and in English. I hear her voice: What of her conversations with the new ambassador, he of Spain, called Chapuys? I speak Latin with the ambassador, I wish to tell her. A language neither you nor your ladies speak or understand. It is the language of Christians.

She hopes, of course, to intercept my messages to my nephew and the pope, hoping to find proof that the fantastic rumors of my desire to kill the king are true. Nothing can be further than the truth, for the messages I send to Rome have everything to do with how much I love the king; how much I wish to save my marriage and so much more, for I am aware of the terrible struggle into which Henry and I are about to plunge England. What will happen not only to us but to the form of Christianity that has been practiced for nine centuries? I ask God to forgive us for our sins, for they are many. We are not only ruining a sacred marriage but a sacred faith, which Anne disdains, evident in her Lutheran ideals and the heretical writings she reads. I know about them. I have spies of my own, and I have told Henry, though he wishes to turn a deaf ear to what I say. Is this not indicative that she has won him over with spells and charms, the devil's tools, for he, as everyone knows, me more than others, despises Luther and those of his sect.

Give me time with him, I have prayed to God. I can retrieve him. I have said the same to my nephew and the pope in letters I have written, though no word comes, and I grow impatient with worry. Order Henry to leave Anne until judgment is passed, I write, and do not tarry in your sentence. If you wait any longer, you will find that you have created a new hell that will be worse to mend than the one they managed to create so far. Henry has gathered an army of scholars, fast at work to prove the legitimacy of his claim. He wishes to hold a Parliamentary meeting and push for the divorce without waiting for a decision from you, Holiness. That is the rumor I hear, and I am fearful of it becoming true. Once you rule in my favor, though, it will be God's law, and Henry will not refute it. On the life of his immortal soul, he will not, for his immortal soul matters to him, despite what he has said about not fearing your excommunication of him. Hurry with your decision. Rule in my favor, for our country is already torn apart and suffering. The people of England do not want to lose their queen, their faith, their church, their pope, their God. Hurry, before it's too late, before he marries without legal consent, breaking the rib of Adam, hurling us all, including our faith, into the abyss. If you, Pope Clement, fail to administer justice you will never free yourself from me. Even from the bottom of hell, where I shall surely reside, I will shout so loud that God will not fail to hear my complaints against you.

38

Henry

He's a funny sort of fellow, that Thomas Cromwell, with his beady, inquisitive eyes and his honey tongue and dangerous intelligence. I'm not sure what to make of him. He came seeking audience with me under the pretense of desiring royal mediation in a private dispute. I didn't believe it. He's Wolsey's man, handling the cardinal's legal affairs and property transactions, things of that nature, though that was when the cardinal owned property and held a voice that mattered, well before he made treasonous decisions resulting in his banishment. I knew he came to plead for the cardinal's cause. I didn't have time for pretense, so I got right to the point, asking, So, how is he? To his credit, he didn't dissemble.

He answered, He cannot be well till he has Your Majesty's favor. I looked at his sober expression, nearly unmoving in the mouth and eyes and said, the charges against him are many, do you not know that? Forty-four charges to be exact, Your Majesty, he said, though there is an answer for each one, and if given a hearing we would make them. I knew if I had asked him to make them then and there he would have obliged me, so I said no such thing. I said instead, you have stayed loyal to your master. I appreciate that about you, sir. The cardinal has been nothing but kind and generous to me, Your Majesty, he responded. I owe him my allegiance, and if I can in any way assist him in his time of need, I wish to do that.

If only it were that easy, I thought. He had too many enemies, including the woman I planned to marry. He was lost to me, to all of us, and he would never return, though I wished not to say that to Master Cromwell. I, in fact, wished to change the subject, and I did. I remember well, Master Cromwell, when you, new to the Parliament—back in 1523 I believe it was—said, rather audaciously I might add, Your Majesty cannot afford a war with France. I would like to know if you still believe that. War was not affordable then, he said, and it's less affordable now. Taxes, Master Cromwell, I declared. Have you never heard of them? They shall break the country, he answered. What is the worth of a country if it doesn't support its king, engaged in a fight? A king, notwithstanding, Your Majesty, must consider the constraints.

What constrains me? I shouted. He was quick to answer: the distance, the harbors, the terrain, the people, the winter rains and the mud, the diseases, the plague, the lack of a stable interior, having only Calais as a stronghold. Should I then be a king who doesn't fight? Have you ever heard of such a one? Fight the battles you can win. Such as? The ones here in England, against waste and corruption. I am speaking of the monks, and I speak from experience, having witnessed it for myself. Go to a monastery and see for yourself the seven deadly sins manifest. The monks live like great lords, selling blessings to people too poor to buy bread. These monks are not scholars, as they profess to be. They exploit children, use them as servants, teach them nothing in return. They sell their worn-out relics to people lying to them that their souls will be saved, and they hold the almighty pen, writing a history that is full of propaganda and only favorable to the corrupt clergy in Christendom. Fight this war, Your Majesty. It is one you can win, and it will increase your power and decrease the power of Rome.

His demeanor and cocksure attitude bothered me, talking to me as if he were my tutor rather than my subject. Still, there's no denying I felt the pull of his talent. He could be useful to me is what I thought, taking care of the daily grind of administrative paperwork and the mess of detail in my struggle for a divorce. God knows, no one else in my council has been able to replace the Cardinal of York, whom I miss every day, despite the forty-four charges against him.

39

Anne

He desired an audience with me. I obliged him, for I wanted to see and hear for myself what possessed Henry to talk about little else but his new man, as he calls him, this Thomas Cromwell, whom he often quotes, who is right about this and that and everything and anyone, speaking interchangeably four languages, about the pope, the church, legal affairs, properties, taxes, monasteries, food supplies, trade and banking, about receiving more than we give, about procuring the annulment through means of Parliament.

I'm telling you, Anne, I listened to Henry say, the man knows. Though he is little to behold in sight, he delivers to the ears music. So, he is to take my place as the chief voice in your ear, I said. He is a man, an advisor, a council member, he responded. You are a woman and will soon be my wife. It is different. How so, different? I wished to know. Oh, please, he said, exasperated. Must we dispute even about this? He will help in every way imaginable, including finding a way for us to marry. Isn't that what you want? Shouldn't you be grateful? And he is of your mind, you must be aware of that. Your religious mind. Anti-clerical, anti-Rome, anti-pope, influenced by the humanist scholars, the radical thinkers. Would you not say that defines you?

And yet for all that I hear he does not smile, I say, even when he jokes. Is that true? I care not a fig if he smiles, he answered. He's useful to me. At what expense? I countered. He wishes to rise, certainly, and he has worked for years under the cardinal. Does that not arouse your suspicion? A man that clever must have motives. Watch him, that is all I say. Henry kissed my head and, leaving my chamber, said, with a smile: We all have motives, dearest Anne.

He enters my room while I sit with my sister and cousin. He excuses himself, asking, Did I interrupt your sewing? No, I answer, it isn't important. It isn't as if I am sewing the king's shirts, as Katherine does. I laugh. The muscles in his face do not move. Immediately, I don't like him, though I hear my father's voice, saying, Gain his trust and friendship. He is on our side, religiously speaking. The more, the better. Do you not agree? Yes, I agree.

I am not in the mood to entertain his central motive, which he makes clear after his preliminary apology. Madam, he says, since the lord cardinal was reduced, how much progress have you seen in your case? None, I answer, as he expects me to say, for he is a man who comes prepared, evident in what he says next. All the accusations against him are misunderstandings. No one knows the workings of Christian countries like him. No one is more intimate with kings. Erase these misunderstandings and restore him to the king's grace. He is the only man in England who can obtain for you what you need.

I smile at his unsmiling face. That is not what the King says. He says you and Dr. Cranmer are the men who can obtain what we need. Do you diminish yourself so much in order to elevate him? He answers: I am a servant of minor means compared to the cardinal. I wipe away my smile. Then why does the King speak so highly of you? I have learned well from the cardinal, he replies. Which is the reason I implore you use your influence on the king and see my mentor restored to his former position, for he is the only man who can deliver cleanly both a good verdict from the pope and the king's conscience.

And yet in two years' time he did nothing to facilitate their occurrence, I snap. Am I, right? That is not his fault, he says. I feel my back stiffen. Then whose fault, is it? Mine? The king's? Yours? Who should we blame? Someone must be blamed. You know that, Master Cromwell. He is not deterred. He continues his practiced speech, wanting me to dismiss those who have slandered the cardinal, saying they are the ones who deserve the blame for having obstructed my cause. Who are the slanderers? I ask. You know them well, he says, and continues before I have a chance to respond. The cardinal's desire is for the king to have his heart's desire, which is what we all desire, to see you and the king married, with the hope soon after to see an heir on the throne.

Then why does he write to Rome, to Katherine's nephew, to the pope? I ask. Why does he send out secret messages? He doesn't answer my questions. You were once the cardinal's friend, he reminds me. You must remember that. All the letters you wrote, endearing yourself to him, offering your friendship. Those letters are still on file. I have seen them. You sent him gifts.

Yes, that was long before he became an enemy to the king and the kingdom, I say. You are partial, Master Cromwell. You cannot separate your emotions from what is real. Therefore, you and I have little left to talk about on this matter. You may go. He hesitates. I feel the stab of his eyes. I stab back. Is your hearing good, Master Cromwell? He bows. Madam, I wish you all the best in your ascendancy. I smile and say: Do be careful as you leave, the stairs going down can be treacherous. He disappears, taking with him that inscrutable face of his, which I expect I will see often, especially in my dreams.

40

Henry

I heard from my representative in Rome that the pope has offered me a proposal. Take two wives, it would be best for all. I get my new wife, Katherine can still call herself queen, and there will be peace in Christendom. He can issue a special dispensation if I agree. I should like to ask him: Will my issue with Anne be viewed as legitimate in the eyes of the Church, in England, and all of Europe if I have two wives? If not, how then can I take seriously such a suggestion when you know my reason for marrying again and waiting long for your approval is to have a legitimate heir. If I wanted to marry illegally and have illegitimate heirs, I would have done so two years ago. I should have to tell him the taking of two wives in England is not as fashionable as it is in Rome, though Kate may not mind since she cares mostly about her title, evident in how her pride will not allow herself to be called lady or sister.

As for Anne, I can only imagine informing her that she is to be queen alongside the current queen, the three of us forever sharing dinners, sitting together during banquets and tournaments and sleeping in the same bed. She might poison me. She is capable, for she has been of late in a rage, chastising me for allowing Kate to make my shirts. I got rid of Wolsey on her account, I remind her. It is not enough she says. She wants him dead, for as long as he's alive he is a threat to her security. Shouldn't I be concerned? She wants Kate and Mary dead as well. How can I ever be queen, she says, when people insist on calling them queen and princess? The people in the streets call me a usurper and many worse names. If they were dead, I wouldn't have to usurp anyone, just replace them, and I wouldn't be anyone's mistress or whore. I would be Queen of England.

She doesn't like the Spanish. I can't say I blame her, but

wishing them all death by drowning in the sea, that is violently dramatic even by my standards. She frightens me sometimes the way she thinks and speaks. If I don't read her books, if I don't promise immunity to a faceless heretic living in France, she tells me it is because I don't love her. She has changed now that she lives with a household, as if she were already the queen. She is more demanding, always telling me what I should or shouldn't do. I am afraid of her temper. Kate never had a temper, at least not until I told her I wanted to divorce her. Too bad her womb and body are old. If not, she would still make an ideal wife. I should not think this way. It is not healthy, considering the tumult my wishing to divorce her has caused.

I shall inform my representative to tell the pope, thanks, but no thanks. His suggestion to take two wives is nothing more than his cowardly way of trying to back out of making a decision in my favor. He knows I have the support of most canonists and theologians in Europe, excepting Luther, who criticizes me for wishing to divorce my wife, though he himself has divorced himself from Rome and has married a nun. What a hypocrite! I don't need, nor do I desire, his support. As for the pope, I have remained patient and faithful with him, though I shall not be much longer, as long as he continues to allow Kate's nephew to pull his strings, for I do not wish to be left on a string of my own, dangling, without an heir, vulnerable to the sharp knives that can cut me down at any time.

41

Anne

My father, appearing to gasp for breath, though smiling warily, reads aloud from Thomas More's latest diatribe, *Dialogue Concerning Heresies*: *The most absurd race of heretics, the dregs of impiety, of crimes and filth, shall be called Lutherans. All evangelical women were foul prostitutes and Lutherans publicly copulated in their churches, defiling images of the saints and the crucifix to bespatter the most holy images of Christ crucified with the foul excrement of their bodies destined to be burned.*

Enough, I say. One day it will be him who is destined to be burned. By the will of God, my father responds. No, father, by the will of man. Surely not from the hand of the king, he says. He loves Thomas More. I shall make him un-love him, I say. That won't be easy now that he is Lord Chancellor. No, I say, and neither was it easy to dispose of the former Lord Chancellor. Yes, my father nods, but he was corrupt to the bone. Thomas More is seen as a scholar and an honorable man of faith. Which, as you and I know, father, is laughable, I say. He blames the sack of Rome on Luther's followers when it was, in fact, men hired by the emperor, his mercenaries, who did it. He is a bitter persecutor of good men and a wretched enemy against the truth of the Gospel. He is a madman, dressed in sanctimonious, self-righteous garments. Ask Thomas Hitton, his first victim burned at the stake for reading the Gospel in what the Lord Chancellor called the rude English tongue. Many believers have followed his death, and many more are imprisoned, having been spied on by his agents and informers, who raid houses, and accuse good, innocent people of crimes against God, the pope, and all of Rome; all of which is a result of the Lord Chancellor's frustration at not being able to find and reel in the man he really wants, William Tynsdale, who More himself has said is nowhere and yet everywhere.

When I am queen, I shall work fervently against him, to stop him from imprisoning men for doing what they should be allowed to do and will be allowed to do once proper laws are established. With the will of God, my father says. No, father, with the will of Henry. I have given him books to read, which I know has already influenced him to move away from Rome, and when he does, he shall no longer tolerate the fanatical practices of his Lord Chancellor. I am pleased to know that Dr. Cranmer, our chaplain, has done much to alter his thinking as well, having given him a newborn perspective. He is a wise and virtuous man, a forward-thinking theologian, one of ours, and soon to be one for everyone, if fortune will allow it. Let us hope Archbishop Warham is not long for this life, for he, like Cardinal Wolsey, has done everything to stall the divorce. He is another of the pope's men here in England. He is old and his ideas are tired. It is time for new men, such as Dr. Cranmer.

My father smiles. Do not speak too loudly these thoughts that live inside your brain, my daughter. They are dangerous. The king, whom you wish to influence, is a fickle man. Never forget that, even when you are queen. Do not worry, father, I say. He loves me and wants what I want. My father embraces me generously and leaves, taking with him More's book, which he promises to burn, far from anyone's sight.

I am left alone in the aftermath of this talk, though I am not finished with the thoughts inside my brain. We are at war, at the dawn of a new day. Cardinal Wolsey is gone; Katherine will follow and soon after Thomas More and most importantly the faith they have followed. The former Lord Chancellor was right. I am the enemy that never sleeps. I shall fly like the night crow that I am. I shall squawk and awaken the senses of this realm.

42

Henry

Already I have passed Parliamentary actions against priests, placing tighter restrictions on them, hoping to reduce their corruption and excesses. They are now banned from keeping shops or taverns. They cannot gamble or hunt and hawk or visit disreputable houses, and they shall be fined for committing gross and unnatural vices. These acts are just the start of those I shall propose to continue necessary reform. Anne is pleased. She says that as I am looking up and reaching, pulling down the pope and all of Rome, I am raising up England. I thanked her for the book, *A Supplication for Beggars*, that initiated my directives. I will, as she implores me, give the writer, Simon Fish, both he and his wife, immunity to return to England, for his words have opened my eyes to the need for what she calls the emancipation from the ravenous wolves in Rome, the priests who own a third of our land and resources. Why should this be, she asked, when you are in the room of God, not them? Hear these words while I read them to you, she said. Hear them and act upon them.

They have gotten into their hands more than the third part of all your realm. The goodliest lordships, manors, lands and territories are theirs. Besides this they have the tenth part of all the corn, meadow, pasture, grass, wool, colts, calves, lambs, pigs, geese and chickens. Over and besides, the tenth part of every servant's wages. And what do all these greedy sort of sturdy, idle, holy thieves with these yearly exactions that they take of the people? Truly nothing but exempt themselves from the obedience of Your grace.

I did not mention to her that Cromwell had already pointed much of this out to me. She wanted the full credit, and I wished to give it to her. I am learning that I must, in any way I can, keep her happy, when I know in fact that she is growing weary of the wait. I thanked her the best way I know how, showering her with gifts: furs and embroideries, velvets and linens and a French saddle. No more shall she say to me: You only give me gifts when you wish to make up to me when I am displeased. For she shall never be displeased again. I shall say to her, A new dawn is coming, Anne. Look up, see it, for it shows what we have long desired, to be wedded, in union, in love, building a dynasty with strong sons and sweeping aside the incompetence of the pope and all of Rome.

43

Katherine

Cardinal Wolsey is dead, Ambassador Chapuys informed me, having died while being escorted to the Tower to await trial for his alleged crimes. I should find pleasure in this news, for the cardinal had done much to discredit my name and reputation in making every attempt to separate Henry from me. I should forever hate him and wish his soul eternal damnation. Yet, I cannot allow myself to feel such thoughts, for I am not a vindictive woman. It is God's will, therefore, that I wish for mercy on the cardinal's soul. He did, after all, following his banishment from court, petition for my cause. He wrote to my nephew and the pope, hoping Henry would tire of Anne, hoping the king would return to me and save both my marriage and Christendom, hoping, above all else, that he would regain the king's favor.

Such is the sorry state of my circumstance that I am grateful for support any way I receive it, even if it was given for selfish motives. I have mercy for him because I know that Henry wishes me to, for he I know has mercy as well. It matters not what Anne whispers in his ears about the cardinal's deceit and betrayal. Henry loved him. He told me so many times, and he missed him greatly after his exile. This he also expressed to me. He never wanted to strip his title and banish him. It was Anne's doing. She is capable of so much harm and destruction. If only Henry would listen to reason. He doesn't though because he is not himself. He is confused. He may attain what he thinks he wants on this earth, but at what price? A time will come when he will wish to reconsider what he has done. For his sake, I hope it is not too late then. I pray for him every day. I shall always pray for him, for aside from sewing his shirts it is what I can best do for him now that I am denied his presence.

She is behind the new anti-cleric laws, for she forces Henry to read heretical books and speak with heretical men, such as Dr. Thomas Cranmer, whom Ambassador Chapuys says met with the king several days ago. He is a shadow, nothing more, a dangerous man, a Lutheran scholar come from Cambridge, the den of Lutheranism in this country; another ambitious man, with motives, who wishes to infiltrate the king's mind with seeds of destruction for the old faith.

My only solace is that Thomas More is now Lord Chancellor. He seeks to find forbidden books and hunt for heretics, to save our faith. He should spy on Anne, for she is but a fox in sheep's clothing. She has fooled Henry. She cannot fool me. Nor, I hope, will she fool the Lord Chancellor, who opposes the divorce. Though he serves the King, he serves God above all. He will not defy the pope. He will not defy me nor the Christian faith of which we have been raised and which we worship. He has sense and reason, and Henry respects him. These thoughts give me hope as I lay in the dark when the last of the candles have burned.

44

Anne

Cardinal Wolsey appeared, fumbling, bumbling, crying as the demons tugged at his crimson sleeves, poking him with their pitchforks, dragging his flabby-bellied flesh into the dark, cavernous underworld to meet his deserved fate. I did all a cardinal could do, he screamed, except honor my king and country, that is. Say goodbye to the world you cheated, the demons chanted. You're going to hell. Can I take my gold with me? The cardinal yelled a last desperate plea. No, they said. You cannot barter with the devil as easily as you can with the pope. Then what shall I do there? He asked. You shall roast like the pig you are. The demons laughed, tying the cardinal in ropes around his chest and legs. They pulled and dragged him as one would an animal, leading him to a dark curtained area. Here is your new home. What shall I eat when I am there? He cried. You shall eat your own flesh, the demons said. There is enough of it. But if I eat my own flesh I shall die, Wolsey pleaded. Yes, that's the point, they said. In hell, you don't die, you continue to eat your own flesh over and over for eternity and you vomit each time you do. And this is my reward for all I have done for My Majesty, my kingdom? The cardinal asked. Wrong, they said, it is not your reward. It is your punishment. Finally, they hurled the fat cardinal into the abyss. I clapped and smiled broadly at the masque, as did the others in my father's house, excepting the French ambassador, Claude la Guische, who looked grim and perturbed. My father and uncle had planned this performance for his benefit to demonstrate to him that the cardinal's reign was over, that his methods and influences belonged in the past, that he and my uncle were now the important court figures with whom the ambassador would now hold correspondence and negotiation.

Did you enjoy it, Anne, my father asked afterwards? I did, I said, revealing to him an interpretation which extended far beyond the cardinal's demise, for it was not difficult to see him as representative of the church the king had begun to despise. I told him I saw in the cardinal's journey to hell the descent of many more: the pope, the emperor, Thomas More, Bishop Fisher, Archbishop Warham, Katherine and her daughter, Mary, the Catholic Church, the corrupt city of Rome. What's missing, I said, is the aftermath. It's not enough to depict the end of the Catholic-Papal era in England. What's important is what follows. I want to see the skies open up. I want to see the banner of heaven, wherein I see myself seated beside King Henry on a throne of green and red velvet and silk tapestries, bejeweled with gems. I want to see and hear angels rejoice for the reformed religion and the freedom that comes with it. I want to see the future, father. Can you make an epilogue and show me that? Next time, he said, but first I shall have this one printed so that the sentiments expressed in it can be spread to many others at court. The king will be dismayed to see the cardinal sent to hell, I said. Perhaps, Anne, he responded, though the king does like a good laugh once in a while at the expense of others, even those closest to him. Including me? I asked. He left my side, forcing me to ponder my own question.

45

Henry

My savior, Thomas Cranmer, handed me a bundle of manuscripts, calling them *Collectanea Satis Copiosa*, saying they were texts drawn from old chronicles which demonstrated that the Bishop of Rome had no rightful claim to exercise spiritual supremacy over the universal church and that, certainly in England, the king enjoyed a plenitude of jurisdiction in all matters. I thanked him and wished for solitude to peruse the many pages. He told me I could expect to receive more manuscripts in the coming months, for he would work immediately on compiling his findings at universities in Europe, regarding my right of an annulment. As he left, he said, Only the Holy Spirit directs the royal conscience, Your Majesty. I smiled and quickly scribbled those words on paper the moment he was gone.

These documents bring me great pleasure, for they support everything I have always believed about myself and my heritage, drawn heavily on Geoffrey of Monmouth's *Historia Regum Britanniae*, the principal source for Thomas Malory's *Le Morte d' Arthur*, wherein I learned the stories about Arthur, the Round Table and the chivalric code, which, for me, is the very essence of English kinship stretching back to Roman times when kings exercised their power by consent of their subjects and not by permission of the pope, having no right to bow to papal authority without their consent. It was the popes who, with guile and deceit, over the centuries, usurped the power rightfully belonging to my predecessors, beginning in 1213 with King John who gave his royal supremacy away to the pope. Why should this one king's actions cause the rest of us to suffer the oppression of Rome for centuries to come?

I am thinking great thoughts. I can secure much more than my annulment. I can do what no king of England has done for hundreds of years, remake the custom of our country, wherein no one should be compelled to go to law out of the kingdom. Why should we be under fiscal or spiritual jurisdiction to Rome? My case is no longer a conflict over strained relations with the pope. It is now about stripping from him the authority which he has no right to claim. It is now a matter of principle, and I shall act on it immediately.

I will dispatch messengers to Rome to inform the pope that I have discovered ancient and inviolable proof that his holiness has no right of involvement in the issue of my marital arrangements. I shall tell him he is no longer recognized as the Vicar of Christ in the English Church. That role belongs to me and any king who at his anointing is gifted with the responsibility to exercise control of doctrine and liturgy.

The English people will thank and praise me as a pious ruler, one who righteously campaigned for reform of the church and in doing so moved our country closer to being the self-sustaining country it is necessary to be. I will erase from their minds their image of me as a selfish monarch who simply wishes to dispatch his wife. I have a destiny to fulfill, I wish to tell them. I hold in my hands the scalpel which will sever the muscles, nerves, veins and arteries connecting the English church to continental Christendom. This scalpel, this instrument, I call royal supremacy.

46

Katherine

The wrath of the king is death, Archbishop Warham said when I asked him to intervene on my behalf. Ask Cardinal Wolsey, if only he could answer from his grave. Ask Bishop Fisher, recently the target of a poisonous attack. Only his predilection to fast that evening saved him from sipping the deadly broth that killed two in his household. Punishment for being my ally? I inquired. That and his refusal to accept the king as supreme head of the church when all the other bishops did. The cook has been boiled alive, having admitted to sprinkling powder on the food that night, though it is believed that someone handed him the poison and instructed his actions.

It is not hard to guess who was behind the attempt to kill the bishop, I said. I dare not speculate and neither should you, Your Grace. Is it not Anne Boleyn, whom Ambassador Chapuys calls more Lutheran than Luther himself, she who supports heretical doctrines and practices, who is responsible for the spread of evil books at court, the principal cause of the spread of Lutheranism in this country, who with the devil's assistance is the originator and promoter of this wretched scheme to see me removed as queen? I must not answer, he said, for the walls have ears, and for the benefit of your safety and security, you, as well, should constrain your voice. Take the righteous, legal course of action. Appeal to the pope and your nephew. Attend mass, say your confession, look inward and speak to God. That is the proper role for you, a woman.

I dared to mention Elizabeth Barton, the Maid of Kent, who does not constrain her voice, speaking her fervent prophecies, saying the king shall lose his realm within a month if he follows through on his promise to divorce me, saying that in abandoning me, God would in return abandon him. Is she not a woman?

I asked the archbishop. She is not the Queen of England, he responded. She is a country girl, a nun, emboldened by her beliefs. She is innocent of the king's tolerance. Her voice will be her undoing. I have no doubt of that, and neither should you.

Then you, as a man, as archbishop of England, must be my voice, I said. Those who make war on me also plan to destroy the church, of which you are its caretaker, and possess its property. You must put a stop to them. I am an old man, Your Grace, he said. God and the pope have granted me my position, but now that your husband is both king and pope of England, empowered by Parliament, I have no jurisdiction to tell him what to do.

That does not stop others, I said. Bishop Fisher and Thomas Abel, my chaplain, who has told the court that anyone helping in the divorce is a traitor to God and the king. Why should you not join them? A chorus of voices grows louder with each additional voice.

He stood and faced me, his dull eyes nearly lifeless. Your nephew is the only one who can dissuade him from his actions, he said. I watched him leave, understanding what he meant, for Ambassador Chapuys had only recently used words to the same effect: Only an invasion by your nephew Charles will put an end to your troubles. Agree to it. If he receives such an appeal from you, he will act on it.

No, I told him. I will never betray my husband, even if it means my own death.

47

Anne

I drink wine, more than usual. I have reason. More than one, actually. First, the picture. How should I feel, react, to a drawing wherein I am standing headless beside the king, the letter *A* beneath me to make clear it is me, while Katherine on the other side of him is fully equipped from head to foot above the letter *K*? Such a drawing I found resting on a chair, in full view, in my private chamber. Who drew it? Who put it there? I should very much like to know, so that the treasonous perpetrator can experience what it's like to be headless. I would, in fact, like to be the executioner to see the head roll, to see the break of arteries on the neck, to see the blood spill from the person's life, to see the person dead to await a worse fate afterwards in the fires of hell, bloodless, faceless, without eyes and ears and flesh to hide her blackened soul, if it is indeed a her, as I suspect it is, for who else but a woman has access to my room?

I am feeling vindictive and vengeful, and I like the feeling. If my enemies—and there are many—believe such intimidation will deter my ambition, they are mistaken. I am resolved to marry the king whatsoever might become of me. I care not for an idle drawing, nor do I care for the false prophecies that abound from the mouth of that madwoman from Kent, who dares call herself a nun, warning me that if I marry the king, I shall destroy England and be ceremoniously burnt at the stake. Why should anyone believe her? She is a country girl, grown up in the provinces, without culture and education, seeking to appease her miserable life with an illusion of theology and God, which she manufactures each time she speaks. I have implored the king to have her arrested, to see her placed on a rack, to hear her squeal. How fast she would change her prophecies. But Henry says, no, she has too many followers, both in the church and among the people. I cannot risk a rebellion. I will invite her to court, sit down and reason with her, make known to her my mind and my good intentions. I will convince her to cease from any more grievous forebodings. I will do it my way.

Yes, his way, meaning the moment she leaves court she will resume her horrid prophecies, damning both of us to the abyss. He is too soft on women. Throw her in boiling water like the poisonous cook, I say. Throw the queen in with her and her daughter, and all the Spaniards, in fact, including the ambassador, that weasel Chapuys, that limping spy come from the south to do Katherine's bidding and the emperor's bidding and the bidding of the Roman Catholic institution which Luther calls Mystery Babylon and Calvin calls the Mother of Harlots.

When Henry anointed himself supreme head of the church of England, I felt as if I had gained Paradise, such was my joy. Now he needs to act like one who is supreme and not be bothered by the pope's bans and prohibitions, his idle threats — thou shalt not do this or that — losing sleep over them. He should listen to my father who told the papal nuncio that the king's council cared neither for the pope nor for popes in this kingdom. As for the emperor, he cannot harm you, I have said, and if he tries my father will have ten thousand men at the ready to meet their arms, and they will be defeated, roundly. Dare them to come here, I wish to say. Maybe you should, so we can finish this business once and for all, and I can rest knowing my head remains on my head, even in the artwork found in the court.

48

Henry

The wheels of the cart came to a stop, mud deep, nearly a foot. My servants pushed, to no avail. I yelled, push harder. Can't you push harder? They did, ten men or more, with every fiber of their strength and still the wheels wouldn't move. What am I to do? I screamed. At which time, I woke up, and for a moment, in that fragile space somewhere between the real and the unreal, I saw her standing in my room, defiantly holding four babies, all dead, in her arms, while the small, living girl stood beside her. It mattered not that I suffered delirium. I spoke to her just the same.

Submit, Kate, I pleaded. Just submit, please. Think of the good that will come of it. Though you and I will no longer be married, the greater marriage of England and Rome will stay intact. I will gladly surrender my title supreme head of the church of England. I will be your nephew's slave and a chum to the pope. You will be my sister, my guest of honor whenever you like, sitting beside me at banquets. Bring Mary with you. We can, the three of us, spend time together, feasting, singing and dancing, just like we had when she was young. We can ride and hunt and hawk and attend mass and say confessions, side by side. We can celebrate every saint and every holiday. We just won't be married, that's all. Still, you will live well, like a queen, though you will no longer hold that title, residing in the finest mansions in my kingdom. Just choose which ones you want, they are yours. I'll even sign that sworn statement you've been wanting me to sign, acknowledging that I knew you had never before been touched by man on our wedding night. I'll do that, give you back your treasured maidenhood, in return for your submission. What more can I do than that? Let us move forward. Isn't it time? Four years is a long time to suffer in strife. Do we not deserve peace, finally? Submit, Kate. I just want to remarry. It's not the great crime you and all of Rome and most of Europe make it out to be.

I could not sleep the rest of that night. My mind raced with excited thoughts. I will appeal to her again, one more time before I move forward with an action sure to shake the world. I will leave it up to her. I will ask her to look beyond herself, to see the ramifications for her daughter, her safety and security, for the relationship between Rome and England, for the survival of the church as she has known it. I will ask her to search inside herself. Look beyond, look ahead. It will only end badly if you don't. You have control. You can end the madness. You can solve the rift and be a savior, not a destroyer. I know you think I am a destroyer, but I am trying to build, not destroy, but if you leave me no choice, I will destroy, and you and Mary and the pope and your nephew and Rome will be left in the rubble. Think about that. You can prevent that from happening. You can surrender to my cause. You can obey my will, your husband. Why should that be so revolutionary? It is normal and healthy for a wife to obey her husband. By obeying me, you are obeying God. Think of it like that. Think of God, think of your daughter, think of the Christian faith. Put all of that before your own needs. Do that and all of our lives will be better, the world will be better.

I wish to tell you all this to your face, but I can't. You will look at me with your woeful eyes. You will beseech me with your words. You will threaten my immortal soul, so I am sending others in my place. Receive them well. Listen to them, and act accordingly to their wishes, which are mine. If you do so, I will always respect and honor you as my sister, and your daughter— yes, mine as well—will always be loved and cared for as if she were still a princess, which, of course, she would no longer be. Do the right thing, Kate. For the sake of our lives and the lives of so many more.

49

Katherine

They came late at night. The Dukes of Suffolk and Norfolk and many earls and bishops, too many to count, though the number surpassed twenty. My, I am astonished to be surrounded by so many powerful men, I said. They bowed, each one of them, doing their due diligence. Norfolk spoke first. The king had sent them to express his displeasure and hurt at the contempt with which he had been treated on her account by the pope, summoned as he had been by public proclamation to appear personally at Rome; a strange measure never before enforced by the popes against the kings of England. Strange measure indeed, I replied. Nearly as strange as a king of England divorcing his wife to marry another. I looked for smiles among the many faces, though none appeared to acknowledge my wit. Norfolk's eyes grew more severe. You can never make the king leave his kingdom and should accept his invitation to have the case heard elsewhere. Otherwise, you might be the cause of great troubles and scandals throughout the kingdom, by which all present, our children, and the rest of our posterity might be thrown into great danger and confusion. Consider, Your Grace, you have been treated honorably as queen. You must now accept that the king is recognized as the supreme chief and sovereign in his own kingdom both temporally and spiritually. As such, you must know that he cannot go to Rome. Therefore, give up this case and submit your will to your husband.

The king, I said, did in the first instance appeal to His Holiness. All I have done is carry it to its logical conclusion by seeking justice. The rest is up to the pope, who, it appears to me with his constant delays, seems to be remarkably partial to the king. The pope's prompt sentence is necessary for the repose and example not only of this kingdom, but also of Christendom at large.

While I willingly recognize my husband as my master and acknowledge him as the chief ruler of temporal affairs in England, I must caution you that the church has only one true sovereign. That is the pope. If any of you wish to argue the king's case, I invite you to pack your bags and set off for Rome. After all, did not my husband, in front of everyone at Blackfriars, give me permission to appeal to Rome? It was in pursuance of the said royal permission that the cause was advoked to Rome, and on it I found my right. None of you can dispute that.

What we can dispute, Your Grace, said Norfolk, is how you have tried to rush the pope into passing sentence. I looked at the duke and all the men, wishing them to know the sincerity of my heart. Had you experienced one half of the hard days and nights I have passed since the commencement of this wretched business, I said, you would not consider it too hasty or precipitate on my part to wish for, and try to procure, the sentence.

The Bishop of Lincoln grumbled before he stepped forward and spoke. He called me a concubine, saying God had punished my unlawful marriage by making me sterile. My maidenhood, he added, was a lie that they could easily disprove. Yes, I responded, disprove with lies of your own, and we all know that ten lies can seem greater than one truth, but it is not, not in the eyes of God. You might remember that I signed an oath before Cardinal Campeggio, swearing to the truth of my maidenhood. My husband refused to sign the same oath. Why, I ask? Because he knows that I am telling the truth and that he is lying. He knows I was a maid on our wedding night, and he does not want to falsely sign an oath before God. Shouldn't that be testament to my truth and honor?

That is a moot point that the king no longer wishes to discuss, Norfolk said. What he wants above all else, Your Grace, is your obedience. Can you give him that? I reminded the duke that while he and the rest of them were subjects to the king, I remained his wife and held the title of queen. As for who I must obey, I said, God, my soul, and my conscience. Tell him that, though I believe he already knows.

Now, if you don't mind, I must get to sleep. I wish to have a clear mind in the morning when I hear mass, say my confession and pray to God that the men of England, such as yourselves, great nobles in the land, will discover compassion in your hearts for one who has labored long as your queen and wishes to die in that labor.

50

Henry

She dismissed the delegation I sent, sending them back to me with their tails between their legs and their tongues tied to the backs of their throats. Perhaps I should send an army to her rooms, with trumpets, cannons and swords, to fight an all-out battle. Even that would fail, I am sure, for Spanish blood does not flow; it congeals into something rock solid and impenetrable. I now realize I must decide the whole affair by other means.

She tells me Mary has written to her, complaining of stomach pains and unremitting headaches. She wishes to see her mother and father. Can I invite her to Greenwich to spend time with us? No, I will tell her. I wish not to spend time with the two of you. If you wish to see your daughter, do it somewhere where I am not, and since I reside sometimes at Greenwich that is not a good place for your meeting.

I must not let Anne know of this business. She does not like to hear the name Mary. When my daughter last visited court, I made the mistake of praising her dancing in front of Anne. That night she wanted Mary dead, for she believed Mary—the way she looked at her—wanted her dead. I tried to reason with her, saying she is just a girl, fifteen years of age, excited to show off to her father, but Anne would not hear it. Mary didn't belong at court, especially where Anne resided. It was bad enough the queen still showed her face. She would not tolerate the two of them in the same place. Was that clear? Yes, it was clear, I responded, wishing to change the subject to something she might like, such as Dr. Cranmer's update on his book called *Determinations*, a compilation of evidence gained from universities to ensure a favorable verdict in my much-desired annulment; such as the latest book Anne is reading from across the channel, though it is surely banned; such as her choice of tapestries and furnishings in the new apartments at York Place, where she hopes to erase all former traces of Cardinal Wolsey, who lived there for nearly twenty years, and where Katherine doesn't come because she isn't invited.

Even these topics did not appease her. She wished to say that Katherine is spreading libel, calling Anne a deviant, a predator, creating a false impression of her. She wanted to know what I planned to do about it. I fear what may be my only course of action, war against Charles. I am informed he told his brother Ferdinand to avoid a war with Germany, for he may have to go to war with England to support his aunt. Imagine going to war to fight for the right to marry whom I please. I can only hope that once we are married, Anne will temper her mood.

51

Anne

He said, I am on my way to becoming absolute monarch and pope in my own kingdom and yet I am the subject of your rage each time we talk. Do not expect me to tolerate your temper much longer. You are under great obligation to me, for I have offended everyone and have made enemies everywhere for your sake. What about me? I answered. Have I not sacrificed and suffered as much as you? You know nothing of the danger I endure from those who do not know, calling me your concubine, your goggle-eyed whore, wishing to kill me. Nonsense, he said, no one wishes to kill you. It is your fear, nothing more, having seen a meaningless drawing wherein your head was missing. I am not afraid of a drawing, I said, and it is not a general fear to which I refer. You should know I don't scare easily. You yourself have called me a lioness, have you not? It wasn't me, he said, it was the Spanish ambassador, Chapuys, who called you a brave lioness. Then why should you say it is my fear, nothing more, only two days removed from a very real threat to my life? I should hardly say that women carrying brooms and sticks threatened your life, he answered, suppressing a smile.

It was more than brooms and sticks, I said. Some had knives. They wished to kill me, I tell you. He remained skeptical. How can you say that when you never saw the women? You only heard they were approaching the manor where you stayed. Yes, I said, thousands of them, come from the streets of London once word leaked out in whose house I resided. I had become accustomed to people calling me names, ridiculing me and dishonoring me in every way possible, but I never thought it would result in violence against me. If I had stayed where I was instead of quickly slipping across the river in a boat, they would have broken the door down, dragged me out and would have beaten me to death or done much worse. What can be worse than being beaten to death? He asked, still smiling, still not taking the threat against my life seriously. What's worse? I repeated his question, feeling the veins in my neck pulse. To be hanged and then burned, as the prophecy says as that an English queen will meet her death. Now, do you believe me?

He laughed, lightheartedly. You are safe, my dear, for you are not yet queen. I slapped at him. And I shall never be queen as long as you fail to act as one who is the supreme head of the church of England. You promise to separate from Rome, saying, I care not a fig for the threats of excommunication the pope makes. You promise to have your case decided in Parliament, and yet each day that passes and you do nothing you only confirm that you do not have the backbone to sever yourself from the pope. If you are king, then be king. Show the pope, show the world, and show that damn woman who persists in calling herself your wife. Otherwise, find yourself another goggle-eyed whore.

52

Katherine

I stand near the open window, Windsor Castle, summer, 1531.
Henry is gone, having left with Anne and his court. Mary, beside
me, tries to cheer me. He shall return, mother. I say nothing. It
has been four days since their departure, four days that I have
been looking at an empty landscape, where even the blades of
grass are still and the leaves lifeless on the trees. I see no horses,
no men in slow or fast gallop, no chasing dogs. I see nothing,
not even birds, as if he took them as well. Mary, bless her heart,
takes my hand as I stand in silence, in recollection and reflection.
At least I have her, I remind myself. She and I ride during the
day; we hunt and hawk, and later dine, sew, read, and pray.
We attend mass, say our confession, walk in the gardens and
speak very little, only that I love her father and her father loves
her. I want to believe her, that he shall return, though with each
passing hour, with each setting sun and each dark-encompassing
night, my intuition tells me otherwise.

He did not say goodbye. He left a note only, *we are gone
to hunt*, brought to me by a woman of my house. He did not
mention four nights or length of time. I know only that he does
not normally take his entire court when he hunts. He normally
returns by nightfall or the following morning. I am worried, and
I cannot easily dismiss the feeling. I send messengers to find
him. I write notes and letters. Come back, I implore. Come back
to your wife and your daughter. We are your home, as sure as
God is our home. Do not alter what God has decided. Do not
allow that woman to bait you like a Spanish bull. You are a man,
not an animal rushing at life with horns. If I disobey you, it is
in obedience to God's will and to my conscience, and you know
I cannot betray either one. Know only that I am your wife. Are
not the babies I bore in my womb, five times, proof? Do not act

in spite because God decided to take our son Henry when only nine weeks old and the others that did not live beyond their births, now resting in heaven. Do not say that God brought their deaths, as punishment for our sins. You cannot mean that, and if you do, have you considered what further punishment He will send you for discarding your true wife and marrying against His laws and His will?

She will never give you a male heir. Heed my word. A union with her will bring a blight to all of England and your realm and more importantly damage your eternal soul. Come to your senses. Come back to me, your lawful wife, who has done little else than serve you for twenty years. Come back to your daughter. See her for who she is, a princess, an heir to the throne, if you would only allow yourself to accept it. My mother, as you know, ruled in my father's absence. Why shouldn't our daughter? You yourself have remarked since her birth on her intelligence and beauty, unparalleled in any child in all of Christendom. You say a woman has never ruled in England. I say, set a precedent. She is, after all, the blood of kings and queens from both sides of the sea. Who better than her to be the first?

Come back. Have your hunting progress, have your mistress, have as many as you like, as long as you drop your case for divorce, for you are my legal husband, and no Act of Parliament can change that, for God Himself decreed our union, and no man can change what God decrees. If I have said this before, both to you and myself, it is because I must say it, for without it I lose hope, and I don't want to lose hope. I want the sky to open. I want God to reach down and pull you from wherever you are and deliver you back to me, back in time, when we were first wedded in 1509 at St. Paul's, happy in our union and excited for life and lives to come as king and queen of the greatest realm on earth. I realize God doesn't intervene in such a way. Just the same, I dream of such an occurrence because it is better than my nightmare, without your presence near my side.

I shall await your response the only way I know how, with patience and love and with an indomitable will to endure. If you do not respond to my message and return to me, you shall leave me no recourse but to seek assistance from my nephew who has the means to persuade you, whereas I, a woman, have none.

53

Henry

That's it, I've reached my breaking point. Go ahead, Kate, write to your nephew all you want, it makes no difference. I will not be intimidated by your threats. How dare you say I leave you no recourse? If it's recourse you want, have this. You leave me no recourse but to remove you immediately from Windsor. Pack up your household, all two hundred people or however many you have serving you. You're headed to Hertfordshire, Wolsey's old place, the More, with its long galleries and bridges extending over a moat. It's the price you pay for being defiant and disobeying me and having the audacity to write, you shall leave me no recourse. See how you like being surrounded by water. I can only imagine what you'll write to your nephew. Send me a note and let me know. Correction, don't send me a note, ever again, unless it's one that states your resignation to your cause. Unless it says simply, I drop my case to have the trial heard in Rome, I consent to the divorce, you are right, I am wrong. Send that, and I will read it. I'll even pin it on my wall and enshrine it with flowers and jewels.

The storm has arrived, Kate. I am not returning to you. Get used to that. I know what you're thinking. How could he leave me without saying goodbye? What man would sneak out the back door after twenty years of marriage? Know this, I tried to talk sensibly to you, for four years. I appealed to you reasonably and could not have possibly made my argument clearer. I am tired of your messages and your beseeching and imploring. They belong where you belong, in the yesteryear. You can fight my leaving all you want, but it will do you no good. It's real, Kate. Anne will be my new queen, though you say it will be over your dead body. Be that as it may, over your dead body or your exiled body, but it will happen. It's already happening.

We're off hunting, enjoying the countryside, riding and dining and making plans for the future.

You leave me no choice, Kate. You could have relented and saved us all from the hardship sure to come. For you, for me, for our daughter. You haven't considered her, have you? Well, now you will have to because as of this day you can no longer spend your days and nights with her. She is to be removed and sent to Richmond until such a time when you comply with my demands. Write as many messages to her as you want. But spare me the details. I wish to return to Windsor, with the woman I love, to go hunting and to eat and drink and try my best to be happy, though I can't and won't be until I wed Anne Boleyn and begin the process of fathering heirs; something you promised me many years ago, taking as your device the pomegranate, symbol of fertility. Well, it didn't work, Kate. You didn't fulfill your promise to me. I am a king. You know how important it is to me to have heirs. If you really loved me, you would let me go instead of clutching at me like a creeping vine. It's selfish of you, Kate. Everyone says so. A king without heirs is nothing, and don't you dare tell me Mary is an heir. That's a joke. She's a girl, enough said. I need boys. If you couldn't give me them, you should be understanding that I need to get them from someone else. Anne is that person. Let go, Kate. Do it for the sake of my realm and for posterity. Perhaps if I reduce your household and your expenditure as you look out over the moat in the damp and chill of an old Manor house it will happen sooner than later.

You will call me cruel. It is like you to deflect responsibility, to say it is I who has made a mess of things, wherein the truth is evident to all who view the situation objectively, which you, of course, cannot, having been raised a princess, sheltered from what's real.

54

Anne

I'm hopeful now we have seen the last of her annoying messages. When will you return, dearest husband? Your beloved daughter Mary and I are sad without you. I am worried, as well, for your health. Are you caring for that wound on your leg? Are you taking your preventives and purgatives for your colds and fevers and frequent headaches? I am surprised she didn't ask him to send her shirts to mend. I should like to tell her, from this point forward I will mend his shirts. Though I will have no such communication with her, and neither will Henry now that he has finally listened to me. The time for negotiation is over, I said, filling for him a goblet of wine. She has blocked every reasonable course of action that could have benefitted her and us. Therefore, do not answer her silly notes again, unless it is to inform her that she is to be sent away, which is the course of action I suggest. Remove both mother and daughter from Windsor and make sure to separate them.

To which he put his goblet down, removed his cap, wiped his brow and said, Separate? That will kill them. Better them than you and me, I said. Do you not agree? He grew silent, except for repeated sighs. Do you want to live? I asked. Do you want to ensure the survival of your realm? If they are exiled together, do you not know that they, with ties to the emperor, will plot and scheme against you? Yes, yes, he nodded, you are right, dearest Anne. I shall have Mary transferred to Richmond, and I shall have Katherine and her household sent to another manor. Another manor? I inquired. Though I wished to say, send her back to Spain from whence she came, back to her pomegranates, though I hear they have grown rotten, which is what happens when they are not picked and eaten. Let her pack with her the Spanish ladies and gentlemen of her house as well and whatever mules she still possesses. Let us become English to the core again, which is what we will be when I am queen.

I shall have to think on it, he mumbled. Think no further, I said. Send her to the More, Cardinal Wolsey's former place in Hertfordshire. Did we not stay at that horrid place for a night while on progress last year? She shall like the quiet of that manor, with its bridge and moat, its damp stone walls and floors that creak at the slightest touch and windows that moan against the unremitting wind. Reduce her household and expenditure. Make her experience what it's like to live the life of a commoner since she prides herself in being close to them. See if this new living situation doesn't soften her resolve. If nothing else, make her aware that times have changed.

He reached for his goblet of wine and drank lustily, as a king should. Very well, he said. I know best that if I don't give you what you want, I will never get what I want.

It is God's will, I said, stopping short of saying, with my influence.

55

Henry

She complains, preferring, she says, to be locked away in the Tower. I know why she says this. I know how she thinks. She wants her supporters to realize the notorious misfortune that has befallen her. She wants them to know I am mistreating her, wherein they will rally to her cause, wherein I will relent to their rallies and release her from her purgatory, the word she chooses to use, as my informers tell me. If I were talking to her, which I'm not, I would say, don't you realize I never knew a supporter who couldn't be drawn to my side with royal offerings, like hawks to the lure? Who are your supporters anyway? Mostly drunken farmers and animal herders who know not the alphabet. Let them do what they do best, shear sheep and tend crops, if there are any left after the deluge of rain, which, as I hear from superstitious naysayers, is due to my abandonment of her. If that's the reason, I say, rain on, for I am not going to un-abandon her, though I don't like the word abandon. I prefer separation. In any case, why should I fear rogue warriors, field mice of no consequence, wielding pitchforks and shovels, knee-deep in mud? I have a greater interest, to defeat her at her stubborn game, of which I can play just as well, for I don't like to lose, be it at jousting, riding or annulling.

Now that she has had time to absorb fully her purgatory, she should understand that pride goes before a fall. I should tell her, consult Lucifer, who defied God. Where did it land him? In a place much worse than purgatory. Let that be a lesson I should wish to say. The master is always right, be it God or king, whether the subject is angel or queen. I am not vindictive, though. I will offer her another chance at redemption, at leaving purgatory and returning to heaven, which is what I call my good favor. If she submits, that is. I am certain, this time, she will. Who would choose to stay at the More if she had a choice to leave? I stayed there for one night and have been brushing off cobwebs ever since. I will send envoys to her, instructing them to give her every opportunity, in her weakened state, to cease her resistance to the divorce. Only if that doesn't reap the desired result should they put a stronghold on her, wherein they should threaten her with a worse fate than purgatory, for I can suggest many a place in England that is hell.

I hope it doesn't come to that. Even a proud Spaniard must possess a breaking point, though in the more than twenty years I've known her I have yet to discover it. I pray the More has softened that pride, for her sake as much as for mine and Anne's. Peace is needed for all of us, including her, whom I do not wish to harm. Nor do I wish to make Mary more miserable, suffering as she is from mysterious ailments. I am accused of using her as bait to reel in her mother. That is what I hear from my informers, who have their ears among the people of London. What nonsense, I should say. I have raised her as a princess, providing her the best tutors, households and manors. How then should she be called bait? If she should be harmed by this business, it is to her mother one should look and point the finger.

I do not call using my daughter bait. I call it using common sense. Kate may sacrifice herself to purgatory and even hell, but she will never sacrifice her daughter's health and welfare. If I know anything about the woman I called my wife for eighteen years, it is this.

56

Katherine

I received the envoys the way I received everyone, in full view of my ladies and gentlemen, for I would not suffer as a lone wolf. My howl must be heard. The four men were unknown to me, and when they bowed before me, I joked: Only four of you? Where are the other twenty? One of them straightened himself and quipped, Pardon, Your Grace? I forgave his ignorance, for he wasn't one of the more than twenty men who had stood in my apartment at Greenwich. How is the king? I asked. Your Majesty is well, was the reply. You are here, I assume, sent by the king to further test my resolve, to see if I have weakened, captive now three months surrounded by water. I will admit that it is enough to weaken anyone, but I am not anyone. I am Queen of England. I do not wilt easily. I, in fact, do not wilt at all. I hurt, yes, and I suffer, though Christ suffered much worse trials. I remind myself of that every day, and it gives me the strength needed to endure. If necessary, I will die as he did, upon a different cross but a cross nonetheless. I am prepared. Now, what is it you gentlemen have come here to speak with me about?

As if they were performers in a masque, all four knelt, perfectly synchronized, in uniformity, before me. Which one spoke I could not tell, for their heads remained bowed, according to the art they had practiced. Your Grace, we are sent by the king to implore you, to consider what is at stake. The kingdom's peace and the king's honor, not to mention your daughter's welfare and your own comfort.

I refrained from applauding their effort. I instead joined them, kneeling with them, though my words relied less on rehearsal. I demanded first that they lift their heads to meet my eyes. This they did begrudgingly, for it was clearly not part of their script. For God's sake, I said, and out of respect for Christ's blood and suffering, I ask of you men, loyal to the crown of England, that you persuade the king to return to his lawful wife. If he refuses, implore him then to allow God, through the pope, to decide what must be done. Do you not see how he has wronged me, I who have not offended him in any way? I beg of you, put him on the right path and save him from himself, for he is lost and does not know it.

I was close enough to the men to feel their breaths and smell their sweat and hear the swallow of their throats. They rose to their feet as if they were conjoined, as one body. Clearly, they were of one mind as well, and that mind was the king's. The words were as well, for these men were hollow to the core, spineless, without wills of their own, full of air, heavy with pretense, the king had blown into them before they left London. Thus, I wasn't surprised by the threat that followed. If Your Grace dislikes the More, consider that His Majesty can move you to a smaller, more remote house or even to an abbey. I rose to my feet to meet their threat with one of my own. Tell the king he can send me wherever he wants, or if he so desires he can burn me at the stake. Neither action will change my position. God has made me queen, and only He or the pope, acting as God, can take away my title.

Think of your daughter, Your Grace, came a voice of malice. The king wishes not to see her suffer for the sake of your principles. If she becomes a martyr, as I, I shouted, then it is God's will, or the king's, not mine.

57

Anne

My great aunt, the Duchess of Norfolk, came to see me. A matter of great importance, she said. Your uncle Thomas says the king comes to him with complaints about your temper, always blaming him for everything that does not favor you. Your uncle did not want to bring the issue up to you for fear you would argue with him, as, he said, you often do. He cannot understand how you shouldn't be content. Katherine is gone to the More. You now occupy the Queen's rooms at Greenwich and possess refurbished apartments at York Place. You have maids, servants, tapestries, embroideries, furnishings, horses, dogs, falcons, clothes, jewels and unlimited expenditure. What could you possibly want more? You must desist in this behavior, Anne. You will be the ruin of our family.

Ruin of our family? How so? I asked. If I do not become queen, neither you nor uncle Thomas nor any of the Howard progeny will see advancement? Is that how I am to be the ruin? I am not your means to an end, great aunt. Tell that to uncle Thomas as well, for I wish not to see his hypocritical face, he who beats his wife and keeps her locked away, a prisoner in her own home, while he administers to his mistress. Should you not say his behavior will be the ruin of the family? Foolish girl, she spat, you know not what you say. He is a man, and as such he lives under different standards. We women must guard our behavior as we guard our chastity. You are guarding that, at least, aren't you? It is your most effective weapon, and you know it is. Leave my business to me and tend to matters which concern you, I replied. You are a Howard, she said, and as such what you do concerns me. Why did you dispute with the king about a present he received? Wishing not to divulge that matter with her, I excused myself from her presence.

Why the king chose to tell uncle Thomas angers me, especially since Henry's behavior that day was unbefitting of a commoner, no less a king. When I learned that Katherine had sent him a gold cup for the Christmas holiday, I asked to see him. When he walked in my privy chamber, I said I knew about the gold cup and demanded that he return it. He said it would cause little harm to keep the cup, for he would put it away and not use it. No, I said, you must send it back. By keeping it, you encourage her.

I do no such thing, he said. Is it not enough that she is exiled to the More? You have the Queen's rooms and a large household. You live like a queen, is it not enough? No, it is not enough, I declared. If I live like a queen, it is only an illusion, for I am not yet queen. If I was, I would sit by your side when you entertain the French dignitaries, but I cannot do that because the French king disapproves of me. I am called a concubine in France, your mistress, nothing more. Why, therefore, should I be appeased by possessing the outward trappings of a queen when I am not one, and may never be one?

Fine, he said, I will have the cup returned to her, but only if you send back the gifts Thomas Wyatt has given you. I know not what you mean, I said. Oh, yes you do, he said. I see the way he looks at you, now that he has returned to court. Give back what he has given you. What shall I give back, I replied, if I have never received his gifts. Oh, but you have, he insisted. Look in your heart, for it is there you will find them. I know about the two of you before I became your new paramour. Suffolk told me. How should the duke know anything? I asked. Wyatt confided to him, he answered. And you would believe a poet? I responded. He lives in imagination only, always chasing after what he cannot have. I am dismayed that you don't believe me. His voice rose. Yet you told me not to believe Katherine when she claimed her maidenhood before her marriage to me. I am not Katherine, I said, I am a maid. His face reddened. Yet you lived in the French court. I lived with Queen Claude, I said, the most pious woman in France. Who was married to Francis, he shouted, the most lecherous man in France.

I stepped away from his rage. I will not dispute any longer with you on this subject. I rejected Thomas Wyatt. He was a married man. He grabbed my arm. As I am, he said. I pulled his hand away. Yes, as you are. He walked to the door, saying, I shall spend Christmas festivities with the French dignitaries, entertaining the new ambassador.

I shall spend Christmas alone, I said, though I have a hundred waiting on me day and night. I have raised you up, Anne, he said, leaving. I ran to the hall and shouted: You still have higher to raise me, Henry.

58

Henry

The beginning of this year, 1532, in the realm of Your Majesty, bodes well, Cromwell began. Why should a foreign bishop share a king's God-given power? The time-honored deference paid by kings to popes is no longer relevant. England is an autonomous realm. Rely upon your Parliament, which can and will, with my advancement, pass this, that and the other against the clergy, sapping their strength and infusing their former power into yours, making it grow as a tree, firmly rooted, branching into the future, whereupon your progeny will grow likes leaves and drop their saplings for years to come.

Less poetry, man, I said. Give me specifics. Which he dutifully did. Break the resistance of the opposition to your new order. Put in place legislation that will cut revenues to Rome. Deprive the pope of the first fruits of all English benefices. Possess the ecclesiastical courts. Give yourself complete authority to appoint archbishops and bishops. Assert your right as high sovereign, possessing the charge of the bodies and souls of your subjects. Attack further the corruption and abuses which have their root in a foreign land. Cut down that tree and plant yours. Do this in the name of your people, for it is what they want, as I with my ears to the ground know, for I hear them in the streets of London. The pope has no right to command the king of England, who is the anointed of God and thus the sovereign of his country's laws and freedoms.

And those that oppose these actions? I asked. He nearly smiled, though I don't believe the man knows how. I will suggest a division in the house. Those for these bills to this side; those against them to the other; let them wear their hearts on their sleeves, wherein you see who are your friends and who your enemies. Yes, I said, a transparent Parliament, with no masks allowed to hide their arranged faces, to learn once and for all which of the clergy are my subjects and which my half subjects, those that take an oath to obey and support the pope. Should they not be taking an oath to me? Indisputably, he said. I like your idea, Cromwell, though the Archbishop Warham will voice his opposition. He will say, Christ is head of the church, and on earth power is divided into the temporal and spiritual realms, governed respectively by kings and the Church. He is, as you know, against anything derogatory to the pope's authority, believing royal supremacy, which you promote, a damnation.

Cromwell was quick to respond. The archbishop, now eighty years of life, fears for his immortal soul, since his mortal life hangs on a short lease. It is what old men say when they will soon expire and meet their celestial king. Pay him no mind. You are the earthly king, and deserve the benefits of such. What of Bishop Fisher? I asked. He will concur with the archbishop and add, as he often says in dispute, the pope is the Vicar of Christ.

Do not bother your mind with this trifling man, he said. This man that vows if he met one hundred thousand deaths, he would still defend Katherine. He should not wish for one hundred thousand. One will suffice. He is old as well, and what he says belongs in the old order. Here are words for the new. When God departed from this world, he left behind him no successor or vicar on earth. Except me, I said. I thought that might elicit a smile from him. Except you, Your Majesty, he responded without the blink of an eye or movement in his lips.

59

Anne

Bitter sweet, I called it, watching him surrender the Great Seal to Henry. If only he had resigned earlier or had never been made lord chancellor, James Bainham would have been spared; first from being chained to a post at More's Chelsea residence, then from being whipped in the Tower, and finally from being burned at Newgate. He would instead be alive, practicing law, married still to Simon Fish's widow. I pleaded with Henry to intervene when Thomas More arrested him. You offered Simon Fish and his wife immunity, I said. Simon Fish died, he retorted. I did not offer immunity to the man who married his widow. He is an innocent man, you know he is, I said. The lord chancellor investigated him and found heretical materials, he responded. The holy scripture in English is not necessary to Christian men, but rather be their further confusion and destruction than the edification of their souls. I looked at him crossly, throwing caution to the wind. And yet you are aware I possess the same heretical materials?

He walked away, shutting his eyes and ears to the truth, still believing he must appease the old faith, as its defender. How absurd, when the opposite is true. The prior in a church, a Katherine supporter, said it in his sermon, my father tells me. The king is the destroyer of the faith. That is your new title, I wish to tell him. Wear it as a badge, proudly. The suppression of the clergy and More's resignation are only the starting points. Further destruct. Rid your realm of all dissenters, and there are many. You need only look and listen. Seek them out, eradicate them. Begin with the Observant friars. The preacher, William Peto. How can you let him get away with what he preached on Easter Sunday no less, said to your face and mine? Under the influence of the wicked Jezebel, Ahab, the seventh king of Israel, built a pagan temple and gave the priests of Baal places in his retinue. The prophet Elijah told Ahab that the dogs would lick his blood, and so it came to pass. The dogs of Samaria licked Ahab's blood. All his male heirs perished. They lay unburied in the streets. Jezebel was thrown out of a window of her palace. Wild dogs tore her body into shreds. He looked right at you and said boldly, If, like Ahab in the Bible, the King of England commits this dire sin, marrying unlawfully his mistress Anne Boleyn, the dogs would one day lick his blood, as they had Ahab's. I still shudder at the words, and I shudder even more that you let it pass. You allowed him with impunity to call you Ahab and make clear reference that I am Jezebel, the means by which sin enters the world and men die on the cross.

The friars must be watched. They are Katherine's supporters. They are subversives, hoping the people of England will rise to the call against their king and his concubine. They must be stopped, I tell you. A good, respectable man gets burned and these preachers are allowed to spread sedition. They are the true heretics. Thomas Abel, the queen's chaplain, as well, with his book, *The Unconquered Truth*, which lashes out at the false persons and false sayings behind your cause for annulment, and the Holy Maid of Kent, whom you believe is harmless, though she daily prophesizes your end. Cromwell agrees with me that they should all be watched. I am beginning to like him and feel more strongly that he is my man, as well as yours, for he is willing to do my bidding, even when you won't.

60

Katherine

It matters not where he moves me or how many times. I will go wherever he commands me, even if it is to the fire, which I half expect, given who he allows to influence him. Alone as I am, excluding the people who serve me, I reflect on where I am, currently at Enfield, a smaller, less comfortable place than the More, if that is to be imagined, and how I came to be here. I recall the splendor of the Alhambra, with its innumerable palaces paved with brilliant white marble, surrounded by lush gardens, adorned with lemon trees and myrtles, with running water coming from pipes and aqueducts, a world of plentitude, for it is where every fruit and flower grew and every fish swam in its waters and every animal grazed in its fields. It is not, however, to this place I return. It is to the vagabond years, when my family moved with regularity, living like nomads, crossing the many mountain ranges that cut and divide Spain, traveling by horses and mules or on platforms borne by animals or men, staying in monasteries, towns and army camps, as many as ten in a month, often fleeing from sudden fires in the tents caused by candles and seeing men and women servants die of thirst in the acrid hills that produced little life.

I remember riding my first mule, aged six, my elder sister Juana ahead of me as our family crossed the River Tagus at Aranjuez. I watched in fright as her mule stumbled and fell into the fast-moving current and disappeared downstream. I held my saddle with all the strength my young muscles could muster, listening to my sister's screams and watching the rush of men who dove in the water to save her. I survived the ordeal, though my sister lost her mind. She became *la loca*, made worse later by her marriage to Philip the Handsome of Burgundy, a cruel, philandering man, the cause of her becoming, as she did that night on a rampart in the La Mota fortress, an African lioness in a fit of rage till the early morning hours. The only reward of that union, the birth of my nephew, now the Imperial emperor. I recall the conversation with myself. I will never become my sister, suffering bouts of jealousy, depression and madness. I will never allow a straying husband to destroy my pride and dignity. I had no way of knowing then that in my future life I would lose my first husband and be abandoned by my second.

It has been more than a year since I last saw him and almost as long as I set eyes on my daughter. I have known abandonment, I remind myself, as well as loss. My mother and father leaving me at Santa Fe, as my entourage led me to Laredo, where I boarded the vessel to England, watching at dusk as the towering Picos de Europa fell almost straight into the Cantabrian Sea. At Plymouth, where we landed, I went straight to church to thank God for keeping me safe on the perilous journey crossing the Bay of Biscay. At London, the English received me as if I was the Savior of the world, greeting me with pageants and much ceremony. One of the pageant actors said: Blessed be the fruit of your belly. Your sustenance and fruit shall increase and multiply. I entered St. Paul's Cathedral, where the choir sung, and I made an offering at the shrine of St. Erkenwald, a seventh-century bishop whose tomb was renowned for miracles. One such miracle came days later when the Bishop of London pronounced Arthur and I husband and wife, future King and Queen of England.

Within six months, I lost not only the boy I wed but my former value. I descended into the realm of hell, mistreated by King Henry VII, who viewed me as a failed commodity, since my father refused to pay him the dowry he owed, made worse when my mother, the greater title holder between she and my father, died, followed by the death of my maternal ally in England, Henry's mother, Elizabeth of York. I became a political pawn, something to be bartered between kings and nations. I became ill, mysteriously so, with unremitting pains in my stomach and head, with fevers, colds and numbing body chills. Bloodletting didn't help, for my blood had dried or seemingly so. My father who had told me when I was little, you are my favorite daughter, seemed not to care. He sent neither a dowry nor provisions for my comfort. I did not eat, caring only to fast and pray. King Henry threatened to send me back to Spain. No, I said. I came here to be Queen of England. I will never accept less, and I didn't.

I think of my mother. Though the sun brought color each morning to the Alhambra, she lived colorless, wearing only black, having in a short time felt the stab of pain pierce her heart three times: the death of my brother Juan, the family's heir, the death of my oldest sister Isabel, and still later the death of the remaining hope, little Miguel, my sister's son. While the natural world carried on in abundance, my mother, unnaturally, took to her bed, unable to recover from so much grief. I should not be like her either, I told myself then and continue to tell myself.

I am steadfast as the Spanish sun. I shall not wear black to mourn what I have lost. I am still queen. I still have a husband, the king, and until Pope Clement tells me I don't, I shall dress myself in royal garments, red, blue and green, in satins, silks and velvets, and wear the royal jewels while dining in the mornings, listening to my servants say, Your Grace, Your Majesty, and I shall smile because it is my nature to smile, even when there is little in my life to induce it.

61

Henry

The news is not good, Cromwell said. Is it ever good? I asked. The challenge is to make bad news into good news, he said. Stop riddling with me, I said, and tell me what is so bad that must become good. It concerns your intended marriage to Lady Anne, which in itself is good, though the obstacle standing in its way is bad. I mean not the pope. I mean Mary Talbot, the Countess of Northumberland, Henry Percy's wife. I mean, more specifically, Henry Percy, for he purportedly told his wife they are not legally wedded given that he, years earlier, had a pre-contract of marriage with Anne. Lady Talbot, since, has petitioned Parliament for a divorce, claiming her husband refuses to bed her due to his love for Anne. So, we are now faced with a he-said, she-said issue, which, if isn't solved, will prevent you from marrying Anne legally.

My grandfather, Edward IV, came to mind. He married Elizabeth Woodville while having had a pre-contract with Eleanor Butler, making, under canon law, his children with Elizabeth illegitimate, throwing the country into a renewal of civil war. This is indeed bad news. I said. I shall have to talk to Anne, though I fear she will have a temper tantrum.

No need, I already did, Cromwell said. She is convinced Katherine's supporters encouraged this newest obstacle, believing, as she does, that they will do anything to block your annulment and subsequent marriage to her. You will be pleased to know that she denies ever having had a pre-contract with Henry Percy. She, in fact, says she hardly remembers him, calling him just another suitor who tried to woo her with words and charm.

That is not true, I snapped, and you know it or if you don't Cardinal Wolsey surely does, though that does little good now, doesn't it, since he is long gone and buried. I cannot deceive myself, believing nothing happened between them when the whole court saw them hanging about like two birds nesting in a tree. So, yes, it is reasonable they had made a contract, and now he feels emboldened to reclaim what he believes is rightfully his. Made that much easier, said Cromwell, knowing the cardinal is no longer around to prevent him from it.

No, but you're around, and you will do it, I added quickly. You will use your tricks of the trade, your dissembling skills and Machiavellian machinations. Isn't that what you call them? I know you are fond of the Italian. Frankly, I don't care what skill you use or what you do or say, as long as he refutes ever having told his wife he had a pre-contract with Anne, as long as he's willing to swear on the Bible in front of witnesses that he never did, as long as Parliament denies her the divorce, as long as he winds up going back to his wife, to live unhappily ever after, as long as he never bothers me again because I plan to marry Anne and wish not to spend my time swatting flies on a wall because that's what he is, just a fly on a wall. I have bigger battles to fight, for the pope as you know is not a fly on the wall. He is a mosquito that buzzes around and never lands, just biting and sucking my blood. That is the worst kind of fight, when you never see the enemy. Does this make any sense, Cromwell? Just a nod of your head will do, for it makes sense to me and that's all that matters. You will pursue this case to its rightful completion and as you do you will tell yourself, I am the king's man, he has made me who I am and what I am. I owe my position and my life to him. Then return to me when the bad news of today is the good news of tomorrow.

I don't know what Cromwell said or did to him. I don't need to know. What I do know is Henry Percy came to my rooms in the presence of the sickly Archbishop Warham, who had conveniently brought his Bible, and in front of me, Cromwell, and the Duke of Norfolk, the Earl of Northumberland, his eyes bloodshot and weary, swore, placing his hand on the Bible, that he never had a pre-contract with Anne, never expressed love to her in verse or in any manner of speaking, never thought of her conjugally, and never considered marriage to anyone other than the woman he had been pre-contracted to marry, Mary Talbot.

Afterwards, to seal his refutation and confession, I watched him take communion. I then laid a heavy hand on his shoulder and said: Go back to your wife and make up with her. Tell her you lied about the pre-contract because of too much drink. Enjoy your life up north and never come back here again, if you wish to retain your title and your lands.

62

Anne

I wore a crimson velvet gown edged in ermine, covered in jewels, and let my hair fall to my waist, wanting it to flow as I myself flowed, stepping as if on air consecrated by the King of England, for it was he who had made this day possible, only a week after Archbishop Warham's death, days after Thomas Cranmer's appointment to the archbishopric of Canterbury, wherein the days shine brighter, opening into a clearing, paved in gold, stretching for miles to a summit, where I, Anna Regina, stand as one of high rank, equal to any man, excepting the king. I looked ahead and peripherally, and saw it all. The Garter Knights in their stalls, the Countesses of Rutland and Sussex, Eleanor and Mary, on either side of me. The presence of Mary, my Howard cousin, behind me, carrying my furred mantle and my coronet; the officers of arms at the castle and a party of noblemen further behind. The King ahead, flanked by the Dukes of Norfolk and Suffolk and Henry's courtiers, including my father, beaming, proud, and my brother George, the white of his teeth, from his smiling mouth, reflecting the filtered rays of the sun, come from the windows high above the chapel at St. George's, Windsor, September 1, 1532.

I knelt before the king, wherein he invested me, draping the long velvet mantle around my shoulders and setting the gold coronet on my head. In his eyes, I saw the sky, blue and infinite, rising high above the common lot of men and women, to where England shall plant its future flag, offering a freedom of thought and religion never before seen. Bishop Gardiner read the patent, bestowing upon me a title never before given to a woman, the Marquis of Pembroke, granting me and any offspring of mine, legitimate or not, lands and annuities, making me the wealthiest woman in the country. I thanked the king, kissed his hand and stood; at which time my admiring women stooped to lift my train as trumpets sounded and musicians played a flourishing processional, wherein I walked down the halls of the chapel, my head held high, so high I thought for a moment it might come loose from my neck.

We heard mass, where a *Te Deum* was sung in honor of the occasion and after, at the feast, I sat beside Henry and the French ambassador. We would shortly leave for France, which had everything to do with the title I received, for it was clear I could not go to France without a title if I should, as expected, meet and be attended by the French women of nobility. I wanted more than a title though and told Henry afterwards when we were alone. I should like to wear jewels fit for a queen, I said. He had already guessed. He said he had notified Katherine to surrender the royal jewels still in her possession. Did that please me? He asked. Yes, it did, I answered, but still I desired more. I wanted to possess the Queen's barges and wanted to see her devices and those of his and her entwined together erased or burned in every palace or building where they were seen.

Consider it done, he said, for now that Dr. Cranmer is appointed archbishop it is only a matter of time, once he returns from Germany, that he will wed us legally in Parliament. As I see it, dearest Anne, the woman I take to France, wearing the Queen's jewels, owning titles and lands, is already my wife and queen, wherein it is my wish to give you all you desire. I moved closer to him. And I shall give you what you have long desired, I said, lifting the top of my gown and laying his hand on my bare shoulder. His heartbeat quickened, as did mine.

63

Katherine

The lone messenger arrived, come from the Duke of Norfolk. The gesture alone insulted me, for I expected, if not twenty or more nobles, at least three envoys, such as on the previous visit. A small man, with a sharp beard, he spoke quickly. The king is preparing to meet the French king and needs your jewels for the woman accompanying him. I smiled, for it is my habit to be polite, even when I wish to rage. You should think I will give you my jewels? I asked, incredulous. They are not for me, personally, Your Grace. They are for the king. I let out a sound, which when made, sounded foreign to my ears, suitable more for an animal without consciousness, which does not define me. They are not for the king, I corrected him. They are for the woman accompanying him. Who is this woman?

He looked at me quizzically, sucking in air. It is the Lady Anne, Your Grace. The Lady Anne? I asked, pretending confusion. Yes, Your Grace, he said. I know of no Lady Anne, I said. You must be mistaken. Lady Anne Boleyn, he said, as if adding her last name would somehow appease me and make me surrender my jewels on the spot. I challenged him further, making him fidget. Do you mean the Anne, who is not a lady, who is the scandal of all Christendom? He moved his head like a bird's. I came not to answer to that, Your Grace. I am here to receive the jewels, as is my instruction from the duke.

Do you know how many jewels I have? I asked. No, Your Grace, he answered. You shall not be able to fit them in your bag, I said, their volume is so great, as befitting my title. I shall have to try, he defiantly responded. No, you shall not try, I said, raising my voice, switching to a serious tone. I will not give them to you. They are mine, and do you know why they are mine? Because I am the Queen of England. I told him what

I possessed — gemstones, pearls, bracelets, rings, beads, chains, crosses and much more — and where they came from; some from Spain in my dowry; some from King Henry VII when I arrived in England; some inherited after my marriage to Henry from his mother Elizabeth and some later from his grandmother Margaret Beaufort when she died; many from Henry, part of the traditional exchange of gifts every New Year.

I lectured him, saying I would consider it a sin and a burden upon my conscience if I were persuaded to give up my jewels for such a wicked purpose as that of ornamenting a person who wishes to defile the faith come from the pope and God; a person who has brought much ridicule to the king by flaunting herself beside a man who is not her husband. His taking her to a meeting across the channel only further brings infamy upon him. If he wishes to have a woman accompany him to meet the French king it should be I, his wife, his true queen, in the eyes of God, as I did in the year 1520 at the magnificence that was the Field of Cloth of Gold, when I danced with King Francis, smiling at his words, though despising his filthy French manners.

He stood wide-eyed, uncertain of his position in the world, wherein minutes before he had been certain of it. In his apparent complicit state, I looked at him beseechingly and spoke sincerely. Do you now understand why I cannot surrender my jewels to you? I do, Your Grace, he answered, barely audible, though the duke will be dismayed to learn you will not give them, as ordered. Tell the duke I do not take orders from him. I allow only one man to command me, and that man is my husband, the King of England. If he commands me, I will obey and give the jewels, though I shall keep the cross I wear now, on this gold necklace, for it contains a sliver of the cross on which Jesus died. I shall never surrender Christ, for he is all I have. Have I made myself clear, or should I write it down for you? His eyes wet with tears, he said, taking his leave, I shall tell the duke what you have said, Your Grace.

64

Anne

She stood in our path as we approached a walled-up garden at the abbot of St. Augustine's in Canterbury. Flanked by Franciscan monks, wearing the habit of a Benedictine nun, her eyes sought us with an excited urgency. I know why you are here, she said. Let us not stop, I said to Henry and our entourage, which included the Duke of Suffolk, my uncle Norfolk, Master Cromwell and many soldiers of the guard. No, the king said, I wish to hear what she has to say. Speak, good maid of Kent. Why are we here? You are passing through, on your way to Dover and then to Calais and France, she began. You are planning something evil, and I am here to warn you against it. Henry's face turned gold-red, his breath heavy, his laugh a mere defense against the quickened pulse of his heartbeat. What is this evil that I plan?

She looked at me. I saw her tongue wag and her teeth bite down, wherein her eyes turned white and her mouth moved rabid, like a dog's. I have spoken with God and the saints who reside in heaven, she said, all of whom empower me to see what others cannot see, nor wish not to see. Hell is fire and damnation, I am informed. It is the devil's den, full of loathing creatures, heretics who sin against God and the pope, women who usurp the crown and marry men they should not. King Henry, beware. Burn English translations of the Bible and remain loyal to the pope. Do not marry this woman, this heretic, this Lutheran, this viper. Your realm will end, your life will end, and God will plague you in the everlasting life to come. Save yourself. Go back to your wife, that blessed woman whom we call queen and shall always call queen, she who follows the righteous path set forth by Jesus Christ and His Holy Mother, Mary. She collapsed to the ground and began to writhe, mumbling to herself, as the monks administered to her.

Henry appeared transfixed, staring wide-eyed, without a blink. I took his hand, which was cold and clammy, shaking in my grasp. Move her from our path, I demanded of the monks. This woman should be whipped, my uncle shouted. It is treasonous to speak of harm to the king. She is a holy woman, sir, one of the monks said. What she speaks is delivered to her. She is less holy than mad, I remarked. Let us return to our lodgings, the king said quietly. I feel as if I shall faint as well. Do you still believe her prophecies benign, or will you now do as I say and investigate her? I said, leading the unsteady king away, toward the busy street, among the goggle-eyed people, whom I did not trust for their continued affiliation with Rome. Trouble me not with this right now, he said. My head hurts. I wish to see my doctor. I turned to Cromwell, who had sidled up to me. We shall speak of this matter, he whispered, when the king is resting and the time is convenient for Your Grace.

Speak, we did, and Cromwell did not disappoint. It should be against the law to foretell a monarch's death, I said. It will be against the law, that I promise you, Your Grace, when Parliament returns after the New Year. Her visions are responsible for why the king hesitates to marry me, I added. I am convinced they hold him back. That will change, he said, when he comes to understand, through gentle persuasion, what you and I already know, that her act is a hoax, a feigned exercise, just as Becket's supposed blood and skull and fingers and bones in the Cathedral are a hoax, created to make unsuspecting people with deep pockets or no pockets at all give money to their cause. The nun is nothing more than a prophet for hire.

Hoax or not, I said, she is dangerous, though the king seems not to think so, still swayed by the endorsements she received years earlier by those he considered good Christian men. Yet, you and I know, he said, these same Christian men of whom you refer belong to Rome and more specifically to Katherine, men such as Fisher and More. The nun must be stopped, for in stopping her we pull out the very roots from which the Roman Catholic Church grows its superstitions and faith in false idols. Stopped, when? I wanted to know. We leave for Calais in two days, Your Grace. Allow yourself to be honored and treated royally. When we return in a month's time, when Archbishop Cranmer returns from Germany and is sworn in, when you and the king are legally wed, when the word pope becomes an anomaly in England and the threat of an invasion by the emperor no longer exists, then we shall move to bring her down and watch the dominoes fall. Does that please you, Your Grace?

It pleases me as much as a promise can, though as you know Master Cromwell, I am still waiting on a promise made nearly five years ago, and until that promise is fulfilled, I will remain suspect of any promises made. I am not the king, he said. I am not restrained. When I make a promise, it is as good as done. I thanked him, taking my leave, saying I could now, with more peace, look forward to visiting Calais for the first time in twenty years.

65

Henry

First, my sister Mary refused to accompany Anne on the trip across the channel, giving as a reason her sudden sickness. Then, Francis informed me that none of the noble women of France wished to receive Anne, not his second wife, for sure, Eleanor of Austria, sister of the emperor, a cousin of Katherine's. That did not displease me, for I would as soon see the devil as a lady in a Spanish dress. It did displease me, however, that his sister Margaret, Queen of Navarre, became conveniently ill when asked to receive Anne, for Anne had so looked forward to that meeting, believing Margaret her dear friend. Francis offered to bring his courtesan, the Duchess of Vedome, to be Anne's counterpart. Imagine my telling Anne that! Anne, dear, this here is the French king's concubine. She shall be your escort, for the two of you share much in common. I had to tell Francis Anne would tear off my head if I made such an insulting suggestion. I instead told Francis we should meet without women in France. Afterwards, he could return with me to Calais and meet Anne, inviting her to talk with him, as he had promised me he would.

I should have made him promise to keep his sons home as well. There they were with their father, waiting for me in Boulogne, seemingly healthy, well-bodied young men, triple heirs to the throne, legitimately had by Francis and the late Queen Claude, deceased after having given him seven children in all. Who did I have by my side to present as my heir? No one. Henry, my illegitimate offspring, came with me across the channel, but I left him in Calais, thinking my meeting with Francis and the French nobles not suitable for a boy only thirteen. He called his eldest son the fair, joyous Dauphin. I had once betrothed my daughter Mary to him when they were both less than three years old. I should have followed through with that arrangement, but Kate didn't want it. She wanted an alliance with her nephew instead. I wound up promising my daughter to a man twenty years her senior. How ridiculous, how wasteful in terms of time and energy spent, and it bore no fruit, for the emperor disappointed me that time, backing out of the agreement to marry another, and on so many other occasions. Francis has already made a union for his son with the pope's niece. If only I could offer a son to the pope in return for a divorce and re-marriage. If that were the case, I would already be divorced, already married to Anne, already with male issue, an heir to my throne.

Why should Francis be so fortunate? Why hasn't God cursed him as He has chosen to curse me? For what reason? For marrying my brother's widow when it was Pope Julius who made the dispensation to allow it. Why, then, wasn't the pope cursed? It is bad enough not to have male heirs. What's worse is to see another king's heirs, dressed in black and silver and crimson satins and doublets encrusted with pearls beneath long gowns of velvet embroidered in gold, wearing stones and rich diamonds; to watch them play superbly at bowls and tennis; to see them ride and joust and hunt and hawk and later, at night, gamble with their father's fortune.

No wonder I have always harbored a dislike for Francis. He has three sons and seven children in all, and he never had to wait for a woman five years, let alone five days. I had to place my feelings aside. Their expression was not my reason for being in France. I had a treaty to complete and favors to ask from the man who calls me his beloved brother, which I'm certain Cain once called Abel. We had to put on a show, which included holding hands while riding, smiling, hugging and exchanging gifts, drinking, laughing and swearing allegiance to one another in a continuous procession of outward affection and love. It is what kings do, to survive, to get what we want. So, it was only after the ceremonial entertainment of three days that I got down to business. Could he speak to the pope on my behalf? He told me, if he publicly supported my divorce it would be to his own detriment, making it clear, though saying it wasn't his view, that on the European continent my wished-for divorce was an evil compared only to Lutheran heretics and Turkish invaders. Still, he would make it a precondition of the match between his son and the pope's niece that Queen Katherine be refused to appeal her case in Rome, that I, his beloved brother in England, be allowed to settle my own marital affairs in my own jurisdiction, using my own bishops.

I returned to Calais with him, and on the last night, after a great feast, Anne and seven women appeared in masks to much music. Each woman picked out a Frenchman with whom to dance. Anne picked Francis, wherein they danced and talked. More than an hour later, I began to wonder. How well do they know each other? After all, she had lived in his court for many years. Her sister had been his courtesan long before she had been mine. What of Anne? Did I really know the masked woman who would soon be my wife and queen?

66

Anne

I told him women in England, unlike those in France, take no delight in being a royal mistress. You are no man's mistress, Francis said. Your sister was the exception, he said, smiling broadly, his teeth stained with purple grape. How unlike Henry he appeared. Dark and devilish, swarthy, active hands, eager lips, more ostentatious in display, a bejeweled peacock; my opinion of him made permanent when I lived in France, as his wife's maid of honor, for six years, that pious, chaste woman, modest, devout, demure and self-effacing, Queen Claude, that bearer of the cross, a regular at prayers, seemingly pregnant all her waking hours and days, delivering him heirs and then some, while he strutted through court clothed in women, wearing them as so many jewels, proud to exhibit himself as a lecher and make of his nobles, both men and women, licentious animals of the flesh. The court she herself never attended in ceremonial role, a queen only in name, though she was the daughter of a king and he a mere duke, made king after her father's death to appease an old law that disallowed women as rulers of their kingdom. I was saddened to learn when I returned to England that she died of the great pox given to her by her husband.

I changed the subject of my sister, asking him if had given Henry his support. He said given the unpleasant realities of his diplomatic and military position, he could not lend his sanction to our wedding. I knew as much. It mattered not, least of all to me. Now that the king possessed me in his bed, we no longer needed any man's sanction. The course of our actions could not be reversed. The king wanted a legitimate heir, and only in marriage could he have that. He would not risk waiting, knowing that at any time I could exhibit a change in mood or appetite within the workings of my body, the first faint signs that our union has begun to bear fruit. He had asked if I wished to marry in Calais, far from the tensions of the English court and even further from Rome. A French prelate could perform the ceremony. No, I said. I have waited five years. I shall wait longer, but it will be on English soil, not here across the channel, as if to sneak in the back door, no less worthy than a common woman. I wish to be married in full view, as other queens before me, as Katherine at St. Paul's and have a coronation in Westminster Abbey. Give me that, I said, if you respect me. Give me my due and proper adulation.

67

Katherine

Be the bearer of good news, I write to Ambassador Chapuys. This year, you have brought to me little but misfortune that befalls both me and my adopted country. How should I feel about the Supplication of the Ordinaries, the suppression of the clergy, the partisan bishops standing before their king in Parliament, telling him he was now both pope and God as well as monarch? You and I know that kings, though they be great, cannot match God in greatness. It defiles the relationship between man and the sacred, taking away our reason for having faith, to bow before that which is greater than us, to humble us, to make us what we were meant to be, small in comparison. I fear for this realm now that Thomas More, lord chancellor, resigned, he who upheld the Roman Catholic Church and made the attack on heresy his passion and pursuit. Can you not persuade him to re-think his position? He cannot be happy living away from court, knowing that the Lord above our heads is angry at this realm. What should he hope to gain other than the quiet and comfort of his home in Chelsea, educating his daughters and tending to his garden? It is not enough for a man of such esteem. He is meant to spread his knowledge and wisdom, using them as influence, more than ever now that Archbishop Warham is deceased, he who refused to disobey the pope and try the case himself, he who is to be replaced by a man, Thomas Cranmer, who defies Rome and possesses no such compunction to try the case as he sees fit when he returns from Germany, where he learns his trade from Lutherans, gathering ideology, falsely rendered, for the execution of a marriage that will scandalize Europe; that the country is being directed as well by an upstart Parliamentarian, Cardinal Wolsey's former agent, Thomas Cromwell, who pursues money at the expense of the monasteries. I remember him as a sullen man, not knowing what to do with himself after Cardinal Wolsey's demise. He re-invented himself in Henry's court. I always suspected he was a man with motives, always lurking in the shadows. Well, now he is at that shadow, both he and Cranmer, mere shadows of the king, appearing and speaking with stealth, without innards, hollow to the core, unsubstantial in their beliefs, practitioners of a faith that has behind it more rebellion than faith, driven by money and promotion in the worst possible ways, through divorce and re-marriage, all to the detriment of the real faith. How blind men are, how ruthless in their sightlessness.

And what does the pope do? He sits by idly like a puppet with knotted strings, unable or unwilling to move, while my nephew wishes only to speak of invading Turks and German princes instead of restoring to me, his niece, the crown and jewels that were given to me by God, and while Henry, my husband, has gone to Calais with his mistress, Anne Boleyn, whom you have said is more Lutheran than Luther himself, that it is rumored they have already married, that she is already carrying his child in her womb, though I refuse to believe any of this is true.

The tide is changing you tell me. I know about the tide and wish to tell you a story. The day I left Spain, more than thirty years now, when I waited on the shore to board the vessel, holding the hand of my dear friend, Maria de Salinas, I watched a lone bird standing atop the sand as the tide rushed in and washed out, higher with each repetition, and yet the bird remained. Why doesn't it fly away before it drowns? I asked myself. Higher still the waves washed out until first its legs and then its beak sank beneath the water. I waited for it to emerge. By then, my entourage escorted me onto the boat. I looked back, standing on the vessel's prow, but did not see the bird. I wanted to believe it rose above the waves and flew off. I need to believe that more than ever, for I am that bird,

Ambassador Chapuys. I stand in the sand as it recedes, as the tide washes over me in a rush of waves. I can only stand firm, for I do not have wings.

68

Henry

She informed me, wherein her doctor made true, that within her womb lay the future King of England, news I have waited long to receive, though requiring immediate action, sanctioned by the advice of the best scholars in Europe who have long told me that Kate and I were never lawfully wed, that I was a free man, that I, to secure the boy's legitimacy, should marry at once. Which is what we did in a private ceremony at York Place, to which few people know for few were there, her brother and sister, one of her women, some of my privy councilors, none other. Dr. Lee, my chaplain, presided and gave us the words, our vows, offered some blessing and prayers, though did not facilitate an exchange of rings, not yet, for we can't yet let anyone know. If word should reach Rome, the pope will refuse to issue the confirming bulls for Cranmer's archbishopric, and I shall not risk that, for his confirmation is of the utmost importance to the permanent reshaping of England. In the meantime, we make the pope and others happy by seeming to delay our marriage, for they, Katherine's supporters, want to believe it will never happen. I have heard the reasons. He will never do it without the pope's approval. He will not endanger his immortal soul, blaspheming God and the Catholic faith. She will never rise above the Marquess of Pembroke. His great folly has ended. He is already tired of her. Amusing it is to play this game of subterfuge, teasing the unsuspecting fools. It is what they deserve, though, for having defied me as they have.

It will only get worse for them when Cranmer takes the case to Parliament, granting me, as he has promised, my long-sought annulment, nullifying my first marriage on the grounds of its unlawfulness and making valid and lawful my marriage to Anne. I shall at last, free of Kate in the eyes of God, become a new man, with the knowledge that I will be the father of an heir, whom I shall call Henry, and hope he will be the first of many. One day, I will take them to visit the King of France and say, Here, are my three sons, just as yours. I will dress them in cloth of gold with silver and black doublets encrusted in pearls and diamonds and collars lined with rubies. They will be tall, more so than me if that can be imagined, and stronger and more able. They will be Tudors, extending the line down through the ages. It is for this reason that I marry, for if truth be told—on the advice of domestic handbooks I have consulted—I should avoid Anne as if she were the plague itself.

Marry not for love, the first of many rules. How can a man command his wife with authority if he had once laid his heart at her feet as her doting slave? Do not choose a wife who talks too much or with sharp tongue, the second of many rules. Silence becomes a woman, and a man ought to make his choice by his ears rather than his eyes, the third of many rules.

I act in defiance of these rules, for now that we are married, now that she bears my son, she will change her behavior and not be displeased with me as she often is, berating me and withdrawing her affection. She should be content, valuing silence, using her ears rather than her mouth, to know that she has made me content. Is that not the role of a wife, according to the masters who know best?

69

Anne

The day of my wedding, I married more than the king. I married ambivalence, for as well as relishing my new position, my feeling of isolation has become greater. Who, now, are my peers? I ask myself. Not my sister, my cousin Mary or my mother. And yet neither are the men of the court either—Cromwell, Suffolk, my father and uncle—who above all else serve the king and in doing so further their interests. I, though queen, shall always be to them a woman first. Perhaps in time I will change their views, for, though not the custom, I feel as empowered as any man, if not in body, surely in mind. The other women around me I do not trust. Lady Rochford, my brother's wife, consorts with Katherine's supporters. I cannot be certain that she spies for the ambassador, who, in turn, writes to the emperor. I know only that she is one I must watch, for she hates my brother and he hates her. I should not look to either of them as an example of how to best conduct my marital affairs. One of the new maids, Jane Seymour, speaks little, averting her eyes often when I address her. She follows the old faith, that I know, for she shrinks at the sight of my Old Testament in English, and if I mention the name William Tynsdale, her body freezes as if she would fall frozen to the floor.

My uncle's wife and my great aunt have only disdain for me, as does my uncle, calling me a parvenu, an upstart, as if I were Cardinal Wolsey, come from a butcher or Thomas Cromwell from a blacksmith. I am neither. I am well bred, raised in the courts of France, made for greatness. They do not yet know that I am queen. I want to shout to their faces: For seven years, I have withstood every sort of insult and frustration. I have wooed and teased the king, tugging at him, urging him on, shaming him when he faltered. I have with unrelenting, hardheaded persistence and intelligence and elusive allure connived and muscled my way toward power. How many women could have done what I have done? I want them to kneel at my feet. I want them to kiss my hand. I want to hear them say, Your Grace, Your Majesty. I want to see them become smaller than they already are, and then we shall see who is the parvenu, the upstart.

You should be content the king says to me. You have now what you have always wanted, to be my wife and to bear my child, our son, the heir to the throne of this great realm. I should expect you to smile more now that you wear both the Queen's jewels and garments and bear as well the title, which is what you have craved. I will smile, I say, on the day of my coronation, when it is official and not just a dirty little secret as it is now, known only to you and me and a handful of others. There, at Westminster Abbey, when I hold the scepter and receive the crown from Archbishop Cranmer, when I can shed the title of Marquess of Pembroke, which, as you and I know, is but a token reward, then I shall smile. I shall, in fact, break the windows of the great Cathedral with my smile, and then later still when I deliver for you and all of England a male heir I shall do more than smile. I shall laugh and shout and cry tears of joy and wear the banner of heaven upon my shoulders for all to see, for then I know I will have truly arrived.

70

Katherine

I am honored, I told the Duke of Suffolk, that the king respects me enough to send his esteemed councilor to me instead of a faceless messenger. His dour expression reflected his desire to not be humored. Your wife? I asked. Not well, he answered. None of us should be well, I said. We should all be suffering for what has taken place in this realm long blessed, though now cursed by the incarnate Jezebel who has bewitched the king. This alone is the reason for your wife's illness, to see her brother defy what God has ordained, to see her queen, her sister and ally, mistreated as I have been so, living with each move, now at Ampthill, further from court, further from my husband and from my own flesh, my daughter Mary. You, dear sir, where is your love for me, as I long remember it, affectionately shown in accordance with your wife's wishes? I pray you have come to deliver me that love, though I can see in the avoidance of your eyes that you have come as a subject of the king, to run his errand in the name of his evil cause, come not as a man in possession of his own conscience but as a child wishing not to receive his father's scolding. Can you not at least look me in the eye and speak?

He lifted his face, looking past me rather than at me, delivering words that cut deep, as if he were stabbing at me with the knife on his belt. You are to renounce your title of queen and allow your case to be decided here in England. If you are complicit, you will confer a great boon on the kingdom and prevent much effusion of blood. Look me in the eye! I demanded. He did, revealing what I expected, a hollowness, born of fear and survival at all cost. Hear me, I said. I shall never renounce my title of queen, and as for my case, it is already decided, agreed to by the king himself in a court of law, and sanctioned by the pope, that my case shall be tried in Rome and only there. He continued as if he heard not a word I spoke. You are to be called Lady Katherine, Princess Dowager of Wales. I reproached him. I have not been a princess since I was fifteen years of age. I am a queen, sir, you know I am, and I wish you to refer to me as that. I cannot, he said, it is by command that no one from this time forward calls you by your former title. Why former when I am still married to the king? I asked, raising my voice. The king has a new queen, madam, he said. That is not possible, I shouted. The king and Anne Boleyn have been married now two months, he replied.

Why was I not informed? I asked. I myself didn't know until a few days ago, he said, when he told his council. The reason for the secrecy? I inquired. That I cannot say, madam. Oh, really? I replied. Well, I can say it, for you see, sir, I am a smart woman. I know the king's mind, his nature, the way he thinks and acts. He waited for the pope to grant his bull of confirmation to Cranmer, that shadow, which I have been informed by my ambassador has been granted. Shame on the pope for allowing the appointment of that man, for he must know that he will act without the sanction of Rome. He will bring England to the devil's den, and nothing will stop him.

Which is why, he said, it is in your best interest to comply with the king's demands. He will treat you better than you can possibly expect. If you refuse, he will stop your money, fire your servants and send you to an even smaller house with a vastly reduced income. He can do as he likes, I said. I am not about to learn how to keep my own house. If I cannot live properly as a queen I will happily go out and become a beggar, but I will always call myself Queen Katherine. At which point, I excused myself, went into my room and locked the door.

71

Henry

Parliament and God are on my side, as the recent events make clear, first with the Act of Restraint of Appeals, validated by Cromwell's words, ringing like bells of liberty in my ears: Your rule is made plenary, whole and entire power, pre-eminent authority, prerogative and jurisdiction, prohibiting the hearing of your nullity suit by the pope, barring Katherine from appealing to Rome against any decision that an ecclesiastical court in England might take. Could such news be better? Yes, by St. George! As Cranmer received the papal bulls allowing him to be consecrated as Archbishop of Canterbury, taking the traditional vow of allegiance to the pope as a mere formality, adding he would not be bound by any authority that was contrary to the law of God or of England, promising soon to assemble a court to pass judgment on my union with Katherine, clearing the way for my marriage to Anne to be made lawful.

Now, if only the emperor would cease to bother me with a meddling ambassador, for Chapuys is a mad dog, always at my ankles with a hard bite. I grow tired of kicking him away, knowing that when I do, he will return mouth agape, teeth sharpened, ears perked, ready again to rush me. What is it with the Spanish? What must I do to make them say, Enough, we are at your command? His latest bite leaves me with a wound that has yet to heal.

I cannot believe, he said, that a prince of your majesty's great wisdom and virtue will consent to the putting away of the queen. God and my conscience are on good terms, I snapped. The emperor will not recognize Anne Boleyn as Queen of England, he said, nor accept any judgment of Cranmer's on your marriage to Katherine. I will pass such laws in my kingdom as I like, I said. To the detriment of everyone but yourself, he responded.

Your Majesty knows that dispensations were issued in such form as to allow your own marriage to be valid, whether or not that former marriage was consummated. I do not want to hear of that, I said. The pope had no right to give a dispensation to marry us because in doing so he sanctioned the worst kind of sin, incest, and because of that sin God has punished me with the loss of my heirs. I am no more Katherine's husband than you are. To yourself alone is that true, he said. Mind your own affairs, I said, and do not meddle and interfere in England. Katherine is the emperor's aunt, he said. As his ambassador, your affair with her is my affair.

Report to the emperor what you wish, I said, as I know you will, the dog that you are, that I mistreat Katherine, that my actions divide my country and split the church, though tell him this as well: I have taken Anne as my wife for one reason, and that is to have a son by her, to which he, as a ruler like me, should understand. There is no guarantee that Your Majesty will have a son, he said, or any living children at all.

Why would I not? I shouted. Am I not a man like other men? Am I not? Am I not? I felt a steam of anger and tears on my face. I wanted to take him by the throat to strangle the Spanish out of him. I shouted louder. Tell the emperor that if he is thinking of invading England, he will lose. At which point, I dismissed the ambassador from my sight, for fear that I would kill him, giving the emperor yet another cause to declare war.

72

Anne

Easter mass, Christ ascended and I, his servant, rose as well. My status made public, evident in the trumpeters who preceded me in the chapel royal, in the sixty ladies attending me, in the mantle of gold, bejeweled, upon my shoulders, in the bowing of the king's courtiers before my presence, in the seat I occupied next to the king, diamonds in his eyes when he looked upon me, in the preacher's words, let us pray for Queen Anne. Imagine that. I had already possessed Katherine's apartments, her barges, her jewels, her manors and wealth and maids of honor. Now, I possessed her title, though as my father wished to remind me afterwards the king's marriage to Katherine still hadn't been formally dissolved. Oh, but father, I said, Henry has already authorized Dr. Cranmer to proceed with a court to pass judgement to nullify and make unlawful his marriage, and I shall stand as the only legal Queen of England. Do not be so haughty, he said. This marriage to the king is not good. I do not sanction it.

You, as well? I replied. Do I not have already too many who oppose me and wish to see me fall? Must I include you, my own father, who had instilled in me my ambitions? Now, I am to throw these ambitions away? I do not understand your animosity toward me, father. I should expect you, above all others, to support my advancement. Has it not given to you and your son, my brother, great advantages? Do not disown my position so quickly, for you know what I have endured to get here, and I shall not surrender what I have earned. Your lack of good will displeases me. Is it not enough that my mother's family, the Howard's, despise me for my advancement? Must you do the same? Give me your blessing. That is all I wish you to say. If I desire criticism, I should walk the streets or the halls of court or listen to the whispers of the chamber women. I should not have to hear them from my own father's lips, he whom I have revered and obeyed all my life.

Except in this matter, he scolded me. I have told you on many occasions I am against your marriage to the king, and I have told you why. You have become too imperious for your own good, railing, with your mood and temperament, against anyone who defies you. You have made the king upset too many times, and you have made enemies, many of whom are now mine as well. Why should you or I be worried about enemies? I asked. They can be converted or abated. He continued to upbraid me. Your royal interference has caused much scandal, which may result in rebellion or worse, such as an invasion from the emperor. Then where shall we reside, if even alive?

You are forgetting this, father. I touched my womb. Does this not justify all and appease your worry? He spit his answer. What if you don't deliver the king an heir? I choose not to consider that, and in any case, I am resolved to risk all, for the cards I have played so far have cashed in well. Not if you listen to the voices crying out to burn you, he said. Not if you listen to the voices of Europe, Luther himself and all Lutherans who despite their argument with the pope believe still in the sanctity of marriage.

Enough of your fatherly advice, I shouted. I will have it no more, for I am now queen, and though I am your daughter I wish from this time forward that you address me in accordance with my title, Your Majesty or Your Grace, if it pleases you better. It pleases me to rot in hell before I call you Your Majesty, he shouted back. Though you wear a crown, you are a daughter of insolence. Leave my sight, father, I screamed. I count you now among those who are sworn against me, though it matters not, for I shall prevail as the mother of the next heir. I am assured you will call me Your Majesty then.

73

Henry

Cranmer and Cromwell, Thomas and Thomas, my men, my advisers, my adherents. How fortunate I am to receive their intelligence, their guile. Cranmer first. The court should be held as far away from London as possible, in Bedfordshire, Dunstable Priory, so as people should not interfere or cause trouble in the streets. Cromwell added, We do not want the rude and ignorant common people to speak of it, for they may riot if they do. Has the Dowager Princess received the order to attend? I inquired. Yes, Cranmer noted, but she has refused. Her reason? I asked. Two, said Cranmer. She has already lodged an appeal at Rome, and she does not recognize the English court. Unremitting insolence, I said. Good fortune, added Cranmer. How so? I wished to know. If she were to appear, she might slow down the proceeding, defending herself. It's not enough that she doesn't appear, said Cromwell. It's best if she heard no news from Dunstable, in case she suddenly decided to appear. We must speak as little of this matter as possible, if at all. I shall set about to ensure the kingdom's silence.

Cranmer and Cromwell, men true to their words. Cranmer concluded the trial far from the ears of men, who are better not to hear or speak. Cromwell swore to have every man's tongue if he did. I received the sentence I long desired. In the eyes of the English church, the only church that mattered, Pope Julius had erred in issuing a bull of dispensation allowing for my marriage to Katherine, for it was contrary to divine law. What appeared to be a marriage for twenty years never existed. She was married to Arthur, my brother, and only to him. Thus, her title as wife and queen are nullified, our daughter made a bastard, no longer princess and successor. No sooner was that settled than Cranmer validated my marriage to Anne as lawful and binding.

A new day has arrived, I should wish to say to Katherine, if I still conversed with her, which, due to the fortune of men and God, I do not. She can appeal to Rome all she wants, but it will be in futility, for it is only a matter of time when men will say, what is Rome? What is a pope? She must face her remaining days bearing the title Dowager Princess of Wales. It is the best she will ever do. Only one queen exists now, and it is Anne, and this truth shall be evident in the coming days when she receives her coronation. The ceremony cannot be delayed, for she is six months with child, with baby Henry, the future King of England.

74

Katherine

I should have attended the court, if for no other reason than to shout after sentence was passed, claiming my marriage to the king never proper, thus null and void: So, I spent half my life as the king's concubine! Is that the judgment you wish me to accept? Are you men so loath to condemn a woman such? Understand that the more you beat me down, the more resolve I have to lift myself up. I shall not slink away like a wounded animal and find a hole wherein to wither away. It is not within reason for one born and bred as myself. I do not acknowledge your decision, for yours is a false court, made by false men, who worship a false God.

The tide flows unnaturally, warning of disaster, made additionally evident by news of Anne Boleyn's impending coronation. She wears my best diamonds and other royal jewels. She attends mass, she a heretic who blasphemes God with her presence at the altar of His son, who died to preserve the honor and grace of the human spirit. Where are those virtues now? She has taken my barge, my coat of arms erased. She has taken my apartments, my seat at church next to my husband, she who receives blessings from preachers forced to bless her, she who takes the holy sacraments, a desecrator of saints and relics and all traditions known to the old faith.

Still, she wants more. She wants to see me dead, my daughter as well, for as long as we live, albeit in vile conditions, she will always look over her shoulder, waiting for the invasion or the occurrence that will supplant her and place me back on the throne. I do not make this up. I hear it from Ambassador Chapuys, who hears it from the people, who speak of the unnatural tide, and the forebodings of which it speaks. The dead fish of marvelous size, nine feet in length, stranded on the northern coast the day

Henry and Anne Boleyn landed in Calais. Balls of fire the size of human heads falling from the sky, making the night seem like day. Plague and famine ravishing people, many hanging and drowning themselves to save themselves from further horrors to come: the sight of Anne Boleyn as their queen the worst, her coronation a testament to evil triumphing over good, the devil defeating God, the world turned upside down, wherein hell stands above heaven and demons rule the angels; fire-eating men favored over those who hold the word of God in their hands, silent in prayer, meek as lambs, killed by the wolves, seekers of vice. Through it all, I am resolved to stand firm, again that lone bird on the beach, swallowed by the waves, wingless, though fortified by what is right and just.

75

Anne

I thought of my unborn child through four days of pomp and ceremony. First the Thames procession, taking me from Greenwich to the Tower, fifty barges, replete with cloth of gold and silver, banners carrying my badge, a white falcon crowned, perched on red and white roses, pennants carrying the king's coat of arms, musicians in all, making the water sing while it blazoned in fire from the mouth of a mechanical dragon. Twenty-four oarsmen rowed my barge, once belonging to the former queen, though as truth now unfolds never the queen lawfully. I alone hold that title, evident in our approach to the landing, where the white stone of the Tower, with its fine turrets and cupolas, gleamed high above the outer wall, when we came to the Water Gate, met with the fanfare of trumpets and a salute of cannons. The king was there to greet me, pulling back my gown to show the admiring nobles my six-month womb, making clear why he spared no expense for my coronation, for the sake of the child I carried, whom I, by the will of God, must deliver safely and in good health to justify the magnificent celebrations.

Though grateful to be honored, I desired more to be resting, to eat apples and pears, cold meats and fish rich in oils and minerals. I wished to be in my apartments, reading my Bible, saying my prayers in silence, speaking to God with no intermediary, making sure at all times how I stepped and moved, talked and laughed, or whether to do nothing other than lie on my back. But the show had to proceed, wherein I processed from the Tower to Westminster Hall, carried in a litter of white cloth, held aloft by sixteen knights, my hair long and loose under a jeweled circlet, while behind me and ahead the envoys of France in blue and gold and the Knights of the Bath in purple and the ladies of the nobility on horses and the long line of bishops and prelates, the Yeomen of the king's Guard, the choirs of children and the pageants performed in my name, the verse and enactments, and the great Holbein's recreation of Mount Parnassus under a vast arch where Apollo and the Muses played instruments and sang my praises as streams of wine poured from the marble fountain of Helicon.

It should have been as if I had received Heaven, though how should that be when the litter swayed left and right, as I held my womb, protecting it from the violence of the motion and the sounds and smells of the streets which caused me nausea? How should that be when thousands crowded the narrow path, behind rails, staring motionless, their hands by their sides, their caps on their heads, their tongues in their mouths, except for those who used words I dare not repeat? I heard my fool: It is because of the scurvy on their heads that they wear their caps rather than don them to their queen. I stared back at them, not smiling, for I do not dissemble or overreach myself to receive their love. I do not need to, for despite their hisses and their cold eyes, I am their queen and soon to be the mother of an heir.

The following day, more faces pressed and measured, more monks and abbots, more bishops and singing children, more mayors, aldermen and nobles, more horses and carriages, trumpets and velvet-clad women, more gold and silver banners and flags, more walking, long lengths on crimson cloth, under a canopy, dressed in purple, edged in ermine fur, my hair again loose under a caul of pearls, wearing my coronation badge, *the most happy*, walking further still to the Abbey's altar, where Cranmer stood, as if an angel, high on a cloud of incense, the only one of many who performed his duty for love and not regret as others, such as the Duke of Suffolk holding the cushioned crown, the Duchess of Norfolk carrying my train, my father, his head bowed and impassive. At the altar, I prostrated myself before the archbishop, lying face down on the cold stone, careful not to press my womb too hard, as he prayed over me, reminding me of the lineage of queens going back centuries. I sat in St. Edward's chair as he anointed me, placing Edward's crown on my head and then another more fitting for my size. He placed the scepter of gold in my right hand and the rod of ivory in my left, calling me Queen of England.

I moved as if dreaming, past the courtiers and the trains of ladies, the churchmen, banners and flags, past the trumpeters and the singing children. I moved into the sky, where I became a falcon, cutting the clouds with my wings. I ascended higher till I was no longer of the earth, no longer among men and women, no longer queen, even. I felt most happy, indeed.

76

Katherine

I lay in bed, my spirits low, after having stepped on a pin, rendering me unable to stand or walk, suffering as well from an unremitting cough. I should have been glad to see my former chamberlain, Lord Mountjoy, arrive, saying he would now be part of my household, as he had always been in Greenwich, though knowing the King sent him gave any feeling of relief pause.

In less than an hour's time, he made his intentions clear. He had come to make sure none of my maids and servants addressed me as Queen Katherine. I should be called Lady Katherine, Dowager Princess of Wales. Anyone who refused to address me as such would be punished by law, according to the report he wished me to read and sign in acknowledgment of it. I read aloud: The marriage between King Henry and Katherine, she of Spain, is now deemed, through the highest court in England, presided by the Archbishop of Canterbury, detestable, abominable, execrable, and directly against the laws of God and nature.

I put the paper down and looked at Lord Mountjoy, whose eyes searched for a place to rest far from mine. No man who swears with his hand upon the Bible wrote these words, I said. Only one in possession of the devil can write such blasphemy. He did not respond, so I spoke more to myself than him. The thunders of the earth do not cast thunderbolts except to strike me. This is yet another one. Still, he remained silent. I lifted the report again, and as I read further, I reached for a pen and scratched out the words Lady Katherine, Dowager Princess of Wales wherever they appeared. In their place, I wrote Queen Katherine.

I signed nothing, handing the report back to him, asking,

Have you not always called me Queen Katherine? Why then should I accept a different title? It is the king's law, madam, he said. Madam? I shot back. Lady Katherine, he said. Hear me, I replied, if you in your insolence are not above listening. I am not a madam, nor am I a lady, and I am not and will never be Dowager Princess of Wales, though at an earlier time in life I had been. I am Queen of England, the king's true wife, despite the recent sentence by a man not capable of presiding over mass, let alone a court to nullify my marriage, and despite the news of Anne Boleyn's coronation in the abbey where she was recently crowned, shamefully showing herself with a six-month child.

You, as much as anyone, know I came to the king a clean maid, without bodily knowledge of Prince Arthur, and thereafter was crowned and anointed queen and had by the king lawful issue. My daughter Mary is the legitimate heir of a legitimate marriage. She is not a bastard, and I am not a common woman, having lived with the king more than twenty years as his harlot. I was born to be a queen, became queen, and shall always be your queen, so I demand that you address me as such and not disrespect the queen for whom you have always served.

He stood impassively, holding the unsigned report in his hand, staring at the scratches in pen I had made. The king shall be displeased, he said. He shall always be displeased, I replied, if his pleasure depends on bringing me to submission when it is not possible that I should ever submit to something detestable, abominable, execrable, and directly against the laws of God and nature. Think of your daughter, he said. Do not insult me, I snapped, for do you think an hour goes by when I do not think of her? I am her mother, though the king does not allow me to comfort her as a mother should a daughter. Tell the king it is he who should think of his daughter, instead of that Jezebel who wears my crown.

I shall, my Lady, he said, though the girl should not be sacrificed for your cause. My cause? I shouted. It is not my cause.

It is his cause. I am the victim of it, and now you are asking me, as others have, to betray and slander myself, to say, yes, I was the king's concubine for twenty years! I cannot damn my own soul, even for my daughter. Cursed be the person who neglects her own reputation.

He left my room, his purpose with me unfulfilled, wherein he should spend the rest of his day and those hereafter listening to the words of my maids and servants, whispered and aloud, making sure they do not call me queen. He will be disappointed to learn that my women, unlike him, act in accordance with their own wills, not with someone else's.

77

Henry

Do not call him pope. Call him Bishop of Rome. Call him but a man, for that is what he is, naked as Adam, apple-stained, marked with the blackest of sin, small, frail and bony beneath his robes and miter, his scarred, knobby flesh, his gout-ridden walk, his sagging jaw and toothless mouth, prone to the curse of Eve and the devil's disease, as are all men.

Leave it to Cromwell. Only he could clear the skies, remove the threat of rain and far worse storms, with words alone. Laugh when you hear his name. Laugh when he condemns you as he has. Laugh to know that others have burned their bulls of excommunication. He didn't need to say who. I had heard of Luther's famous bonfire, his exorcism, his freeing the German people from Rome and the old faith. Call the pope a magician if you will, for he uses tricks as his predecessors before him, though that was during a time dark as dirt.

This now is England, magnificent, brilliant, a fire of light, on the cusp of reform, where men are ruled by intelligence and reason, not superstition. Pay no attention to tradition, for it is concocted in mythology, spun in lies, wherein a king who was cut off from the sacraments of the church was, in feudal law, deprived of his rights of lordship; wherein his people no longer owed him obedience; wherein his kingdom could be seized, with the pope's sanction, by another ruler.

Disregard all, for they are nothing but sleight-of-hand tricks, performed to make you believe he is right in declaring your marriage to Anne null and void, that your unborn child, still in the womb, will be illegitimate in the eyes of Catholic Europe, that your only recourse, for the salvation of your soul, for its eternal burial and celestial placement, is to abandon your newest wife and return to Katherine, for if you don't Emperor Charles now has the justification to invade with the blessing of the English people who cry out: The Tudor claim is not a strong claim. If Richard III could be dethroned, why not this king? Do not fall victim to the threat of the pope's magic and unnatural deceit. The emperor wishes to avoid war with England as if it were the plague, or worse still, the German Protestants, and Katherine has been heard to say, she would rather die than be the cause of it. Remember this, Your Majesty, and never forget it: God knows your righteous heart and always prospers your affairs.

I looked at Master Cromwell and said: You and He have much in common.

78

Anne

My servants wear on their liveries my motto, *the most happy*, though I should not say I am happy, for while I possess much I do not have that which I desire most, that being peace.

Perhaps in death, in salvation, in God, only then. For how should I achieve it here, surrounded by dissidents? The latest, a paper found in my apartments, words written in fine penmanship, the art of a monk I am certain.

When the Tower of London is white and another place green, then shall be burned two or three bishops and a queen; and after all this be passed we shall have a merry world.

I asked Cromwell to search out the author and the person who placed it in my sight. Must I live like a mother hawk? I said to him. Must I day and night guard against predators who wish to harm the child I carry by wishing ill will upon me? It is that nun, I said. She incites the commoners and the friars and monks, persisting in her mad prophecies. On the day of my coronation, no less, boasting of superhuman powers enabling her to command the wind and waves and to intervene to free souls from purgatory, claiming to have observed devils conversing with me, filling my mind with evil, saying in the end I would not only converse with devils, I would live among them in hell, at which time Mary would be queen. I hear the king's daughter is cheered in villages on her way to mass, the people rejoicing her as if she was God Almighty come down from heaven. I shall not have peace until the nun is gone, arrested and properly punished, until Mary is no longer a threat, until Katherine is moved still further away, until she falls off the map of England, into the sea where she belongs.

Cromwell, under promise to me, is tracking subversives, Friar Peto, said to be hiding in Antwerp. Thomas Abel, the notorious chaplain, invisible to the eye, though the words of dissension he writes blindingly clear. Two Observant Friars, detained and tortured, made to confess they secretly visited Katherine in Ampthill. The loose-tongued priest from Leigh, Lancashire, who said: I will take none for queen but Queen Katherine. The king should not be king. Katherine herself, every note, every letter, every visitor that passes to and from her.

I am mollified to know Mary Tudor, the king's sister, one of Katherine's most outspoken allies, has succumbed to her sickness. Henry wished for me to attend her service and pay my respects to her and her husband, the Duke of Suffolk. I did no such thing, using as my excuse pains in my womb, my need to rest, to avoid crowds and unwanted excitement. She refused, against the king's wishes, to escort me to Calais and attend upon me there. Why should I respect her when she been nothing but a voice of dissent in my rise to the crown? I shall not miss her.

Now, if only others would follow her, Lady Willoughby, Lady Salisbury, Katherine's oldest and closest confidantes. These women and those they incite to call me names and deride the crown I wear may have small teeth, but they bite the most. Have all dissenting women of the kingdom beaten, I said to Cromwell, until they learn to say the words Queen Anne, with or without smile, I do not care, as long as they say it. Do what is necessary, for I must, in peace, bear this child. I know all too well the dangers of childbirth, having observed in my mother and sister the loss of babies. Heaven help me if that were to happen.

79

Katherine

It shames me to say I pray to God for another woman's misfortune. Do not deliver her a son, I say. She is not worthy. It is she, not Henry, who is responsible for the mistreatment I endure, living now in yet another residence, smaller, darker, colder, in Buckden, further still from court, in the damp, rainy Fens, the landscape barren and desolate, where she wishes, I believe, I will meet my death and threaten her no more, for she knows that as long as I live, as long as Mary is the legitimate heir to the throne, the ground upon which she walks shakes to hold her frame, as she knows from the reports she hears from Cromwell's spies who surround me.

She knows the day I left Ampthill for Buckden, along the more than twenty miles my entourage traveled, people lined the roads to see me, to show their respect, waving, weeping, wishing me luck, shouting my name, calling me queen, desiring the worst for my enemies, offering to take up arms in my defense, ready to die if only I would give the word to my nephew and allow his invasion, of which they would support, and in doing so restore what I had lost and eradicate the madness of the realm. I did not want war I wanted to say, even if it meant my restoration. I did not wish to be irredeemably damned, knowing I could be the cause of bloodshed and the possible ruin of the king.

She hears these reports, and she knows, despite what she wears, where she lives and with whom she beds, that she is a queen under false pretense. Ask the people lining the roads, I should wish to say to her. Ask my maids and servants who wear upon their liveries the initials *H and K,* and who shall always call me by my deserved title. Ask the history of the earth, which holds the bones of so many kings and queens here and on the continent. Ask God, if you aren't afraid of his wrath. Ask Christ who died for your sins, though you dishonor his act with your hauteur and arrogance, made evident in your latest demand, that you wish me to surrender the triumphal cloth, the christening gown, into your possession as you prepare for the birth of your child.

I will do no such thing. That gown I brought from Spain and used it for the birth of my own children, who, though all but one died, were legitimate in the eyes of the only church I have ever known. God forbid I should ever surrender the gown to you and help your horrible cause.

80

Henry

She held her swollen womb and flashed her dark eyes, the muscles of her mouth twitching. I worried the child might burst from her. Such was the torrent of her anger. I am your wife, she screamed. I have suffered and sacrificed much for your sake, and now you betray me. I will not tolerate your wandering eye, your affairs of the flesh, your bold displays of infidelity, while I am burdened with child.

What you have done *for my sake*? I shouted back. Whatever you have done for me, I have done for you greater. Have I not recently approved the arrest of Bishop Fisher and Cranmer's interrogation of the nun, both at your insistence? Have I not kept my daughter, whom I adore, away from court and move her mother often to new residences, further each time, to smaller houses with reduced households and incomes, to satisfy you? Did I not, in fact, for your sake, tear the English kingdom from Rome, isolate ourselves from the rest of Europe, divide the country, at the risk of invasion and civil war, to make you queen? You should know I can just as easily bring you down as quickly as I raised you up. Shut your eyes to my affairs, I demanded, for they are none of yours. Endure as those worthier than you.

She stepped back, cupping her hands to her face, her voice carried by less breath. Worthier than me? I know not what you mean. I believe you do, I stammered. She removed her hands from her face and found renewed breath. Do you mean Katherine, the Dowager Princess, who was never lawfully the queen? She said, as if spitting in my face. Yes, Lady Katherine, I said, she knew how to look the other way and endure in silence what she didn't like, for she had no choice, and neither do you. I am king of my realm, and as king I shall act accordingly.

She called me words which I dare not repeat for they

offended me upon hearing them, from a woman purportedly devout of God, and I wish not to offend myself again with their recollection. I threatened to take back the gift I had only a day earlier given to her for her childbearing preparation, the great French bed I had purchased as part of a ransom in the French war nearly twenty years earlier. She threatened me with further rage. Take the bed, take the jewels, take my gowns, the barges and manors, the annuities and all the members of my household; take everything I possess, for you have taken that which is my greatest commodity, my heart, and have trampled upon it. If you truly loved me, you would not treat me thus.

Loving you has nothing to do with what I do, I said. Mind your own affairs, which you can control, such as delivering the child in your womb. This upset of yours cannot be good for the delivery. Think of that. All other thoughts you should put out of your mind for they will do neither you nor the child any good to think of them. Now, if you are finished with me, as I am with you, I have business of far greater concern to which to attend.

She sat and wept, covering those eyes that had always held me in their sway, making me bend my knees to serve at her altar. I stood over her momentarily before leaving, feeling a shift in balance and rather liking it.

81

Anne

I did shut my eyes, though to keep them open would have done me little good, for the room, days on end, was dark, tapestries hung over the closed windows, no light, no sun, no foul air from the summer heat, no pestilence and plague, no politics of men, no Henry, just women, my sister and cousin, midwives and servants, running in and out, like specters, perfuming the walls and floors, feeding me, replenishing me with drink, wiping sweat from my forehead and cooling my arms and feet, careful not to speak too loud, for I wished to hear the prayers I recited to myself and sometimes aloud, whispering to me when my pain became sharp and stabbing.

Your time is soon, Your Grace. Your child, your male heir, as we all hope and pray, for which the doctors and many astrologers say is as certain as the stars that shine in the night, wherein, you, his mother, will be shaped in glory.

They did not know what I knew, for they did not live in my dream, where Lady Rochford handed me my child, swaddled in white linen, and I heard against my chest his rhythm of breath with mine and felt his tiny fingers holding tight to my finger, his eyes closed, his face red as his father's. Henry, I said, my son, alive and vital, my vindication. Call the King, I said. Here is his son, his heir, whom he has long waited to see. Silly, Anne, Lady Rochford said. She started to laugh, and soon all the women in the room began to laugh. I shouted for them to stop.

I awoke to silence and facelessness, wet in my clothing, under a satin canopy, screened on all sides with lace curtains, and afterwards heard my screams and the commotion of the room, the shuffling of feet, the ripping of sheets, the clanging of metal objects in the metal basins, and a cacophony of voices, high-pitched and deafening, disembodied and threatening, sounding to my ears like the storm at sea I had endured when I was still a girl, sailing across the channel, believing I would die, and here it was again. Would it never end? The unremitting wind and rain, the roar of the waves, the tipping of the vessel left and right, up and down, the creaking of the starboard, the moan of the stern, the cry of the gulls.

I clutched at the cloth on the bed and released. I heard a whimper and the return of natural speech, one of the women, I knew not who, saying, It is not what we had hoped.

I shivered. Is my baby alive?

Yes, alive, came the answer, though nature did not conform to our wishes. You have given birth to a girl. Would you like to see her?

I shut my eyes and wept, realizing my ordeal, far from over, had just begun.

Yes, I want my child, I said. I wish to hold her and never let go.

I held her up until the time Henry came to my room, his face long and weary, his smile not convincing. You and I are both young, he said, and by God's grace boys will follow. He said nothing else and bothered not to look at his daughter. He left as he had arrived, in a rush of wind, followed by his councilors, whom I thought I heard laughing in the hall.

82

Henry

Walking out of her room, I held an eerie thought. She could have as well been Katherine, twenty years earlier. For hadn't I also said to her, Boys will follow? They didn't, of course. Just a girl and stillborn babies. Am I to see a repeat with Anne? If so, I would like to know now so I can make a change to avoid reliving what I don't want to relive ever again.

Cromwell interrupted my thoughts, saying, the celebrations, Your Majesty. Do we proceed as planned? No, I answered. We cancel everything, the jousts, the fireworks, the bonfires, the cannon salutes, the river procession, the fountains with their free-flowing wine. We keep the christening, that's it, though I won't be there. Make sure it is handled well, befitting a princess, with Cranmer as the girl's godfather and anointer. What shall I do with two princesses?

One shall have to be demoted, he said. Yes, I wonder which one. I shall have to consult with Anne. He looked at me quizzically. I am joking, of course, Cromwell. You will have to inform Mary that she can no longer refer to herself, nor can anyone else refer to her, as princess. She will not like it, which is why you must tell her. I have long endured her mother beseeching me to be fair with her. I don't need the two of them ganging up on me. He said he would inform Mary of her changed title, organize the christening, and do whatever else was necessary to promote better health for both me and the realm. I thanked him, and he left.

What a man, that Cromwell, he and Cranmer, Thomas and Thomas. The only ones who fulfill promises. Not Katherine or Anne, neither one able to give me a male heir, not my physicians and the many astrologers I paid for their assurances, not Wolsey who failed to deliver me the divorce and chose in the end treason over loyalty, not the emperor who failed me twice, not Francis because as a Frenchman he knows only deceit and debauchery, not the pope who can hardly buckle his own shoe or feed himself, let alone pass a sentence, not the German princes who want my soul made heretical in return for their support in my fight against Rome.

I dare not lump God in that group, but I do wonder what plan he has for me. He must know that for seven years I turned the world upside down, seeing my country and court divided, factions forming, mostly against Anne, for I am not a fool. I see and hear. My courtiers do not like her, nor do women, noble or not, French or English, nor do the foreign visitors, such as the German diplomats, whom she said mocked her at her coronation, nor do her own relatives, the Howards. I have lost allies because she has none. To think, without a son to show for the price, what I have risked and sacrificed. Forty-two years of age, graying in the hair, gaining weight rapidly, wounded in my leg, beset with headaches, poor eyesight and weak hearing, and what have I to show in my accounts? Two daughters, that's all. A king at my advanced age more should be able to face himself in the looking glass and say, I am a man, am I not? Are not my sons proof of that?

So much for that, for I am forced now to do what I have always done, keep trying and waiting, though my patience wears thin, as does my hair, as does my performance, which is not what it once was in my lusty youth, made worse by my waning desire for her. Where is the Venus I once saw, that sensuous smile, that embodiment of grace, with the power to mesmerize me and make weak my knees, so easily bent to worship her as one does a goddess of myth? I grieve now for the loss of my great folly, the ecstatic madness she had loosed in me, which I had nourished for so long in words and letters, in songs and gifts, in dreams and prayers, as she called forth my tenderness and made a net of my future wherein she sat alone. Why now do I find myself eager to keep my distance, always wishing to ride and hunt without her? When did her presence become for me a blast of hot air, making me wince, wherein I see only her bad-tempered self, forever goading me with complaints, for which I desire to shut my ears?

I possess not the answers and know only that I surrendered much to make her my wife and cannot entertain thoughts of abandoning her. Not yet, least of all, after one birth. She has much childbearing left, I remind myself, and fortune may still smile upon us. As for the present birth, Anne wants to name the child Mary. Why, Mary? I asked. So, when I say the name Mary I see and think of her and not your daughter, whom you know is a bastard and not deserving of the name. Deserving or not, that is her Christian name, I said, and I will not have two daughters named Mary. I possess enough confusion in my life. She shall be named Elizabeth in honor of your mother and mine.

Princess Elizabeth, she said. Yes, of course, I responded.

83

Katherine

God answered my prayer, delivering to Henry's heretic woman, no more a wife than I am a courtesan, a girl. I am now certain that God looks after me and will in time restore my title and return my husband to me, for Anne Boleyn's birth is a sign that He has abandoned Henry for having abandoned me. I know now and can rest with this knowledge, that she will never deliver him a male heir. He will know, it is just a matter of time, that he sacrificed his true, most loving wife, for an empty promise, cast as he was under her charms, which in time will manifest to expose her for who she is, that being a witch. I should not be surprised, nor should anyone, if he soon realizes the error of his way and by one means or another seeks to rid himself of her.

Return to me, I should wish to say. Acquit yourself of trying other women to help bring you your desired heir. It shall never happen, for you have offended God. Recognize that your daughter Mary is your heir. If you would only accept that, how much you would please the emperor, the pope and all of Catholic Europe, once again joining our countries, Spain and England, as they were once joined when we were married lawfully before God. Those you have offended will welcome you back with open arms if only you would accept your true wife and daughter and disband your English church, which is not a real church of God. It is a church of men, created to fulfill ambitions, much like your Parliament, not a church to worship God, the true God who resides, and always has, in Rome, where your loyalties and the salvation of your everlasting soul should lie.

I shall celebrate with my maids and servants the news of Anne Boleyn's failure to deliver a son. Perhaps Lord Mountjoy will join us, he who keeps to himself knowing that his mission with me is futile, for all continue to call me Queen Katherine. I shall toast to my daughter Mary, who is the true princess, born in wedlock, blessed by the pope and the rest of Catholic Europe. The child Elizabeth will forever be known as the bastard child, born in sin by the king's whore. The girl, like her mother, will be looked down upon and called such names that will make me pity her, for the fault is not hers that she was born into the world by a woman like Anne. I pray that God will pardon her for the sins of her mother, though not spare the mother from what she deserves, punishment by exile or, God forgive me for saying this, by a much worse fate, as is the custom for one who does the devil's work.

84

Henry

I tried to be generous with her, offering to set her up in her own household with more than a hundred servants under Lady Salisbury, who has always been her governess and guardian. All she had to do was accept her change in status, show graciousness and allow herself to be called Lady Mary, for her sister Elizabeth now held the title of princess. Cromwell said she reacted violently, throwing herself on the ground, crying that there was no princess in England except herself. I was displeased to hear her reaction. I was further dismayed having received her letter, hearing in her words the same proud and stubborn voice of her mother.

I know well my rightful heritage, father. I came into this world a princess, born of a king and queen, ordained by nature and God, and I have graced this world, seventeen years now, as a princess. How then can I toss it away on a whim? I refer to Anne Boleyn, your whim, a woman without noble blood, whom you allowed to seduce you, to take from you your reason and virtue, your goodness, your Christian heart and soul, and take from me the loving man I knew from birth. Where now is your love for me and your wife, my mother, the only true Queen of England, whom you have abandoned and exiled and have forbidden to visit with me? Do you not see how your actions have ruined our lives? I ask you, father, to search your conscience and examine your own conduct before you act further in removing my title and the title of my mother. We are your true family, not Anne Boleyn and the baby Elizabeth. She is a bastard child and will always be one, and Anne will always be just a pretender to the crown. Heed my words, dear father, before you further damage all that you ever cared about.

To think that I should be so scolded by my own daughter, who often complains of illnesses that doctors cannot cure, becoming, I am told, thin, while foregoing food, taking preventives, losing teeth and hair, suffering headaches and stomach cramps. I cannot allow her sad state to sway me. Her words, her adamant insolence and disobedience, leave me no recourse but to teach her a harsh lesson. I will disband her house, send Lady Salisbury away, reduce her expenses. Let her feel the sting of my wrath for a while. Let her stay awhile without her favorite governess, with few servants.

I will wait for her to bend her will to me and say, I accept the title Lady Mary. I accept whatever you decide, father. You are king, you are master, I prostrate myself before you. Let her say that and I will make sure she lives as a princess, though in title she be not one.

85

Katherine

I sit at my desk with only words to console Mary. Daughter, I write, I heard such tidings today that I do perceive, if it be true, as I fear it is, the time is come that Almighty God will test you, as he has long tested me, and I am very glad of it, for I trust He does handle you with a good love. If the King has instructed you to stop using the title of princess, you should reply with the same mix of obedience and rebellion that I use. Answer with few words, obeying the king, your father, in everything, save only that you will not offend God and lose your own soul, wherein you stand by the decisions of Rome and act in accordance that your parents are still lawfully married and that I, your mother, am still and will forever be Queen of England.

To fortify your resistance, pray often, at all hours of the day and night and read scripture. For entertainment, dance occasionally and play the lute, for I know these acts bring you joy. Above all, your maidenhead should remain protected, your body kept from all ill and wanton company. Repel any attempts at marriage, for your father's mistress cannot be trusted, desiring as she does to diminish your right to succession. Write often to Ambassador Chapuys. He, other than God, is your greatest ally in England. Listen to what he says and let his words guide you, for he corresponds frequently with your cousin Charles, the emperor, who we must trust will not allow your father to continue his mistreatment of us.

Here are two books I wish you to read in addition to scripture. The first, *De Vita Christi*, offers peace to a troubled mind, asking of it to imagine scenes of Christ's own life. Read and do as I myself do, practice what the writer, Ludolph of Saxony, preaches in words. Close your eyes, picture yourself blind like Celidonius, touched by the hand of Jesus, washed in the pool of

Siloam, seeing as if for the first time. Become Lazarus, wrapped in linens, head to foot; hear Jesus say, take off the grave clothes and let him go. Remove the linens and see again the color of the trees and sky and walk free, rejoined with me, your mother. Picture that you stand on water, like Jesus, and calm the tempest. You will not drown. Your faith will keep you safe. Just as with your faith you will endure anything. Say as I say in the dark of night: Give me the cross that Jesus carried. Give me, as well, the whips and nails and scorching sun upon my skin. Make me bleed and die, if necessary, if it be God's will. The book is a miracle, if you allow it to be, as I know you will, for your soul is the saint's soul, Mary, Mother of God.

When you complete that journey and understand that we are not alone in our suffering, that Jesus suffers with us, and for that we should be thankful for his example, read next *The Letter of St. Jerome*. He writes that paradise greets those who stick to their principles, as we do, for God Himself does not compromise. Here is but a sampling.

The Savior likes nothing that is half and half, and, while he welcomes the hot and does not shun the cold, he tells us in the Apocalypse that he will spew the lukewarm out of his mouth.

In other words, dearest Mary, a moment for all or nothing, a belief that you and I can pass any test given to us. Know that with God in my heart, as he is in yours, I write this letter to you in recognition that we share the same painful ordeal, and if things come to that extreme, wherein God decides it is our time, we might next meet in paradise, with our Lord, our Father in Heaven. If it is you who shall begin, know that I shall follow, wherein from that time forward we shall never again be separated. I have never written words with a better heart and with more devotion than these you read. Your loving mother, Queen Katherine.

86

Anne

Though I am queen and have a princess daughter, whom I call my great consolation, I live with the thought that I am no closer to doing what my coronation had set out to achieve. I must again be pregnant and next time bear a son. If not, I shall forever stay weakened. I see the sideways looks of the king's courtiers and the women at court and imagine what they think:

She did not fulfill her promise to the king and to the country. The birth of a girl does not justify the troubles of the past seven years. Only a son can do that. Delivering a girl is something her predecessor did. She is no better, just a pretender, with much to prove. The birth of a girl does nothing to prevent the emperor's impetus to restore Katherine and Mary. A son would have forever put to rest such an action.

It would do much more as well. Restore the king's love for me, wherein he treats me with care as he did before we were married. Now that I am done with being churched, I long to have him visit me at night. He need not stray any longer, seeking to satisfy his needs with others. I am ready to take his seed and bear the son he has long desired. We shall then have a prince and a princess, and I shall have what I desire most, security, peace and love for children, at rest being a mother, a wife, a queen, truly blessed and held in esteem by those who have long opposed me.

Until I have my son, I shall love my daughter, for I find in her sight and smell, in her sound and touch, such great joy, the likes of which I could have never imagined. I wanted, at birth, to hold on to her and never let go, though that was not possible. She was taken from me to be christened, and she is taken from me to be fed and nursed. I wanted to feed her myself, but Henry laughed at such a suggestion. Queens never suckle their own offspring, he said. It is not the custom and never will be. She must have a nurse for that purpose.

When I can, I keep her near me, lying at my feet on a velvet cushion, and, the few times we are left alone, I speak to her, looking deep into her tiny blue eyes. You are a princess, born of Anne Boleyn, never forget that. Though you are a girl, you will be educated by the best scholars come from Cambridge and one day surpass the achievements of men, for you have within you your father's title and heritage and your mother's desire for new learning and the new religion. You will be a pioneer, dearest Elizabeth, my child, my love, my vindication for now, until your brother is born, to which to that end I have much work to do.

87

Henry

Anne kept saying, See, I told you so, did I not tell you she was a fraud and should be stopped and punished? Yes, yes, I said, you told me. You were right, yes. Though I wish not to give her any more credit, for it was Cromwell and Cranmer, Thomas and Thomas, who did the investigations and interrogations, and it was their work at trial that landed the mad nun in the Tower prison along with five of her colleagues, monks and priests who, according to my chief adviser, incited her to speak her prophecies, which, for the record, never came true, evident in my being married to Anne for ten months, not having died a villain's death after one month as she had forewarned, evident in Anne continuing to wear the crown here on earth, in this realm, dripping with diamonds and gems on her satin and velvet gowns and not naked in hell, burning with devils, as the nun said should happen, evident in how my daughter Mary has not supplanted me on the throne and is in fact not even a princess anymore.

Cromwell said it was just a matter of finding and shutting off the fountain from which the nun's warnings sprang. Look no further than Edward Bocking, he said, monk of Christchurch Priory, who produced a book detailing Elizabeth Barton's revelations, and had seven hundred copies made, ready to be distributed and read, a clear act of sedition, though Cromwell discovered what was happening and ordered that all copies be seized and destroyed. It didn't take long for my advisor to work his magic. I don't know what he did or said to the nun, but in the words of Cranmer who was with him the nun quickly confessed, saying she never had visions in her life, that what she said was feigned of her own imagination, only to satisfy the minds of those who influenced her, and to obtain worldly praise.

Cromwell takes her out of prison to tour the kingdom, to stand in front of people and confess her fraudulence. Yesterday she made a confession in front of two thousand people at St. Paul's Cross, where temporary platforms and public seating had been erected. He invited me to attend, though I declined. Just give me a report, I said. I now read her words.

I, Dame Elizabeth Barton, do confess that I, most miserable and wretched person, have been the original of all this mischief, and by my falsehood have grievously deceived all these persons here and many more, whereby I have most grievously offended Almighty God and my most noble sovereign, the King's Grace. Wherefore I humbly, and with heart most sorrowful, desire you to pray to Almighty God for my miserable sins and to make supplication to my most noble sovereign for me for his gracious mercy and pardon.

I leave it to Cromwell and Parliament, which meets in January to determine her fate, though I'm certain Anne will have something to say about the nun asking for mercy and pardon. I expect she will say, send her to the hell she wished to send us, let her rot with Satan. Let her and her friends stand as examples that those who deny Queen Anne's right to rule, and the birthright and legitimacy of her daughter, shall perish.

88

Anne

It is done. Mary is now at Hatfield, in the capacity of Elizabeth's servant, as I had suggested to the king. Disband her manor at Essex. Conserve expenditures and make clear to her on a daily basis that she serves the true princess, the legitimate heir of a legitimate queen. He allowed me this satisfaction, knowing I suffered the absence of my daughter, only three months old, taken from me as custom dictates, miles from the pestilence of London to the healthy country air, to be cared for by Lady Bryan and a household of nurses and servants. I wept to have her taken from my arms, though I consoled myself knowing I would visit her, speak to her as I was wont to do, and remind her that I and no other was her mother and would always be, despite our separation.

I am not surprised to hear the task of removing Mary was fraught with difficulty, that when my uncle Norfolk went to escort her to her new home, in her new position, she raged nonsensically, crying that the title of princess to which he referred belonged to her by right of her royal blood, and to no one else, that she would never call her sister princess, nor would she ever call me queen. To which I said to my uncle: She deserves to have the Spanish blood slapped out of her. He responded to me coldly. Madam, he said, I shall leave the slapping to you. That action was not part of the job description given to me by the king.

Do not insult me, uncle, I said. If I make such a suggestion, it is with good reason. The girl is insolent, is she not? His eyes were gray, the color of stone. Many others are insolent, and I do not slap them. If you are insinuating me, dearest uncle, I should remind you that I am Queen of England, which makes you my subject. Subject? Do not make me laugh. You are my niece, and shall always be my niece, though I wish not to remind myself that you are a relation.

A time may come, good uncle, when you may call upon our relation to save you from the king's anger. Until then, he said, it is better I do not answer to you about matters concerning the king and his daughter. You shall tell me that the job is done, as you were ordered to do, I said. By the king, I remind you, he replied, his eyes straight as arrows. It is from him I take my orders, not you. Never you. Let us have that understanding between us. Tell me that the job was done, I demanded, that Mary now resides in Elizabeth's household as her maid of honor. Yes, I will tell you that much, he conceded. The job is done. I owe you no more information than that. He took his leave. I shouted after him: In time, you will owe me much more.

89

Henry

I wished not to hear about my wife's insolence, I told Norfolk. If he and his niece could not get along, it was their business, to which I would not interfere. I just wanted the report from Essex and Hatfield. He complied, telling me in his own words, as I sat and listened.

I told her she was being moved to Hatfield, to serve her sister, who now owned the title Princess of Wales. She became hysterical, saying she would never acknowledge Your Majesty's mistress (her words not mine), nor would she ever call Your Majesty's daughter Elizabeth princess. She said I had wasted my time traveling from London, for she would never renounce her title, given to her by royal right. Wrong, I told her. I did not waste my time, for I am not here to make you renounce anything. That is the king's business, and it is within his authority to remove your right and give the title to whomever he wished. I have not traveled here to dispute with you over lineage. My business is to make sure you pack your belongings and arrive in Hatfield before nightfall. She fell against a wall and screamed that she would not obey such a ridiculous order. I looked the other way, waiting for her to finish her rant, which continued for some time, becoming a tearful beseeching on her knees, which I allowed her to do, saying nothing as she did. When she finished her weeping, I said, I am determined to see my desires and commands executed, and as such you're going to Hatfield one way or the other. It's best you comply peacefully, riding your own horse rather than strapped to another's, like a sack of grain.

She wiped her tears and asked for time, saying she must first inform Lady Margaret Douglas and Lady Margaret Pole, her best women and confidantes, as she called them, allowing them opportunity to pack as well for the journey to Hatfield. That won't be necessary, I said. Your best women and confidantes have been reassigned. A woeful, moaning sound escaped her lips, followed by words of hysterical protest. Lady Pole has been with me since childhood, she cried. My father cannot take from me the woman who has been as a mother to me, in the absence of my true mother. Yes, he can, I said. Your father can do as he wishes when it pertains to one so obstinate as yourself. Perhaps if you obeyed the king's will your circumstances would be different. Lady Douglas is to serve Queen Anne's household and Lady Pole is being sent to her children. Anne Shelton, sister to Thomas Boleyn, aunt to Queen Anne, will command the household at Hatfield, including the servants, Princess Elizabeth and, in particular, you.

She looked like a rag doll as she flung herself awkwardly over a chair. Am I left with nothing? She asked. No, not nothing, I said. You may take as many dresses as you like, but not your jewels, for they now belong to the new princess. She wept profusely, to no avail. The next morning, dressed in her finest gown, her eyes swollen and streaked with red, she rode between me and my contingency to her new home, where upon arrival she refused to pay court to baby Elizabeth, acknowledging her as princess, as I commanded.

I will treat her as a sister only, she said. Expect nothing more of me. Before I left, I asked if she had a message she wished me to deliver to Your Majesty. None, she said, except I, the Princess of Wales, his daughter, ask for his blessing. I told her she needed to obey Your Majesty in all matters, for to disobey her father, the king, daughter or not, invited grave consequences. If she knew nothing else, she must know that. To which she replied, I will obey my father on some, not all, matters. Only those just and fair. Relinquishing my title doesn't qualify.

Though dismayed by his report, I thanked him for his duty, going so far as to say the queen, his niece, thanked him as well.

He laughed from the side of his mouth and bowed, taking his leave.

90

Katherine

I gathered my servants around me in the great chamber so that they could bear witness to the encounter soon to ensue as the Duke of Suffolk and a contingent of men faced me. I will not move to Fotheringhay, I said. It is old and not in very good shape, and I will not go to Somersham, especially there, for it is worse than where I currently reside, even more damp and cold, further in the Fens, more surrounded by water and marshes, more pestilential. I know it is what Anne Boleyn wants, to see me catch cold and die to avoid murdering me at her hands, for I hear the rumors of her evil intentions, both toward me and my daughter. I am not worried for myself. I can lock my doors and guard myself. It is Mary for whom I worry now that she is under the care and direction of Anne's aunt, who surely wishes her harm.

Suffolk rolled his eyes and sighed. Shall I convey to you in person, duke, what I wrote when I heard of your wife's passing this summer? It is not necessary, he said. I already read your words when they were delivered. Dear Mary, sister of Henry, I recited from memory, may her soul rest in everlasting peace and join with God, as she much deserves, having supported me till the end of her life against her brother's mistreatment of me and his abandonment of the faith his family long practiced. Again, I appreciate your words of condolence, he said, but it is not for them that I am here. No, of course not, I said. You are to be congratulated for having taken a new bride. He shuffled his feet and made further breathy sounds, for he knew I did not condone of his actions, marrying as he did his thirteen-year-old ward, the daughter of my good friend, come from Spain with me, Maria de Salinas, now Lady Willoughby. The girl, Katherine, named for me, had been betrothed to Suffolk's son, Henry. Now she found herself married to a man nearing the age of fifty who should be more her grandparent than her husband. I did not spare my sarcasm, saying, I am sure you wish to be back home with her rather than here face to face with an old woman, close in age to yourself, who is about to defy your orders.

To which he said, It is to your own detriment and that of your daughter's if you defy my order, for what I say originates from the mouth of the king. It originates from the mouth of Anne Boleyn, and you know it, I said. Do not use pretense with me, dear sir. These good people who surround me do not wish to hear your lies. They call me by my rightful title and have vowed their allegiance to me, willing to fight alongside me rather than see me moved again to an even worse house, for I prefer to be hacked to pieces rather than accept the conditions of the king, wherein he disbanded me and married another against the laws of the only church that matters, in front of the only God who matters. You can be treated better, he said, your daughter as well. You don't have to live in the wet marshes of England, and she doesn't have to suffer the humiliation of being her baby sister's maid of honor.

The price for that concession is too high, sir, I replied. In any case, I have my order, he persisted. I laughed, looking around me at those who still revered me as Queen of England. Do you know me as one who bends her will to an order? It will take force to make me move, perhaps even bloodshed, and though it may be my blood that spills it will puddle and come to rest on your conscience, sir. There will be no bloodshed, he said. I assume that means you will leave me in peace. It means no such thing, he said. Only that you will be made to comply.

Have you not ears, Suffolk? Did you not hear me say I will not comply unless you wish to force the issue and take up arms and drag me by my hair, half-naked, thrown on a litter through the village, where men and women shall attack you with whatever implements they hold in their hands, sticks and stones or even their bare knuckles? If you are willing to endure that, fine. Otherwise, I shall not comply to your demand, for a move to Somersham is tantamount to the taking of my own life, for I would surely die there in that pestilent house surrounded by marshes and bog water. I cannot do that, for the taking of one's own life is a sin against the laws of God, and I shall never fail God, though the men he has put on earth have failed me. Why should you want this trouble, you who have a new bride, barely out of the cradle, with whom I am sure you wish to begin procreating, though you shame yourself by doing so, as you shame yourself accosting an old woman, one whom you once called your queen, having taken a vow of allegiance toward her? Where is your decency? Desiring to take me to a house that will kill me dishonors the memory of your wife, Mary and your newest mother, Lady Willoughby.

I shall have to write to the king, he said, and tell him you are the most obstinate woman that may be. You do that, I responded, and tell him if he wants, he himself can come here and tie me in ropes. He has after all, done worse. I shall do worse, he said, before I leave here, if you do not come with me of your own volition. He followed through on his promise, locking up Thomas Abel, my chaplain, in the porter's lodge, forcing some servants to swear an oath never to call me queen, and sending others away. Then, to prove the seriousness of his intent, he ordered his men to pack my luggage unto a wagon. To no avail, though, for I shut myself in my room and locked the door, forcing him to address me from a hole in the wall.

Think carefully about your actions, sir, I said. You have three choices. One, you can break down the door, though it might cause more harm to you and your men than to the door. Two, you can break down the door to your own detriment and then, while escorting me outside, you will be set upon by a mob of angry villagers, who will not stand by idly to see such cruelty brought upon their queen. If you fight them, you risk a rebellion which is sure to spread. Three, you can leave peacefully and save yourself the humiliation of hurting yourself on a door and saving yourself and your men from bloodshed.

Fine, he said through the hole, I will leave, but you should know that in refusing to obey these commands, the king will reduce your household further, and new servants with no loyalty to you will be brought in to spy on your every thought, word and deed. You will be, in effect, a prisoner in your own house. What, am I now free? I asked. Or have I been the past two years? It will be an imprisonment much worse than what you've known, he declared. Do what you must, Suffolk, but know this: You can imprison me in this or any other house, but you can never imprison my will, my conscience, or my soul.

91

Anne

I am again pregnant and wish to enjoy the carrying of this child, a boy with God's grace, though how can I ever be at rest while Katherine and Mary live? I tell the king of my frequent dreams, wherein they wish to see me dead. Do you wish to see me dead rather than them? I ask. His response is always the same: They are just dreams, for which we should not worry. But worry I do, for dreams or not, what I see and hear could as easily bear fruit in this conscious life, evident by how I still shake to recall the latest.

Mary stood over me, toothless, balding, grinning. What do you want? I cried. You cannot have my son. What son? She asked, her mouth spewing fog and fumes. Here in my belly, I said. She walked closer to me. I see no baby in your belly, Lady Anne. Call me Queen Anne, I demanded. Lady Anne, she repeated. My father's mistress, nothing more. See for yourself that you have no baby in your belly. I looked down and saw and felt that I was flat. Where is my baby? I shouted. You have taken him. Give him to me. She left the room, wearing still her hideous grin. I jumped out of bed in only my nightgown and stepped outside, in the hallway, that soon became a street, that soon brought to my eyes a marching of guards, speaking Spanish, including Katherine and the emperor, leading me to a place I knew well, the Tower, where I stayed before my coronation in apartments lush in tapestries and cloths of gold and silver. Now, I sat on a cold, stone floor, in a room barren of even a stick of wood or a window to bring me air, imprisoned, listening to the cries of a baby. Mary entered wearing a crown, her teeth and hair restored, her grin wider than before, holding a silent baby in her arms. Is that my son? I said, pleading, my arms reaching out. Give him to me. She handed me the child, blood-soaked and dead. I dropped him and screamed.

I woke up, on my lips the words: I am her death and she is mine. I must write to my aunt at Hatfield, I thought. I am disturbed by the reports she sends, telling me of the belligerence she witnesses, how Mary wants to be treated differently, demanding separate and more expensive meals than others in the household, shouting at all hours for her independence to walk and ride as she pleases, complaining of one illness after another, claiming that my aunt, under my orders, wishes to kill her, refusing to acknowledge her sister as princess or me as queen, saying to all who she encounters, I am Princess Mary, the only legitimate princess in England. I have told my aunt to box her cursed bastard ears whenever she says this. Get her to acknowledge my title and that of my daughter's. I don't care if she says it freely or reluctantly, as long as she says it. My aunt wishes not to harm the girl physically, she says, worrying that if the girl, in her already fragile state, dies, she will be blamed. She will not die from a slap to the head, I have said. If anything, it will awaken her senses before she has none.

She is not deserving of respect and kindness, I will write. She is a bastard, not a princess. I know my aunt, a mother of six, with a natural heart of gold, will say that even a bastard born of a poor gentleman deserves honor and good treatment. I will remind her, though, that Mary is not an ordinary bastard. She is a dangerous one. She must not be allowed freedoms. She must be supervised and watched at all times. Do not let her fragile health influence you, I shall add. She is spoiled and manipulative. Forbid her to write to her mother or receive letters, and never allow visitors, especially Ambassador Chapuys. I do not trust him, for I know he communicates with Katherine and the emperor, plotting with them to have Mary freed from Hatfield into their waiting arms to initiate war against us and crown her queen.

I shall end with this note: I know you have told me you are a mother, not a jailer. Let me put it to your straight, dear aunt. I am your queen and you serve me and Your Majesty above all others. I care not whether you perform your position with enthusiasm and love. I care only that you perform it well.

92

Henry

I visited briefly with baby Elizabeth, held her in my arms, marveled at her features and coloring, which so resemble mine. I called her princess. She smiled, as if she knows who she is and who I am and what her future holds. Though I was glad to see she is healthy and happy, I did not travel to Hatfield with the intent of visiting only her. I aimed to speak with Mary, set her straight, let her know her behavior would only make her situation worse until she comes to accept that she is no longer princess and acknowledges her sister's title and Anne's as queen. That visit never happened, though. Anne altered my plans. See only Elizabeth, she said. She is your legitimate daughter and princess. Do not see Mary. She will plead and beseech with you, make you soften your resolve against her, wherein both you and I will suffer for it. Have Cromwell talk sense into her. He is more suited for the job, for his emotions will not interfere with his objective. You know what I say is true. Honor my request, if you care anything about my condition.

Yes, of course, her condition. How could I refuse her request, knowing if I did, she would become upset and rage at me? I must, above all else, think about the child she carries. I want a son, and he must be healthy, and if it means I should forego seeing my daughter, my first born, to settle Anne's nerves, then it is a sacrifice I must make. While I held Elizabeth, I thought of Cromwell and how he would work his magic on Mary. He had broken the Maid of Kent's will; he had made the pope a nonentity in England; he had passed bill after bill in Parliament to give me greater authority in church and state matters. What couldn't he do?

I soon found out the answer when he came downstairs, looking dour, and faced me, long after I had given Elizabeth back to her nurses. Well, I said. Speak to me, even if it is not what I want to hear. What did she say? She prays always, he said, for the day when she can be reunited with her mother and father, the three of you dressed royally, sitting on your thrones at court, she being called by courtiers and foreign ambassadors from near and far the names and descriptions she had inherited at birth, Princess Mary, Princess of Wales, the most blessed child in all of Christendom. I sighed. She won't let go, will she?

She knows you are here, he said, and wishes to visit with you, to kiss your hand, to let you know she desires your affection. Did you tell her that was not possible until she renounces her title and acknowledges Anne as queen? I asked. She made it clear she will never renounce her title or acknowledge her sister as princess or Anne Boleyn as queen, he answered. She will never turn her back on her mother, whom she calls the only Queen of England, or on God. She called my travel to Hatfield and my visit with her wasted labor, for she would sooner receive worse punishments and die a martyr than relent to my demands, come from you.

It's her mother who puts such thoughts in her head, I said. Why else should she choose to die when she is young? I would give her the world if only she would bend her will to mine. Did you tell her that? Yes, he said, I told her if she wanted your love, she needed to earn it by showing her obedience to you. She said she could not do that without dishonoring herself. She believes she is right and no matter what threats I made to her she would not alter her belief. I told her that the only right in this world is what you, her father, says is right. She replied sharply that Lady Anne, never queen, pulls your strings and makes you say what you believe is right, knowing in your heart it is wrong. She wants you to know she is not a puppet. She moves and talks without strings, unlike those, like myself, who serve you. I told her I was not a puppet either. I am, however, loyal I said, and as his servant I shall tell your father you wish to persist in your disobedience. She said, tell my father that what he calls disobedience is nothing more than my obedience to God and my conscience.

Those are her mother's words, I shouted. As I reminded her, he said. To which she said, I can think of no better person to parrot. My gosh, Cromwell, such insolence from one so young, I said. She is, Your Majesty, he replied, like her mother, a stone that cannot be moved. Oh, really, I said. Stones may not move, but they can be broken. He cautioned me. You may have to chip away at this one, he said. Meaning what, Cromwell? Her punishment is still young, Your Majesty. Time will wear down her defenses. Time hasn't worn down her mother's defenses and it's been seven years, I responded. Why should Mary's defenses be any weaker?

I left, disgusted. As my men and I mounted our horses, I looked up and saw a girl on the terrace, looking down at me. I wanted to believe it was someone else, but her small thin body gave her away, as did her hands clasped in prayer and the movement of her lips. I thought I heard her say, Father. I stared at her for a moment. It could have been longer, as if time had stopped and we had become frozen in tableau. Finally, I felt myself move. I bowed to her and put my hand to my hat. My courtiers, including Cromwell, did the same. I turned and quickly rode away.

.

93

Anne

I dressed for the occasion, wearing a French hood, a red ermine kirtle, gold damask gown and furs, and around my neck and on my fingers pearls from Egypt and gems from Turkey. When Mary entered the room, escorted by my aunt, Lady Shelton, I still held Elizabeth in my arms. You are well? I said to Henry's daughter, though I could see in her bleary eyes, cracked lips and pale skin that she was far from well, despite appearing fashionably dressed, minus the jewels she no longer possessed. She looked away. Lady Shelton answered for her. The Lady Mary suffers from illness in her stomach, head and teeth, she said. That is too bad, I replied. She is becoming all bones, my aunt continued, for she does not eat, believing the food not suitable for her. I have done everything but force the food in her mouth. I handed Elizabeth to the day nurse and dismissed the servants. I sat down and asked Mary to do the same. Lady Shelton asked if she should stay. Not necessary, I said. I would call her if needed.

A table, with a flagon of wine, two goblets, and assorted cakes, had been set for our meeting. I lifted the bottle and a goblet, asking her if she wanted wine. She refused to look at me. I placed the bottle and goblet down and lifted the tray of food. A pastry or cake? I asked. She sighed, clutching at her stomach, rubbing it. I shall take your silence as no, I said, setting the tray down, aware that my hands shook. The presence of Henry's daughter near me had that kind of effect, due to her royal smugness, her Spanish bloodline, which could be traced to kings, queens and emperors, which had a way of announcing to me, you, Anne Boleyn, are nothing compared to me, you who are born in the English backwaters, among provincial commoners. Which, of course, is not true, though in my mind I believe she thinks that.

I am glad you have agreed to see me, I said. My letters to

you have gone unanswered, and I wish very much to extend my previous offer, to have you come to court and live there beside me as my daughter, to see you to live in better health. She turned her head to meet my eyes, appearing to study them. Do you not believe I care about your health? I asked. She frowned. I prefer to believe what is true, she said. I smiled back at her. Pray, tell me, what is true? You wish to kill me by poison or some other means, she said. My mother as well. I took a sip of wine to steady myself, to arrange the expression of face I wished to convey, cordial, welcoming.

To the contrary, I said. I wish for peace between us. You need only acknowledge me as queen and my daughter, your sister, as princess. If you do, I will intercede with the king on your behalf to see you are better treated than ever. I shall be pleased to have you at court, received honorably in a position not much below mine, and you will once again have the affection and favor of your father. I know of no queen in England except my mother, she said, but if you wish to speak to my father on her behalf, I would be much obliged. I took another sip of wine. It is only your stubbornness that rejects my lawful marriage to your father, as decreed in Parliament, I said. She spat as she talked. I care not for Parliament. Only for the laws of God.

I suppressed an urge to raise my voice. Fine, I said, if it's the laws of God you want, is it not proven in the Bible and confirmed by the bishops of England that in marrying his brother's widow, your father, along with your mother, committed incest, an act offensive to both the laws of God and man? She shouted at me: My mother was a maid, and my father knows she was. I shouted back: Six months of marriage, and we are to believe your mother was a maid? As much as is to be believed you were a maid before cohabitating with my father, she responded. My chastity is no business of yours, I said, feeling the calm exterior I had hoped to maintain leave me. As your opinions of my mother are none of yours, she said, saliva escaping from her mouth.

I sat forward and swallowed hard, determined to break her pride. Is not the proof of their sin evident in your mother not producing a male heir? Having had six pregnancies and only one living child, and that a girl? She leaned forward as well. And you, Lady Anne, what have you produced, other than a single girl? Call me Your Highness, I demanded, and render me the respect which is my due. Her eyes became blood red. Never shall I call you anything but what you are, my father's mistress. I could call you a different name, but as a Christian, I must refrain.

You shall speak differently when I deliver the male heir that is now growing inside me, I said, caressing my stomach. You cannot be certain of that, she said. Boys will follow, I said. Your father said those words to me while I lay in bed, holding my daughter after her birth. He said those same words to my mother after I was born, she said. Which turned out to be false, I said. I, however, have received from the finest astrologers, assurance that the child I carry shall be the heir to the throne. It is God's will, not science's, she said, to determine the birth and sex of a child, and if God's will be fair, as I know it is, you shall never deliver a male heir, for you have broken his commandment, marrying my father while he was already married to my mother, as decreed by the pope in Rome.

I stood up, pushing my chair aside. I have made you an offer, let that be known, I said. She stood as well. How dare a usurper to my mother's crown tell me to submit my will to her. You wear the crown unlawfully, no matter how it fits your head, and all the jewels, gems, furs and gowns in the kingdom, which you stole from my mother, cannot make you queen. I took a step toward her. Let it be known what you speak is treasonous. She did not move. What I speak is true, she shouted. Do not come crying to me for mercy when it is too late, I snapped, for it is only a matter of time, unless you change your attitude by first obeying your father, and, by second, respecting me as your queen and superior, that you will suffer ill effects, even worse than those you suffer now.

Her eyes began to tear and her voice, high-pitched, became slurred. I, unlike you, am a Christian woman and understand how to suffer, taking as my example Christ himself. Know this, though; I shall outlast you, for when my father tires of you, as he will, you will be banished as my mother has been, and in your place, will be another. God has told me she will return England to the traditional faith, the religion of my mother and father, wherein I will once again see my rise as princess. England will never return to the traditional faith, I said. Rome and the pope no longer exist to us. If you opened your eyes and saw what was real in place of your illusions, such as your mother still living as queen and you as princess, you would see the world around you changing. Get used to it. God, let me inform you, also speaks to me, and he tells me He has chosen me to be Queen of England in order to restore the true religion.

She rushed toward me, like an animal loosed from a cage. The voice you hear is not God's, it is the devil's. I raised my quivering hand, then settled it, suppressing the urge to slap the Spanish out of her. If it were up to me—and it shall be when my son is born—you would be sent away to a convent or married away to someone of modest means, and your husband will not call you princess. He will call you lady, if you are so fortunate, though in time it is more likely he will call you wretched, for that is what you are, a wretched, cursed bastard, for all your disobedience and disrespect. Her face became a smear of tears and dark smudges, which she rubbed as she talked wildly. As you are the unloved mistress of the king, so like your sister, who was my father's whore. Mistress Anne, that is what you are and will always be, nothing more, a former lady-in-waiting to my mother, who is of royal blood from Aragon, Castile and Spain. What are you in blood? A Boleyn. Upstarts without spines.

I grabbed her arm. I am queen, and you shall say it. She pulled away from my grip and with both her hands grabbed the sides of her head. I pulled her hands down. Say it, I repeated. She moved away. My mother is the only queen I know, she shouted, covering her head again. I threw the goblet to the floor, breaking it. You shall say I am queen, or you shall not live. I am prepared to die a martyr, she said. Do you not see that I am? So be it, I said, brushing past her, calling for my aunt, calling for Lady Bryan, calling to see my daughter again, to hold her close to me, to forget that Henry has a daughter with a woman whom I despise.

94

Henry

I do not want to see that annoying little man, I said to Cromwell. He is a flea in my ear, belonging on the hide of a mule, somewhere in Spain. Can you not dispatch him there? I expected Cromwell to laugh, to let down his guard, or let fall that mask he wears, which, according to many, is used for effect. He stayed on course, straightening his face, aligning his lips, saying, The ambassador is linked to the emperor, who is linked to Katherine and Mary, who are linked to you. Thus, I'm afraid his audience with you cannot be avoided.

How short he is, I thought as he entered. What a twisted frame, what an unsteady walk, what gimpy, tiny legs, what an awful twitch of his lower lip when he speaks, curling his r's and hissing his s's, making the English language a rope tied in knots. I could crush him with one blow if it didn't result in retaliation. If only I could rid myself of the emperor and eradicate his aunt and make her daughter (mine as well) submit to my will. All these Spanish bulls rushing at me. I am not a matador. I am an English king, forced to find ways to sidestep them, to not be run over and trampled by them, to come out looking like the mangled man who faced me.

So, what can I do for you ambassador? (As if I didn't already know!) He tells me I mistreat Katherine and Mary, formerly queen and princess of England, in case I had forgotten. I give him a brief history lesson in case he has forgotten. Nearly one year it has been since my marriage to Katherine was determined in an English court to be unlawful. She should have never been called queen. As for my daughter Mary, well, even if she were legitimate, which she's not, her disobedience merits disinheritance. I tell him how she upset the queen on her visit to Hatfield, the queen who is now with child, my heir. The child she carries is everything to me, I continue, so don't bother me with trifles, such as my treatment of a woman who was never legally my wife and a daughter who is a bastard. They are treated as they deserve to be treated.

To which he was not in the least deterred from rushing at me with his horns, pointing out that Parliament could not make Mary a bastard, that legitimacy cases could be decided only by ecclesiastical judges, and, besides, Mary was legitimate owing to the lawful ignorance of her parents, wherein I myself had considered her as the true princess until the birth of Elizabeth. It was bad enough he tied the English language in a knot. I wouldn't allow him to tie me up as well. What are you saying, man? According to English law, Mary cannot succeed. There is no other princess except my daughter Elizabeth, until I have a son, which should happen soon, wherein the whole business of who is the rightful princess will be made a moot point, sure to disarm the imperialists, don't you think? He said he wished not to speak of uncertainties, for until the day came that I had a son the debate over who had the right to succeed would continue. In the meantime, he wanted better conditions for Mary, asking that she be allowed to live with her mother, raising the possibility of unpleasant rumors if she fell ill. Such as what? I demanded. People will say she was poisoned, he said, a mad gleam in his eye. Catholic Europe will be up in arms, forcing the emperor to do what he has till now restrained from doing.

Do not blackmail me, ambassador, I shouted, hoping I will act out of fear instead of sense, for I am not a man given to rumors as you Spanish are. As it concerns Mary, know this. She is well and in a good place, and I shall dispose of her as I wish, without anyone, least of all you, laying down the law to me. I need not give you nor anyone else of your side an account of my affairs, especially those concerning my family. A daughter owes some obedience to her mother. I grant that. But it is to her father she owes her greatest obedience. Mary, by refusing unquestioned loyalty to me, has forfeited all due consideration of her situation. Placing her with her mother would mean that she could never be brought to see reason. Thus, your request shall not be met to your satisfaction. You may now sulk out of here as you sulked in, and in your next report to the emperor make sure to say hello from me.

95

Katherine

I am on my knees. Thank you, God. Finally, His Holiness has passed the sentence I have long dreamed, seven bitter years, to hear: The marriage of Henry and Katherine always has and still does stand firm and canonical, and the issue proceeding stands lawful and legitimate. To which, in His Holiness's words and those corroborated by Cardinal Campeggio, Henry is ordered to resume cohabitation with me, his lawful wife and queen, to hold me and maintain with me such love and princely honor as becomes a loving husband for it is his kingly honor to do so.

I wait for his message, his summoning me back to court, as I am certain he will, for he cannot deny the words come from the holy fathers, those who meant so much to him, despite his recent break with them, due only to those who have filled his brain with dissent for that which he once loved, that which earned him the title Defender of the Faith. That does not disappear on a whim. What does disappear is the whim itself, the infatuation with Anne Boleyn, the false marriage, the bastard child. Just passing whims, unlike his beliefs, which ground him. I know in my heart that he wishes to be grounded again after having lived for too long ungrounded, leaving him vulnerable to those who influence and use him for their own interests and advancements. Anne Boleyn is one such person, Cranmer and Cromwell others. He doesn't need them any longer. I will tell him he has me, he has our daughter, and our hearts are brimming with forgiveness and love. That is our only concern, not what has happened, but what will happen once we are together again, attending mass, saying our confessions, riding, hunting, giving the greatest banquets England has ever seen, bringing the court back to its original glory when courtiers and foreign visitors delighted to be in our presence, not like it is today, more suited to a funeral, everyone's faces low, turning their heads away from the concubine queen, spreading dissension. I know, for Ambassador Chapuys tells me.

I shall sleep well tonight for the first time in years, for not only does the sentence mean that Henry must return to me. It means I did not sin, that my marriage has always been good and lawful, that my daughter is not only legitimate but the true heiress to the English crown, that my arguments, though labeled mad by many, were sound and just, that God is the real judge of our actions, that I have been vindicated.

96

Henry

I am laughing. How else should I react to the pope's sentence, ridiculous as it is, stating, my marriage to Katherine always has and still does stand firm and canonical, and the issue proceeding stands lawful and legitimate? To think, it took him seven years to write those words. So, if I am to understand the rest of his judgment completely, I am to do the following, in this order: first, rid myself of Anne, the concubine, and the bastard Elizabeth, and, second, return to Katherine to once again become a loving husband and family man, restoring Mary as heiress to the English crown. Lastly, I must pay the costs of the trials and deliberations, both in England and in Rome. I must do all of that if I hope to avoid excommunication (yet again).

How should I rid myself of Anne? Do I poison her with the poisons she is said to possess and wishes to use on others, such as Katherine and Mary? Would I not then also kill my unborn child, whom I expect to be a boy, the heir to the throne? Do I, more mercifully, send her away to live out her days in Hever with her bastard children, visited by her father, brother and sister on Sundays to share a meal, good ale and merriment? Sure, I can see either of these acts enforced, though it took me seven years to marry her and see issue from her, all the while turning the world upside down to make it happen. But if getting rid of her is what I must do to save myself from excommunication, then it must be done. Afterwards, I can ride a white horse to Buckden to save the damsel in distress, Katherine, carrying her away from the damp Fens, returning her to Greenwich and most importantly to the jewels I took from her. I should beg her forgiveness for seven years' worth of mistreatment and pray with her day and night, in between eating the host and cleaning the statues of saints, for at her age, well past the ability to give birth or dance with me, for lack of a better term, there would be little else to do. But why should it matter as long as I loved her, as it is honorable for me, as king, to do, and she loved me? We would have our ailing daughter, replete with headaches, stomach cramps and toothaches, near us to live happily ever after, without a son, though why should I care about something as trifling as that?

I shall burst a few blood vessels if I don't stop laughing. Take a breath, I tell myself. Calm down. Rely on your faculty of reason, and if that doesn't work simply write a note to the pope to inform him that his timing couldn't be more absurd, for on the very day of his stupid sentence, Parliament has passed the Act of Succession, which in its preamble states that the pope (that's you) could not encroach on the great and inviolable God-given rights of kings (that's me), declaring further that my marriage to Katherine is not just void and annulled, but *utterly* so. A word Cromwell insisted on using for its definitiveness. You will also read that Katherine shall be from henceforth called and reputed only dowager to Prince Arthur, and not queen. Meaning that Mary is pure, unadulterated bastard. As for the present queen, know this: My marriage to Anne is declared true, sincere and perfect ever hereafter, our children vested as successors to the imperial crown of England. Now, does that sound like someone whom I should like to discard?

I might not laugh if you had made your sentence years ago, when it may have been relevant, when you were relevant, seen as supreme, second to God. We know now that none of that's true. You are as irrelevant as a fallen leaf, scattered by the wind, a weightless, deteriorating man, who can barely decide what shoes to wear, let alone decide on a king's annulment. The only ones, I imagine, who take your sentence seriously are Katherine and Mary, the emperor and Chapuys, the little charging bull. In other words, only the crazy Spanish. We English no longer care what you say or do. Don't be offended if I don't send you payment for the trials and deliberations. Charge my account, if you want, though for the record, it, like you, expired long ago. As for that excommunication, you know where to stick it.

97

Anne

You should be pleased, should you not? Henry asked me. The Act of Succession is done for you, to make known to the people of this country that you alone are the true queen and all issue which proceeds from our union should be titled successors to the crown of England, and you shall be their regent if I were to predecease you. It is not enough I said. I shall remain hated, and you know it. If you really want to please me, have every man and woman in the country swear an oath to this newest act. Make them sign their names to prove their loyalty, if not their outright respect for me as their queen and the issues I bear as heirs. Have Cromwell, your Mr. Secretary, as you now call him, do that, ensuring those who do not sign are convicted of high treason. I wish to know with certainty who is for and who is against our marriage and my title. Only then, by abolishing those against us, will we have peace. Only then will the child in my womb know security. I know if you dare refuse me you will not refuse your heir.

That was how it started. Since then, many have been arrested, refusing to sign the oath, sent to the Tower: Bishop Fisher, Thomas More and Thomas Abel the biggest catches in Mr. Secretary's net, all Katherine supporters. They might ask the nun from Kent and her five associates, priests and monks who encouraged her mad prophecies, what happens to those who are defiant to law and make threats to those who wear the crown, though that should not be possible since they were executed the day before last. When I told Cromwell I wished to know the manner of their deaths, he said, It should satisfy you enough, Your Grace, to know they are dead. Let me be the judge of what satisfies me, I said. I wish to know that an example was set.

He obliged me, describing how they were taken from the

Tower and lashed tightly onto wooden planks, hitched onto horses, their wrists tied together as if they were praying, while dragged through the streets of London, five miles to Tyburn. On the scaffold, the nun told the assembled crowd she had been the cause of her own death, which she justly deserved, blaming her misfortune on being a poor wench without learning, exploited for profit by those condemned to die with her, men who had filled her head with praise and foolish fantasies. She was hanged and beheaded, her head impaled on London Bridge. The men suffered worse, having been hanged and revived, having their entrails removed and waved before their faces, before being hanged a second time and beheaded, their heads placed on various gates throughout the city.

Does that qualify as a strong enough example? He asked. Are you now satisfied? I will be, I answered, when I receive word that Katherine and Mary have signed the oath, and if they refuse that they are arrested as the others and met with the said punishment as laid out in the newest act, death and the forfeiture of land and goods to the crown. Dissension shall end, Mr. Secretary, and loyalty shall begin. By whatever means necessary, he said.

98

Katherine

They came, a contingent of bishops, new to me, Anne Boleyn's appointees, except Edward Lee, who now held the archbishopric of York. He had once been a friend. Now, he stood before me as a messenger, void of manners and proper respect. He knew only duty to the king, which required of him a cold heart. The sentence from Rome is meaningless, he said. The newest act in Parliament renders it so. Do not say meaningless, I replied. God's judgment has great meaning to me, even if it has none to men who choose to turn their back on Him. We are not here to dispute God's judgment, he said, especially when the pope, whose authority we no longer acknowledge, issues it. We are here as emissaries of the king, who, as anyone loyal to the crown knows, is ordained by God. It is, therefore, the King's laws which command us. You, as an obedient subject, must allow yourself to be commanded as well. This house is not suitable for your health and well-being. You can, if you choose, live a life of elegant retirement, if only you will accept the Act of Succession. He took from his bag a paper. It is the oath, he said. Sign your name to it and swear on it, as every subject must.

I will not disrespect my hand to hold a pen to such a vile paper, I said. I am not, and will never be, Henry's subject. I am his wife. Though you say the pope's sentence is meaningless in relation to this newest act, I say it is rendered even more meaningful, for it gives me the impetus to choose to keep my name where it belongs, in my principled soul, not given up cheaply for sale, like so many others who sign and sell themselves to live as cowards. I will do as those imprisoned in the Tower have done, friends of mine, good Christian men, Bishop Fisher, Thomas More and Chaplain Abel, who value conscience above all else, even life. I will sign nothing. I am married to the king lawfully and my daughter Mary is the rightful heir to the throne. Anne Boleyn has married him illegally, and whatever children they have will be illegitimate, and neither this Act of Succession nor your demeaning of the pope's sentence will change that truth.

Do not be surprised, as you appear to be, because I am small and have always conveyed a cheerful public temperament that I now speak loudly, with great choler. I am in agony. Can you not see that? Are you so dead in your brains that you cannot understand a woman's pain, she who has been unjustly treated?

He didn't blink as he said: Understand, madam, that if you do not sign and swear to the oath, you are subject to the same punishments as everyone else. The same punishments as the Maid of Kent? I shouted. Shall I be dragged through the streets on a cart and hanged in a public square and then beheaded and seen by all on a pike on London Bridge? It is that I wish for instead of pining away here, alone, unnoticed, to die in secret. Tell the king I am prepared for martyrdom, like the certain fate of my friends. Only I desire it in public, as a final show, one that proves my right, shows my courage and exposes the cowardliness of my killers. Tell him I would like nothing better than that. For what else do I have since he has cast me out of Eden, wherein the serpent, Anne Boleyn, is left to feed on the apples, the good Christian men and women, who fall from the tree?

99

Henry

I will not make her a martyr, to give her what she wants, a public spectacle, to rouse the masses, to alarm her nephew, to turn his Imperial army against us. I shall stay the course, keep moving her, reducing her household, keep her hidden away from those who wish to continue their support of her, though they sign their names to swear to an oath they do not in their hearts believe. Chapuys informed me she agreed to move to Kimbolton without a fight, asking to be allowed to keep her confessor, physician and apothecary, as well as two menservants and as many women as I in my kindness would appoint, for she was often sickly and required their attendance for the preservation of her poor body.

I granted the request, with a condition of my own, that he stop accusing me of mistreating her. Did not my concession to her terms, along with the yearly expenses I pay, exceeding four thousand pounds, prove that the Lady Dowager is being well treated in everything, though she behaves disobediently to me? Let it be known that I could have forced the issue and sent her to Somersham, which she called a swamp of death. Kimbolton is a stately manor, far enough from the damp and cold of Buckden. It is an improved condition. Make sure to tell the emperor that.

I shall, he said, though I am certain you are concealing your true motive for sending her to Kimbolton, which, as my informants tell me, is a fortified castle, a stately well-kept prison. Am I wrong in saying that? If she is a prisoner it is because she chooses to be one, I snapped. She can be free, remember that, ambassador, if she swears to the oath and signs her name. That is all it takes. You may as well ask God to give you heaven while you live before you have properly earned it, he said. That is a more likely occurrence than the sight of her signature wherein she denounces herself as queen.

I dismissed him, though I desired to put my hands around his throat to put to an end his pestering of me. As for his calling Kimbolton a well-kept prison, I can make that happen. I have appointed two officers of the crown, Sir Edmund Bedingfield and Sir Edward Chamberlayne, northern men, hardened by their disputes with the Scots, as her governors. They are instructed to make sure she does not receive anyone or go anywhere without their consent, and to intercept every message she sends and receives. These measures, with the hope of good fortune, I pray, may yet wear her down until nature does what I cannot do, lay her defiance down to rest with God, unless He, unable to tolerate her Spanish pride, as I, sends her elsewhere.

100

Katherine

This house, like none other where I've lived, is divided. The governors and their servants keep to their side of the house. I have two rooms across the courtyard and great hall from theirs, my own chamber women, Spanish speaking. Only they cook my meals, in my presence, using whatever means they can, in the very room where I sit all day and sleep at night behind a door bolted shut. It is where I pray with my confessor and where my doctor and apothecary treat me for the cough I have had since Buckden, the result of living so close to the damp Fens. I trust no one from the kitchens who wish to serve a nonexistent woman called Princess Dowager. I speak only to the contingent of people I brought with me, those who call me Queen Katherine. All others I call my jailers. I do not give them the opportunity to be my poisoners.

I have lived here less than a month and already the king has sent another emissary, this time the Bishop of Durham, to speak *sense to me* as he phrased it in his attempt to make me swear to the oath. I asked him: Who is Queen of England? He answered: Queen Anne. Is it because her name is on the oath that she is queen, and only that? I further inquired. She is queen according to law, he said. How can that be when I am queen by law? I replied. You, madam, are Princess Dowager by law, he declared. How dare you come to my rooms with your insolence, I snapped. Take your oath and leave, for I will never relinquish the title of queen. I shall retain it till death. That may be sooner than you think, he said, in light of your refusal to sign, for your defiance of law and your disobedience to the king. Hold your tongue, bishop, I said. What you speak are the wiles of the devil. By right, the king can have no other wife. Let this be your answer to the king or to whomever sent you, his Mr. Secretary, Cromwell, or his shadow, the worshipper of a false God, Cranmer. He dared to laugh at me. You shall not speak so bravely, or with such obstinacy, when you are sent to the scaffold. And who will be the hangman? I asked. If you have permission to execute this penalty on me, I am ready. I ask only that I be allowed to die in sight of the people of this village. I will leave that for the executioner, he said. Now, if you will not swear to the oath, I shall gather your servants and administer it to them, as I am requested by law to do.

He did just that, with my blessing, for all my servants, including my trio of men, were naturalized Spaniards, who spoke in their native tongue. I heard him say to them, their hands upon the Bible: Do you swear to acknowledge that King Henry is head of the church? Each answered: *El Rey se ha heco cabeza de la Iglesia.* The bishop seemed pleased, believing they had cooperated with him. He left not knowing what we who speak Spanish know, that they had merely acknowledged that Henry had made himself head of the church. A small victory, I thought, in this war of attrition.

101

Anne

I want Elizabeth closer to me I told Henry. Why should I, in my condition, be made to travel to Hertfordshire to see my daughter, the Princess of England? Bring her here to Greenwich. Can you not make Eltham Palace her home, moving her household there? Was it not where you yourself grew up with your mother and sisters, happily as you have said? If that is true, should not your daughter, your true princess, share the same experience, knowing her mother and father are but an hour's ride away? Think how pleasing that will be to her and to all of us.

Her transfer from Hatfield did not occur without drama, as told by my aunt. Mary locked herself in her room when she heard she would have to move to Eltham Palace and continue in her role as maid of honor to Elizabeth. She refused to eat for days on end, saying she would prefer to die of starvation than follow her sister and continue in a subservient role. I quickly dispatched a note to my aunt, instructing her what she must do. The girl should be dragged out of her room by her hair if necessary. If she resists further, tie her in ropes. I care not for her health and safety as long as you get her in the litter, next to you.

As it turned out, one of the gentlemen servants carried her in his arms into the litter while she kicked her legs and screamed that she was the only princess in England and her mother the only queen. My aunt tells me she cried the whole time on the journey to Greenwich, saying: The Lady Anne wants to kill me. Do you not see that? Do you not care? My aunt says she did not answer the hysterical girl. She let her blabber to herself: I want to see my mother, who alone knows how to cure me of my illness. I want to return to my own residence with my own maids and servants, to my beloved Margaret Pole, Lady Salisbury. Let me at least see her if you will not let me see my mother. My aunt closed her eyes and ears to the belligerent girl, though she should have knocked her on the side of her head to shut her up.

No sooner had Elizabeth arrived at Eltham Palace than I visited her, and on the same day I went to the royal chapel to give thanks and saw Mary. I assumed she saw me as well, for she quickly left. Lady Rochford, who was with me at the time, told me afterwards that Mary had curtseyed to me on her way out. I did not see it, I said. Your Grace must have looked elsewhere at that moment, she said. Hearing that buoyed my spirits. Was it a sign that Mary was ready to concede her title and acknowledge mine? Her respect for me, only that, is what I have long desired, and if her curtseying to me was true, I wanted to acknowledge my appreciation of it. I decided to send her a brief, conciliatory note. I salute you, Lady Mary, with much affection and crave your pardon, for I understand that at your parting from the oratory, you, according to Lady Rochford, made a curtsey to me, which, if I had seen it, I would have answered with the like. I receive your curtsey as a sign that you wish to acknowledge me as queen, and if this is true, I wish to be so much more to you, if you will let me.

The next day, I received a response which read: Lady Rochford was mistaken. If I made reverence, it was to the altar, to my maker, and to the only queen I know, who lives far from this place. It is not proper etiquette, as I have been taught, to bow to one below me in title.

I tore her note to shreds and yelled at Lady Rochford for having deceived me. I wanted to rage further, go to Eltham Palace and, with my fists if necessary, force Mary to kneel before me. My ladies calmed me down. You have a child inside you, Your Grace. Think of what is best for him. Lie down, listen to your songbird, sent from Lady Lisle as a gift for your impending birth. You yourself have said it never ceases to bring you joy with its constant music.

Yes, of course, I, said. I will listen to my bird, and dream of the heir inside me, wondering how he shall look, how tall, how strong, how able in thought and deed, to lead this country as none other ever has, not even his father. And while I listen, I shall hold my dog. Where is he? Give him to me. He ran to me, jumping into my arms. My Purkoy, I said. My favorite dog, the most beautiful spaniel that ever was. I kissed and hugged him, feeling his loving fur next to my skin. I should like to write to Lady Lisle in Calais, I said, ask about her husband, the Governor, who was so kind to me when I was there. I will thank her for the bird and the dog, for thinking of me as my time approaches. I will not mention the monkey she sent, for I cannot abide the sight of it. It is a beast which belongs in a jungle, not in a woman's room. Perhaps I should give it to Mary, for as a Spaniard, she is familiar with what is ugly.

102

Henry

She became sick and took to her bed, to give birth I thought. I had no idea her confinement would end in the death of another child and the sound of weeping women within, heard in the corridor where I stood. Was it a boy? I asked Doctor Butts, not wishing to enter Anne's room, to see her pained expression, concealing her deceptive eyes. No, he said. A girl, premature. If only I had known, I could have gone to Calais as planned. I could have met with Francis. I could have strengthened my position in the world of politics and men, made myself useful. I didn't do any of that, though. I thought it reasonable to stay behind to see the birth of my son, to celebrate with banquets and jousts, to gloat and rejoice, to say to myself in the looking glass: I am a man, like other men! But I can see now that such an act is not reasonable with God. It was not enough that I had rid myself of the woman I had no business to marry twenty-five years earlier, wherein I committed the worst kind of sin, incest. He wants further retribution from me. He wants me to rid myself of Anne, as does the rest of Europe.

How should I make myself blind and deaf to Him as easily as I have the pope? Can you not absolve me from my sins? I wish to say to Him. Have I not paid enough penance? And if it is for my forebears I suffer, why should it be? I had nothing to do with their crimes. Release me from the curse I have inherited. I have lived holy. I hear mass, I confess myself before your priests. I give alms, I take pilgrimages. If I have sinned by taking another wife without the sanction of your emissary on earth, it is for the sake of my crown, my name, my legacy. You cannot ordain me as king and then treat me as you would a fallen angel. I am not Adam, your first born, your original sinner, he who ate the apple. I am the supreme head of the Church of England. I am

King! Why, then, do I feel like a commoner, made to hang on hopes and dreams for twenty-five years, having suffered the deaths of five children, forced to live with the shame of not having a son, anguished by my father's voice in my ears: *I leave the Tudor dynasty for you to carry on. Do not disappoint, though you be the second favorite of mine.*

Do you not know how these words haunt me, night after night, making of sleep a river I must swim upstream, against current? What is it that you want from me? The relinquishing of my title and a return to Rome, to the pope, made to kneel at the altar of the emperor? Give me a son, and I shall say, Yes. Do you hear me? I am prostrate before you. Send to me a son, and I shall surrender to you the England I have these past three years reformed.

103

Katherine

Thank you for the news, I write the ambassador, about Anne's failed pregnancy and my daughter's refusal to sign the oath. I cannot tell you how pleased I am, especially with the latter. Knowing she has been ill, it has worried me that her weakened state would make her succumb to her tormentors' threats. I can only imagine the wording of these threats, for I have heard them myself, that she, as I, will stand on the scaffold, alongside others who defy the king's law, and lose her head. This I thought would never happen, until recent events, the birth of the bastard Elizabeth, the Act of Succession, the imprisonment of religious, scholarly men and the execution of the Maid of Kent. I now know the world around us has gone mad, wherein anything evil is likely to occur.

I will in my next letter congratulate Mary for her continued defiance, for showing her teeth to the devil, making known to her what I have discovered in my loneliness, kneeling and praying on bare stones that I flood with tears in such great quantity that one might think rain had fallen upon them; that martyrdom is an expression of love. One need only look to Jesus, the greatest martyr. His suffering was his passion, as it must be ours, for with it we experience freedom and purpose. Just think, Europe has not seen martyrs for centuries. We shall buck the trend, and it is a beautiful thing indeed, for it holds the promise of an afterlife filled with eternal happiness. Better this, surely than a sinner's death followed by eternal damnation. I will tell her that it matters not that we are separated now, for we shall see each not very long hence when the storms of this life shall be over, and we shall be taken to the calm life of the blessed. Knowing this, it should comfort her as she endures the trials that God in his glory has given to us, to make us stronger, to embolden us to His truth, for it is only the obedience of His truth wherein we can release ourselves from our imprisonments.

We are the fortunate ones anyway, unlike our friends, the Observant Friars, who I am saddened to hear, as you report to me, are now taken from the monastery and brought to the Tower in cartloads, where they face torture and certain execution for their collective refusal to swear to the oath. Have you news of Friar John Forrest? He visited me often since my exile, always aware that his movements were watched. Such was his courage and his steadfast belief in me as his queen that he cared not for his mortal being. I wish to send him a note in the Tower, if it were only possible, to tell him to be brave and stay firm. Learn to suffer for Christ's truth, and to die for His Holy Father. He, of course, already knows this, as do all the friars, the true soldiers of Christ, who do not shy away from their torments, understanding that through them they receive eternal reward. Should you have recourse, please send word to him and all of them that the Queen of England reveres and respects their unyielding loyalty to me and to God and that I should also follow their leads, not failing in my task until death, as otherwise I should imperil my soul, and I pray as well the Princess Mary will do the same, as a good daughter should.

104

Anne

I needed good news and thought my father would be the bearer of it as he entered my room. He had returned from Eltham Palace, where he had gone to administer the oath to Mary. I could tell by his weary expression, though, that what he had to convey would not please me. She refused, he said. Did you not try to force her? I asked. Your aunt, Lady Shelton, tried, he answered. Tried, how? I demanded to know. She shook the girl violently, he said. How violently? I said. Did he kill her? No, he said, not that violently. Then violently is the wrong word, I responded. It is not the wrong word, he insisted, for to see and hear your aunt you would know why. She shook her, throwing her to the ground, shouting: Stop saying you are a princess when it has been made official that you are a bastard. If I were the king, I would kick you out of the house, for your disobedience and defiance. I would make you lose your head. To which Lady Mary cried, picked herself up and left the room, saying as she did: I am prepared to die a martyr, like my mother.

If it were only that easy, I said. If only she wasn't the daughter of Katherine, aunt to the emperor. She will not hold out much longer, he said. That I can promise you. She is very ill, so small and nearly all bones, that nature may do what the king has not the stomach to do. That might be just as good as her signature, might you say? That would be much preferred, father, indeed. Get better, he said. Soon the king will come to visit your bed, and you shall once again carry his child. Carry? I asked. Deliver, he answered. A healthy boy. If it were only that easy, I said. Why do you say that in reference to everything? It must be that easy, he replied, if you wish to remain. I turned and heard him leave.

I reached for Purkoy, who had been lying by my side. He licked my hand, and as I brought him closer to me, he licked my face. If custom would allow, I would make sure Elizabeth were lying on the other side of me. I might then be happy to have both my beloved daughter and beloved dog together with me to offer me solace at this troubling time, when few others show me love, for the king is gone. I do not mean he is gone hunting or riding. I mean he is gone to me. He has someone else. I do not know who, and I must not ask or complain. It is not a concern of mine, he should say. I must look away, I can be lowered just as I was raised, I must be satisfied with what I have.

And what is it that I have? Wealth and land and gowns and jewels, though no friends, just a dog and a daughter and a bird that sings to me. This, then, is my life as I lie in wait for another opportunity, subjected to the whispered words I hear through the walls: The king is unhappy. He wants a son, and if she can't give him one, who then will? I watch and suspect. Can one of the ladies who comes in and out of my room, serving me out of duty, be my betrayer? Is there more than one? Is the king trying them to see who he might wish to be my replacement? Is it my cousin Madge? Is it the small girl who doesn't speak, she who darts her eyes away when I look at them? That Seymour girl?

105

Henry

The pope, aware of how Bishop Fisher, old as he is, sits in the Tower prison for upholding his faith and the true authority of Rome, has made him a cardinal, Chapuys informed me. I laughed, loudly. He shall have to wear his miter hat on his shoulders for he will not have a head. Tell that to Pope Clement, for in his senility he seems not to understand that the actions of England are of no concern to him. He promised to convey my words to the Vatican, though he wished to speak with me on a different matter. Let me guess, I said. You wish to give me lessons on how to treat my former wife, though she was never my wife, and my daughter, who, born to a woman who was never my legal wife, is not my legal daughter. Am I warm or cold, ambassador?

He straightened his crooked lips. The Lady Mary is gravely ill. Again! I sighed. He frowned and spoke hurriedly. Lady Shelton, tired of hearing of Mary's unremitting head and stomach pains, called to the house an apothecary to administer to your daughter's complaints. Upon taking pills he gave her, her condition worsened. She shivers and shakes and is day and night nauseous, unable to hold down food or drink. Both Lady Shelton and the apothecary fear that unless Mary is treated, she may die wherein they will be accused of poisoning her. Your daughter is in need of a physician, and I suggest you send to her your very best, Dr. Butts.

I sighed again, purposely, before responding. Do you know that when she was a child she never cried? Never, not once do I recall. Now, all I hear are her complaints. I will send Dr. Butts under one condition. That you write to her mother and tell her she is the cause of the girl's troubles, which are, in my opinion, phantom illnesses, self-inflicted, the result of her mother filling her head with thoughts of martyrdom. Make clear to the dowager that she should desist in telling her daughter to be defiant towards me and more specifically to the Act of Succession, which Parliament did pass into law. She should instead be demanding that her daughter obey me, her father, in all matters, though they may not be to her liking. She must swear to the oath, and in doing so acknowledge me as the supreme head of the church, and Anne as queen and her sister as princess, that she herself is illegitimate. Promise to convey this message to her mother, and I will immediately dispatch Dr. Butts to see Mary.

He swallowed his Spanish spit and conceded that Mary should not sacrifice her life, young as it is, so full of promise. He would deliver to Lady Katherine my words. Do not deceive me ambassador, as you are wont to do, in your correspondence with those of your homeland. You know what I say and wish for you to convey is nothing more than common sense. The sooner Mary alters her behavior towards me, the sooner she will be treated better and thus feel better. Neither you nor I need to be doctors to understand this certain outcome. He bowed, and thanked me for my concern for my daughter's health and welfare. Do not sound so surprised that I care, ambassador, for you have no idea how much her condition distresses me. He bowed again, and without another word left my chamber.

I should have known better to send Dr. Butts. He is soft, as they say, particularly on women, evident when he came to me after seeing Mary and said her illness arose only from sorrow and trouble; and that she would be well at once if she were free to do as she liked. But she can't be free to do what she likes, I said, until she does what I like. Did you tell her that, doctor? No, he said, I am a physician, not king. I listened to the words from her heart before I made my diagnosis. I care not for her heart, only her obedience, I said. Yes, of course, he responded. In any case, in my opinion, if you wish to see her health improve, I advocate you send her to her mother. She will be cured in no time at all.

I care not a fig for your opinion, doctor, I shouted. What you request is out of the question, for there would be no way of getting her to renounce her title and claim if I were to send her to the source of her defiance. In my opinion, and let me make it clear my opinion is the only one that matters, the matter of her health and any solution for it is entirely up to her. Until then, she will never be free to do what she likes.

106

Katherine

You should not be saddened to hear, Ambassador Chapuys wrote, that Pope Clement has passed from this earth, succumbing to his many illnesses, not least of all his suffering negligence in delaying for so the sentence he passed much too late to save your marriage, resulting in the subsequent humiliation you have endured, making more serious the threats against both yours and your daughter's life. Cardinal Farnese, his successor, has already been anointed as Pope Paul III. You will be heartened to know he is a more decisive man than his predecessor, wishing, as one of his first acts, to follow through on the bulls of excommunication against King Henry and Archbishop Cranmer, to which he will make demands on the emperor, engaging him to your cause, as you have long desired in your letters, demanding that your nephew do more, that he study his conscience, change his attitude and be more affectionate both to you and your daughter. This I have communicated diligently, making urgent to the emperor your troubles and the manner in which you live and are treated, conveying what you wrote to me last, that you have come to realize that it is absolutely necessary for him to apply stronger remedies to the evil. I am certain that once Pope Paul publishes the bulls it will incite the emperor to war, for he will know that no one, especially not France, will come to the defense of someone who has received excommunication. Take heart in these changes and know that you are not abandoned, as you have long believed. Pope Paul III shall apply a remedy to these matters with all speed, wherein you and I shall see an end to the damnation of souls and the unnecessary seeking of martyrdom for those who sit in the Tower prison and elsewhere. I am hopeful as well that this pressure will force King Henry to amend his treatment of you, allowing you to see your daughter, to care for her, as you have long desired. Believe that this will happen, for without faith we may as well not have breath, for it is only faith that sustains us during these troubling times.

Visit me, I write back. Seek permission to do so, for I am not well and desire to see you, my ally, my countryman, while time and failing health allow it. You will be shocked to see how I have aged, though I care not, for I have long surrendered whatever vanity I once possessed, wearing, beneath my clothes, the hair shirt of the third order of St. Francis to remind me of the frailty of the flesh. Bring, if you can, almonds and good wine, for I cannot drink what is served here, as you should understand, and I crave more than ever almonds reaped and harvested in Spain. Bring, as well, fabrics and linens, for I spend my time, when not in prayer, sitting with my few ladies, embroidering and fashioning altar-cloths for the churches in the district. Make your intention known to the king. He must not refuse you, as he has refused my request to see my daughter. Plead with him, beg him, use the new weight of knowledge you bring from Rome as your collateral in the pursuit of this important persuasion. If he refuses, be so bold to visit anyway, for you, the emperor's ambassador, cannot be harmed, not while the threat of invasion hangs like a dark cloud over this realm.

Make your leaving a spectacle, bringing with you as many men as you can, no less than sixty, wearing much color and bright textures on your garments and feathers in your hats, carrying flags and banners and making much noise with gaiety and merry-making, taking with you your minstrels and trumpeters, and making sure to ride the finest mares of the Spanish guard, so that the clack of their hooves and their snorting, their whinnying and braying, chase the birds from the trees to gather in the sky as if a storm was preceding your advance, ensuring that your departure becomes the main gossip in London on that day and for months to come. If you are stopped and prevented from seeing me, even that will serve its purpose, for it will tell the people of England that I, their true queen, am a prisoner. As you ride in the streets and on the roads, announce to everyone, of which there will be many, I am certain: We travel in much ceremony to see the exiled Queen of England, Katherine.

107

Henry

Why did he go when I never gave permission? I asked Cromwell. Neither did you refuse, he answered smartly, as he cannot help himself. He took that to mean it was okay. It's okay if I say it's okay, I shouted. If I say nothing, it means it's not okay. How can that be misinterpreted? The ambassador, in his devotion to the Dowager princess and Lady Mary, is a forceful man, he said, not wishing to moderate himself. Well, under my rule, I said, it is essential for each man to moderate himself. Is that not clear? Unless that man is king, he replied. That is true, Cromwell, given God's ordinance. Why, then, should Chapuys have the audacity to act as he pleases? He is just an ambassador. The emperor's ambassador, he said. Does that give him special privilege? Your question is rhetorical, Your Majesty. Whatever that means, Cromwell. You're sometimes too fancy with your words. Just give the report. Your man, Stephen Vaughan, shadowed Chapuys' motley gang of Spaniards, did he not? Yes, and lived to tell about it, he said, nary a hint of a smile, as one would expect from a normal person who spoke wit.

Here's is what I learned, Your Majesty. Acting on your explicit orders, a messenger from Kimbolton intercepted Chapuys' contingency to tell them that by order of the king they would be refused to enter the manor or in any way speak with Lady Katherine. To which Chapuys said he needed to see the order in writing. Only a Spaniard would dare be so impudent, I interrupted. Indeed, Cromwell said, for his impudence proved itself further when he ordered his men to continue toward Kimbolton. Does not that little Spaniard know he can be charged with treason? I asked. Oh, I'm sure it has crossed his mind, Cromwell said, as a sure way to incite the emperor to act against us. He does understand his limitations, though, as the continuance of my story will show. When he and his men arrived five miles from Kimbolton, another messenger arrived to warn him that he would provoke the rage of His Majesty if he appeared at either the manor house or the village.

He wished to incite the mob of people loyal to Lady Katherine, I said, especially if they were to learn he was refused entry to see her. Is that not true, Cromwell? That is most true, Your Majesty. It is likely that the ambassador and Lady Katherine planned for that to happen. In any case, that night Chapuys and his men camped in the hills, wherein they received from the manor a shipment of venison and game, with much ale. They ate and drank and later played their instruments and sang and laughed, behaving, as Stephen Vaughan so poignantly said, as one would expect Spaniards to behave, like beasts in the wild. That's fine if they want to act like Spaniards, I said, but I prefer they do so in their own country, not here, where we practice civility. Agreed, Cromwell replied, for in the morning their incivility proved itself. They rode to the manor gates and made exchanges with Katherine's ladies, leaning out from windows, shouting Spanish to the men below. To which the men responded in the like language.

Did not your man, Stephen Vaughan, understand what they were saying? I asked. He does not speak, nor does he understand the Spanish language, Your Majesty. The thought of that horrid language ringing out in the East Anglian air disturbs me. Does it not disturb you, Cromwell? It is distressing, indeed, he said. Though not as disturbing as what happened next. They brought with them a fool, a small, funny fellow, who wore a padlock dangling from his hood. This little man got off his horse and ran to the moat, crying out that he wanted to get to the women. He got himself in the water as far as his waist. The women and men alike feared he would drown. On Chapuys' orders, some of the men dragged him out, but not before he hurled his padlock across the moat. Take this, he shouted in broken English. Next time I will bring the key. Village locals, who had come to see the commotion, laughed, as did the entire contingency of Spaniards. Though they were explicitly told they could not enter the manor, no one said they couldn't stand outside its gates and play their instruments and drink their ale and wine and sing and dance, creating, as they did, a spectacle.

Do you think Lady Katherine had herself a good laugh over this, Cromwell? If she did, Your Majesty, it is probably the first laugh she has enjoyed in years. She gained a moral victory, perhaps, nothing more. Yes, we can stand to lose a battle or two, I said, as long as we win the war. Is that not correct, Cromwell? I stand beside you, Your Majesty, to serve you and give my life, if necessary, for your just cause.

108

Anne

My sister stands before me, tells me she is pregnant, that she is newly married, done in secret, having exchanged vows sanctioned by God, to a soldier serving in Calais, a man named William Stafford. I care not for his name, I shout. You insult me and your father by marrying a common man. I have been widowed five years now, she says. Can I not decide for myself what is best for me? No, you cannot. I am Queen of England. You serve my household. Your business is mine. I am your master. You are my sister, she says, and younger than me I should like to remind you. Age matters not when status and title are involved, I say. Unless you annul this marriage at once, and I shall help you do it, you will suffer repercussions the likes of which you may not find recovery. Father will cut you off from your allowance, and I shall ban you from court. You will be forced to live in a forsaken abode in the country without the means and amenities for which you are accustomed. Have you considered that? You will come to me begging for crumbs before long, and I shall turn aside from you, as you are now turning from me in your defiance.

I wish not to dispute with you on the subject of my marriage, she responds. I came only to inform you, hoping you might be happy for me. Happy for you? I cry out. To see you ruin your life and ruin my reputation and that of your family? Ruined? She fires back. No, not ruined, saved, for this you should know, sister: I might have gained a greater man of birth, but I assure you I could never have had one that loved me so well, and if it means I shall have to beg for bread I am determined to live a poor honest life with him, for our love is enough for me. Desist speaking of love, I shout. You know not what you say. It is fool's gold. It will not feed your stomach or put clothes on your back.

It will only lead to hardship and misery. You speak, sadly, for yourself, sister, she says. I am not married to a king, like you. I love him for the man he is, not for the wealth and title he can provide me.

I want to strike out at her, but refrain. Are you saying I possess only wealth and title and nothing more because I have been fortunate to be christened queen? Yes, she answers. Do you ever think what your life could have been if you had been allowed to follow your heart before King Henry consumed you with the promise of being raised higher than any other woman? Well, you have been raised, though now you wait for him to lower you because you know he has it in his power to do so. You have told me so, that he has told you to be content with what he has done for you, which he would not do now if your courtship were to begin anew. Those were your words. You cannot deny them. You are queen, dear sister, but look what you have lost in order to have gained. Your eyes have lost their luster. I see now only suspicion in them. Your lips, which once smiled so easily, have now become pinched shut. Your cheeks have fallen. You have aged and lost your beauty, waiting, as you do, to deliver a son, with little other hope in your life. Thus, you should not criticize the choice I have made, for noble reasons alone. You are in no such position to speak of the love between a man and woman, though you are queen.

Get out, I shout, and do not return. You are finished here at court, banned, both you and your husband and whatever bastard children you deliver, and from this day forward I will forget I have a sister. As she leaves, I search for my face in the looking glass. I force myself to smile, to raise my cheeks, hoping that my eyes, the greatest commodity of my youth, return to me.

109

Katherine

I stand near the window, open it, and weep tears of hope, if not joy, though of the latter I have had little familiarity in my recent life to know with certainty its sensation. Ambassador Chapuys' letter, decreed by God, has given me this hope. It is the reason for the shining sun, which has long been absent in the sky, and the birds that soar above the clouds, towards it, like so many angels loosed from heaven, made golden in its rays. Mary, I whisper. You may not have to die a martyr. You may be free to ascend and take your rightful place where only queens and angels of God tread. Hear the ambassador's words; read them for yourself. The Admiral of France, Chabot de Brion, visited court. He met with the king, though also with the ambassador, for there has been much discussion between Francis and Charles for an alliance between France and Spain, and you, Mary, are part of the discussion. The French king does not acknowledge the Act of Succession. He accepts the late pope's validation of my marriage, and in doing so announces Elizabeth's illegitimacy, for she is the child of a concubine, who married the king unlawfully, and having done so is called such names in France. You should not hear these words, for you have been raised a Christian woman and understand the importance of behaving as one.

The French see you, Mary, as legitimate and heir to the throne. Discussion takes place about a proposed betrothal between you and the Dauphin. Yes, as you were once betrothed to him when you were just a baby, which I protested loudly against, for I did not want an alliance with France. Though now I am in much favor, for it is proposed by Charles, the newest pope and King Francis, all of whom stand as sentinels to the Catholic faith, the foundation of which lies in Rome, and this alliance of power and faith will force your father's hand to admit he made a mistake in marrying Anne Boleyn, for as the ambassador writes, for which you already know, she is hated by the world, and your betrothal to the Dauphin will result in the tilting of the earth, wherein night turns into day, our abandonment into freedom, and Anne Boleyn's time as queen into exile. She deserves far worse, though I should be happy enough to see her gone from court and England, perhaps to Flanders, where she and those of her religious beliefs belong. She is to blame for our hardships and for your father having to face the worst punishment a king can face, that being excommunication. I hope if matters turn out as they should, the pope will forgive him his sins and afford his immortal soul the comfort it deserves to have.

110

Henry

Tell your king that will never happen, I told Chabot de Brion. Mary will never marry the Dauphin. She is illegitimate. I stand by Elizabeth as our successor, as made clear in the act passed by Parliament, and it is she we wish to betroth to France. If not to the Dauphin, we shall consider a match with her and the king's third son, the duke of Angouleme. Offer him that and tell him to desist with talk of Mary. I shall do as you request, he said. The smile on his face seemed practiced, leaving me to conclude what I've always known about the French. They are not to be believed or trusted. Your tone is not reassuring, I said. I do not speak for the King of France, he said. What he decides is entirely his doing, based on beliefs and principles he holds. Are you sure it's not based on beliefs and principles the emperor holds? I asked, matching his practiced smile with my own. After all, why would he suddenly propose a marriage agreement involving Mary, with her evident handicaps, and not Elizabeth, whom he knows is in our favor?

Has he not kept up with news in England? Does he sense that our sails will change direction, caused by a sudden, unexpected wind? Or is it that he wishes not to stand alongside one who faces excommunication, believing if he does it will damage his immortal soul?

He is well content with the status of his immortal soul, he answered, for no one in Christendom has done as much as him to preserve the Catholic faith. If you do not believe that, ask the heretics who daily face persecution and punishment in my country. Yes, I said. Offer him my congratulations. Your tone is not to be believed, he said. We have much in common when it comes to our tones, I declared. Though we differ greatly when it comes to loyalty. Your king has long called me his brother and cousin, his friend and ally, and has long been on record saying he will support me in my fight against the emperor and Rome. Yet now he betrays me. Explain that, if you can, Admiral. He is bothered by the alteration in the succession, he said. He respects the late pope's sentence on your marriage to Katherine, refusing to acknowledge your marriage to Anne as lawful, believing any offspring of hers is illegitimate. Thus, in his eyes, Mary has a better claim to the English throne and wishes to pursue a marriage agreement with her and the Dauphin. Tell your king that here in England we do not see through his eyes. We see through my eyes, for I am the king of this realm, and as long as I am, Mary will remain a bastard and Elizabeth shall be my successor, that is until my son is born. Tell him that, if you will.

111

Anne

Cromwell said when Pope Clement passed away the devil died. That is not true, for the devil lives. He resides in France, in the guise of French authorities, obeying edicts from their king, Francis, who, upon hearing that the new pope planned to finalize plans to excommunicate Henry, unleashed aggressive action against reformers there. I hear from a refugee, part of my father's network, that Francis has emboldened priests to encourage mobs to take to the streets, to start a reign of terror against any who speak out against the pope or the Catholic mass or are found reading the Gospel on their own, shouting, Death to the heretics! Francis has declared war, saying: Let all be seized, and let Lutheranism be totally exterminated. Even Margaret, the king's sister, whom I have always valued as a friend, with our shared evangelical leanings, is under siege. All her chaplains have been seized, and she is being accused of being the greatest heretic. I hear she has fled Paris with many of her fellow believers, seeking refuge in her kingdom of Navarre. I have done what I can to save many, most notably the poet Nicholas Borbonius, who, now in England, wishes to commemorate me in his latest verse, recently sent to me.

A poor man,
I lie shut up in this dark prison:
There is no one who would be able
or who would dare to bring help:
You alone, O Queen: you, Oh noble nymph,
both can and dare: As one whom
the King and whom God himself loves.

When Chabot de Brion arrived in London as Francis's envoy, I had hoped to address with him the issue of France's persecution of innocent men and women. I had known him when I lived in France as a young woman and later we were reacquainted when Henry and I visited Calais before we were married. I quickly learned, however, that personal familiarity counted for nothing when it clashed with diplomatic interests. His disdain for me and what I represent to him and his country were evident from the start. He did not greet me, nor bow to me, nor bring me a gift from his king, nor speak with me, unless it was Henry who told him to do so. Even then, he offered little more than perfunctory courtesies, feigning pleasantry in the most unfaithful way, smiling, showing the glint of his teeth, like sharpened knives. He wished neither to speak of the proposed betrothal of Elizabeth and the Duke of Angouleme, changing the subject or turning his head from mine each time I mentioned it.

What did I do to deserve his disdain? I wondered. Did he not know that I was in many ways as French as him? I was educated there, learned its customs and fashions, bringing them to England, and I have always favored the reading of the Gospel in French rather than English. Yet, my attitude and love for France will change, unless the French accept my marriage to Henry and treat Elizabeth as the legitimate heir she is, deserving of the highest marriage to the Dauphin and if not him then to Francis's third son. I must do what I can to make this happen, for I know Henry's mind. He sees the union as a dynastic necessity. Outside of giving birth to a son, which would put to rest all debates of legitimacy and bring me great favor with the French and the rest of the world, it is all I can do to ensure my survival.

112

Henry

I am forced to acknowledge what I have long heard whispered into my ears, though it could have as well been shouted for the breadth of its clarity. Outside of delivering me a male heir, my wife, Queen Anne, is a liability. As long as she remains queen, minus the all-important birth of a son, my diplomatic situation is bound to worsen, or so it appears, given France's reaction to her and its involvement with the pope and emperor. England cannot stand alone, defenseless in a world where defense is everything. I don't need Cromwell to tell me that, which he has on several occasions, though he has stopped short of conveying the real reason of his concern: That my marriage is politically unsound. I did my best to make it sound, passing the Act of Succession; though, while it has tamed the majority in England, it has done little to bring love from across the channel. Anne is disliked, I am told, as if I didn't already know, by the Spanish and French ambassadors; by the German princes and even Luther, whom I detest as much as I would a rat. Why should he, of all people, denounce my marriage? He, who married a nun, and lives in worse sin. I should like to tell the world to go to hell, but as Cromwell reminds me, I can't do that, for I need the world. Without it by our side to anchor us, to hold us up, England would fall into the sea and never again emerge.

It is a game we play, like chess, he says. They move; we move; a dance of balance; power against power; pawn against pawn; and when there are no pawns left, it is the bishops and knights who fight with their castles, and when they are gone, we, the kings and queens, stand alone, facing the opposing kings and queens, caught in a stalemate, unless like now the board is tilted in one's favor as it is for Francis now that he has additional pawns, knights and bishops to support him. Thus, I find myself unable to move. Oh, but you must, I am told. Norfolk especially tells me. She is to blame for the diplomatic mess. She has not given you a son. She lacks the quiet decorum suitable to a queen. She complains of your love interests. You complain she never gives you peace. She must be made expendable, unless she delivers you an heir, and soon enough. Oh, really? How so, while Katherine lives? For it would be expected of me to return to her. No, that shall never happen. I must wait. She will die, sooner than later, for the dropsy already has its hold on her, as I am told by those who live by her, her wardens, out of necessity. When she is dead, perhaps then, and only then, can I act.

113

Anne

It was not an accident, I said. My dog did not fall from the window. You know well he didn't. Someone threw him and meant to kill him, and whoever did wishes to kill me next, and I suppose you, who have ceased to love me, as you had promised to do from the earliest days when you hunted me like prey, will stand by and allow it, leaving you free to carry on with your favorite woman of the court, that great betrayer of my household, whom I call Judas.

You are hysterical, he said. Calm yourself. You are pregnant. Think of the child you carry. Is that not more important than your dog? You can have another dog. I do not want another dog, I shouted. I will never want another dog. I wish to find who killed Purkoy, and throw that person from the window, even if it turns out to be the woman you love, she who detests and disrespects me each day. I wish then to see what you will do as a test of loyalty either for her or me, though I know which side you will take. It is the side you have taken for months, dishonoring me with your disloyalty. I shall not listen to you further when you behave like this, he said. When I behave like this? How should I behave moments after learning from my husband, rather from the cowards of my household, that my favorite dog, a second child to me, has been found dead on the ground, beneath my chamber window?

His face reddened. I would expect you to show more gratitude to me for informing you with as much gentleness as I could rather than leaving you to learn of the misfortune on your own. I let my rage burn. You expect me to say: Thank you, Your Majesty, for telling me my dog is dead? I expect you to act with more grace and decorum! He yelled. Is that how your favorite woman of the court acts? I countered. Perhaps I can take lessons from her, if only you will allow it. Will you? Please, Your Majesty, I want to learn from the very best, and she, by the way I see you look at her, even in my presence, must be the very best.

He raised his hand to my face. I demand you to desist your foolish talk! I took his hand and held it tightly. I demand you to leave that woman and return to me, your wife, who has suffered much for you and who has borne you a princess daughter? He threw me aside. Do not tell me what you have suffered and what you have done. It is what you have not done that is your undoing. Shut your mouth, as I demand you do, and stop complaining to me. Keep silent and care for that child in your womb. If and when you deliver me the son you promised when we married, you may see a change in my affairs. Until then, leave me be, or I will use words to bring you down, as you deserve to be brought down, words too harsh even for one as yourself.

What are these words? I screamed. Do you wish to call me, as does my uncle, great whore, or as King Francis says, the king's concubine, who will never be accepted as lawful and legitimate in the eyes of France and Rome and throughout most of Europe, as is true also of her daughter? Or do you wish to say, what you have already said, that you can lower me as fast you raised me, that if you had to do it all over again you would not marry me? You told me those very words. Whatever else you may say to me cannot be half as bad.

He rushed to the door and turned to me, his eyes fire red. If someone did kill your dog, as you believe, I can see why. That is what I wish to say. As he left, I ran in the hall after him and raged for all to hear: She, your favorite woman of the court, is the great whore, not me. She is your concubine, and I wish her to burn in hell.

114

Katherine

Two nights ago, one of my servants cursed Anne Boleyn, using a word I strictly forbid in my house. I chastised her, to which she asked my forgiveness, saying she meant only to say that Lady Anne was surely the devil manifest and deserved to burn in hell. I told my servant to hold her peace and to pray for Lady Anne, for the time would come when she, my servant, as well as I myself and others of the kingdom, shall pity and lament Anne's case. You do not mean that, Queen Katherine, my servant said. She has usurped your title and has taken your husband, the king, for her own. As God touches me with his presence, I do mean it, I replied.

I spoke no further on the matter with my servant, though I have since thought about my response and the reason for it, the result of Ambassador Chapuys' latest letter, detailing the events at court and, in particular, the state of Lady Anne, who daily rages at the king for his unfaithfulness with a young woman of court whom Henry's courtiers refer to as his new favorite. Chapuys wished me to know this information, apologetically he emphasized, only because the woman in question holds strong Catholic beliefs and is believed to whisper in Henry's ears her support and reverence both for me and Mary. I look forward to writing back to the ambassador to ask, knowing he will understand my wit: Should I be mollified, dear friend, to know that Henry, still my lawful husband, loves a court woman who reveres me?

I shall not labor my heart over this, though, for I have long settled with myself my responses to Henry's affairs. I vowed early in our marriage that they would not be my ruin, but instead my strength, wherein I relied upon the manual from my childhood, which I still possess and read, by the Franciscan monk

Eiximenis: Girls should carry rosaries and spend a part of each day praying. Girls should be discreet, contained and exercise self-control. Weaving, sewing and praying were appropriate pastimes. Their greatest enemy was the madness of love. It is the reason I pity Lady Anne, who does not possess my strength, who allows herself to be tortured and tormented by jealousy, as many before her have been. I would, if we were friends, offer her my book by Vives, who wrote of the madness of love these words:

It is a relentless and uncontrollable tyranny. It is better to die than to give way to it. If a woman allows herself to suffer from it, she must do so in secret. Her jealousy must not be excessive and violent or upset the peace of the home and become an intolerable burden for her husband. If it is of that type I think she must be given medical treatment. Above all, a woman should bear in mind that her husband is master of the household, and not all things permitted to him are permitted to her. Human laws do not require the same chastity of a man as they do of a woman.

Thus, I learned to disassociate myself from Henry's affairs, convincing myself the women were not real, that they could have been so many dogs in the fields, just animals, acting as such, separate from the spirit, wherein I have always lived, where Henry has always resided to me.

Ambassador Chapuys informed me of Henry's diplomatic mess, the poor relations between France and England, evident in Francis's calling off—perhaps never considering seriously—the betrothal of Elizabeth and his son, the Duke of Angouleme, reflecting yet another impediment to Henry's dynastic ambitions, for the Catholic world knows she is a heretic and should consider herself fortunate that she no longer lives in France, where people such as herself are arrested and persecuted.

Does this not bode well? He wrote. Does it not signal that Anne, as has been whispered, is a liability? That Henry knows the danger she presents, politically speaking, and will thus look to rid himself of her, unless the child she carries in her womb this time proves to be a healthy son, the outcome of which Chapuys doubts, citing as proof God's disallowance of it, for Henry possesses too many unredeemed sins. Besides, her womb has suffered as has her mind and body, which has aged and lost its beauty. What child, let alone a son, stands a chance under such conditions? It is not to be, he wrote.

I shall write back to him, to thank him for the news, though I will add that I do not despise Lady Anne, as does the rest of the world. I now have only pity for her shameful life, which I am certain if she had a chance to do again, she would do differently, far from court, far from the man crowned Henry VIII in 1509, the day I was made Queen Katherine.

115

Henry

Cromwell stood before me, a beacon of light in a world of shadows, bereft of trusting friends and allies. You are now Vice-Regent, Vicar General, in all matters spiritual, I said. Offer me hope, for I have lived long now with despair, and I am afraid I shall die from it, unless you have a plan to save me. He did not appear to breathe or move, except where it mattered, in his brain, eliciting a stream of thoughts and words issuing from his beautiful mouth. We must divest the church of England from the abuses that have corrupted Rome, and in doing so sever any lingering allegiance to the papacy. I mean to have every monastery and convent visited and reported upon, with a view to its possible closure and the appropriation of its wealth, including its vast lands, by the Crown. These religious houses have a higher loyalty to some foreign power. It is for you, Your Majesty, to take back what they have, for they have not earned their assets and holdings. What they possess belongs to the realm, to you specifically, to your loyal subjects. Such as yourself, I interjected. Yes, Your Majesty, he quickly replied. Such as myself, and others who wish to see you as you deserve to be: the richest king ever in England.

To those who say we are destroying the church, Cromwell, what do we say to them? We seek to renew, not destroy, he answered. We say that, for that is the truth. The truth, as we see it? I asked. He did not blink. Is there any other truth worth honoring, Your Majesty? Consider the results: England will be made better for it, once it is purged of liars and hypocrites, fat monks who sit on fortunes, who hold to a monastic life that is not necessary, not useful, not commanded of Christ or part of God's natural order, where good Christian men live out in the world, not in buildings susceptible to decay and ruined by lax stewardship. We shall correct and reform what is wrong. And become rich at the same time? I smiled, then laughed, hoping he would laugh with me, but other than a glean in his eye he showed no expression of joy. He remained all business. Brilliant business, I might add, offering a royal panacea, as if on a platter, to what ailed me. I had, in fact, forgotten what ailed me as he spoke, as I surrendered myself to the music of his words and the calm and reason—the persuasiveness—of his voice, emanating from that masterful mind of his.

We need not seek to justify our actions, Your Majesty. God and sense guide us. The monks are in the business of creating dread among the people with their tales of ghosts and curses and all their foolish relics and superstitions. They claim to have relics that can make crops grow, stop the rain or make it rain, cure people of diseases. They profess to have meats from the Last Supper, torn linens worn by Christ, nails from the crucifixion. Has anyone ever asked: How is it that these relics came to England when Christ died so far away? But the foolish farmers and commoners continue to buy these relics. So, why should it be such a sin to put a stop to all this? And these lies they sell are only a small part of their disgrace. They're not Saint Francis. They eat well, while the poor they serve starve, and they partake of the flesh, keeping women and virgins, saying they were given license by the pope to have whores, claiming it is within their God-given nature to do so. I ask, Your Majesty: Aren't they supposed to rise above their nature? What's the point of all their supposed prayer if it leaves them insufficient when the devil comes to tempt them? All the more reason I say to shut them down and cast them out.

Where shall these monks go, Cromwell? They will join the world, Your Majesty. We will make it simple for them, and it has nothing to do with God, religion or suffering. We shall ask them: Who will you have, Henry Tudor, your king, or Alessandro Farnese, the newest pope? There is no gray area on this matter. None, I echoed. None at all.

116

Anne

I shall not forget nor forgive Cromwell's dismissal of my request. If only he and not my brother had gone to France, this matter of Elizabeth's marriage proposal to Francis's son would be settled. Everyone listens to him and sets in action what he says, kings notwithstanding. I count myself as among those who listened and relied on his words. I shall no longer, for I now know where he stands, or where I stand to him, as I stand to Francis and the French, who disdain the name Boleyn, evident in my brother's early return, his long face and hollow expression, the result of my proposal having been rejected yet again, wherein he couldn't look me in the eye to tell me they continue to favor Mary as a marriage match to the Dauphin.

He was too sick to travel, the king told me. He Cromwell, sick? Impossible. Men like him do not get sick unless they manufacture the illness for a purpose that suits their needs. He would not be too sick to travel to a monastery, to close its doors on the monks, to melt their leaden crosses and possess their property. I do not object to these visitations, I told him. I am glad for them, though I wish to see reform more than I wish for closures, if they can be avoided. He looked at me with his practiced look of superiority. They possess land and property they do not deserve. So, this is about lining your pockets in gold, I said. Not mine, as much as the monarchy's. How should it survive without it? And you yourself, madam?

How should I survive, indeed? It is not a question of money, though. It is of loyalty and friends, both of which appear to be short in my supply, made even clearer still by Cromwell's lack of support, leading to a truth that leaves me feeling desperately alone: that he, the king's Mr. Secretary, is against me, as others are, and wishes as Francis and the French, to see me fall from the great height I occupy, hoping there is greater advantage in it for him. My uncle shares that view, excepting that he, unlike Cromwell, does not hide his feelings. He has called me a whore and damaged goods. He has told me the king wishes to rid himself of me, and he will be first in line to applaud the act when it happens, and make no mistake it will.

If nothing else, I can rely on my uncle's honesty and his acts of vengeance against me, such as his bringing to court, into my household, my cousin Madge, a frivolous girl who writes idle poems in her prayer book, though far from idle in her devotion to Henry's advances, quickly becoming his newest mistress, as my uncle intended, to induce me to further suffering, to make the child inside me an un-child, as the previous one, to reduce my value, to make me expendable, to see me replaced, banished, exiled or worse. I have told him he shall vanish first, perhaps by being dropped from a window, like a dog. He showed his guilt in his anger. You are a woman, he yelled, though you disgrace your sex. You are wrong, uncle. I am Queen of England, and as such I sit high above you. You are queen in name only, he spat back at me. In every other manner you are despised. You must know that. Look around you.

I do look. When the French envoy, Palamede Gontier, arrived at a banquet, I sought him out, sitting beside him, though I was too afraid to speak aloud to him for the room was abuzz with eyes and ears, pinpricks on my skin, stinging and searing, causing me edginess, though even more so an acute awareness of every movement, gaze and sound, seeing and sensing, inward much more than outward, my uncle, Cromwell, Henry, those still in alliance with Katherine, Ambassador Chapuys and Nicholas Carew, even Francis from far away, Catholics to the core and thus my enemies, and I theirs. Why should the King of France's envoy care to listen to me about the unfair persecution of good men and women in France, denounced as Lutherans? Was not I and my daughter part of their legion? Did not the French believe this as much as Elizabeth's illegitimacy? The world closed on me, the air reduced, stifling, as if many hands clutched at my throat. I gasped, shook and quivered, jerking my head from left to right, behind me.

I was once considered French, I said. Now, I am no longer French and yet to the English I will never be English enough. What am I? I am lost, nearly ruined, in more trouble than before my marriage. He turned, readying himself to greet the courtiers who advanced toward him, though offering some final words before doing so. Your husband shall protect you from whatever fears you have. Do you not understand? I said. It is my husband whom I fear most.

117

Katherine

I wrote to Henry's Mr. Secretary. Speak to the king and beg him on my behalf to be so charitable to me as to send his daughter and mine to where I am, for I myself will be her nurse, allowing her to come to my bed for her nightly comfort and watching over her during the day, when necessary, to ensure her recovery from illness.

Kind, Lady, he answered. I wish to help you, if only I could, though the king will not allow what you request, believing it is you who fuels your daughter's obstinacy towards him. It is best that you obey your sovereign's command in this matter and bother him no further.

I made a further appeal. If only she can be moved close enough to be in regular contact. I pledge not to visit her even if she is just a mile away. I just want to know she is near me. The times do not permit me to make visits and, even if I wanted to, I do not have the means.

Kind, Lady, he wrote, it is not politically expedient at this time to move your daughter. Rest assured that her illnesses are being carefully examined by the king's doctors. Please cease from writing further on this matter, for you should know, better than most, that when the king grows weary from those who defy him, he grows ever more disturbed in temperament, making your requests all the more less likely to be received in a favorable way.

I continued my plea, writing directly, not in vagueness about political expediency. No such plot to smuggle Mary out of England exists. Hear that and believe it from my mouth and in my words, for if it did exist, I should know and yet nary a word of such an abominable act has been spoken. How should my daughter escape in her condition, which, as I read in reports mercifully sent to me, states that she is in grave danger and could, if she does not receive her mother's love, which even Dr. Butts has said is the surest cure, could result in her dying. Good sir, I beseech you. You, I have heard, more than anyone, have the power to persuade the king. For the sake of an old woman, still your queen, who has suffered more than any Christian ever should, I beg you to honor what I write and ask of you. It pains me greatly that I am helpless in caring for my child, who is in need of my love more than any medicine doctors can give her. I assure you my intent is sincere. I offer my own person as surety, so that if such an escape by her, with the aid of foreign help, was attempted, the king may mete out justice to me as if I was the most treacherous woman ever born.

118

Henry

Oh, so I have lost my reason, have I, ordering many of the saintliest men in England to their deaths? What is that I hear from reports, moving swift as birds from across the channel or from the farmlands of England, in the bleating sheep, or seemingly so, as I wake from sleep to hear them, the words of my accusers? I am consumed with bloodlust, monstrous and depraved. I should like to shout at the stars that glare down on me like the eyes of the world, passing sentence: Am I not fulfilling the prophecy that I would start my reign as a lamb and finish it as a raging lion? Yes, for that is exactly how I aim to be from now on, now that my spirit is not at rest, that shadows are lengthening over my life, that darkness is closing in, cut off as I am, due to no fault of my own, rather due to the queen, who is mocked and laughed at by Francis and dismissed by Charles, and I, through association, have been made to suffer.

I shall have none of it! I shall roar louder to see more arrests, more executions, and if a few monks should die as examples to others, so be it. I have nothing to do with the manner of their deaths. That is left to others. I know only that those who sit in prison and defy me must know that what happened to the monks could happen to them. We have treason laws for a reason, to see that they are obeyed, and if people of this realm, no matter their position, criticize me or slander the queen or challenge royal supremacy they are not obeying the law. Sign the oath or perish. It is plain and simple. The Carthusian monks have shown no respect to these laws or to me and the sovereignty that I hold or to the marriage I made.

If they have been brutally slain, dragged by horses through the streets of London and hung and disemboweled, their quartered bodies paraded among the people, their heads rotting on pikes, it is the result of their doings, not mine. Though it couldn't have been too bad for them, if what Thomas More says is true, that as they were being tied to the hurdles at the Tower they were as joyful as bridegrooms going to their marriages. I hope for their sakes they are married well in heaven, though those who defy me should never see the face of God. That is the more likely truth. Fisher and More are to blame for their deaths, holding to foolish principles, persistent in their belief and longing for an England that no longer exists, its branches joined at the trunk of Rome.

Those trees of yesteryear are dead, as both Fisher and More will be if they have not learned from the defiance of the monks. They must know they are either with me or against me. I shall not wait much longer for their answers.

119

Katherine

Tell me it is not true, I write to Ambassador Chapuys. This report that Mary should be smuggled out of England and taken abroad, that she should get out of Eltham by night or while going out to sport, that she would ride to the Thames at Gravesend and take a boat to then board a Spanish warship waiting at the estuary. Heed my words, as your queen, as Mary's mother. Put a stop to such a plan, for it is madness. You must know it is, though you write that Mary herself favors the plan. If she says she does, it is only out of confusion and illness that make her say that. She is distressed, as she should be, as we all are, by recent events, the brutal execution of the Carthusian monks, men who, as you know, were friends of mine, both temporal and spiritual advisers to me all these years during my grief, men who till the very end of their lives held steadfast to God and conscience. Now they exist forever to us as martyrs and saints. May their souls rest in peace, for they died for their defiance against the king, for their exhortations that most of the people of England, three quarters of its population, are against the new acts of royal supremacy and Henry's claim to be head of the church, and only swear to oaths out of fear, not loyalty, for what they really wish to see is me and Mary restored to our rightful places.

Does this not prove that there is no need for senseless, dangerous action? Allow the fire that is raging to die out on its own, for fire can only burn so long. She who now wears the crown will die in the flames she herself has lighted. The French will see to it for they disdain her, evident in their favoring Mary, not Elizabeth, in the succession. Let that, the hope it embodies, buoy our spirits for now, without having to upset the king further by an action that could result in Mary being captured, wherein she will end up like the monks. How should you feel if that were to happen, knowing you could have prevented it? And even if she is not captured, she is sure to die on the journey, for this is no time to travel on the sea, when storms rage daily. I know not from where this idea was born. Surely not from my nephew, for he is not a man to take such risks. If he were, he would have already helped me during my exile and confinement, which, as you know, is little more than an imprisonment. Mary has already suffered enough, has she not? I know you will say that is justification to have her smuggled out. What should happen then? I do not want an army coming here to England. I do not want to see more death and destruction on my account. Already there has been too much. If only you knew the guilt I carry.

120

Anne

I no longer carry child. It matters not what happened. I had little time to cry. Such was the desperation I felt that I had only one recourse, to fight for the status I held, and for my very life. I sought the service of a psychic, he of great reputation, who confirmed to me what I always believed. That I will never conceive a child, a healthy son, as long as Katherine and Mary live, for they are the fountainheads (his word, not mine) from which springs all dissent, all slander and rebellion, in the kingdom, wherein people are speaking out against the throne, against me in particular, against Henry, against our marriage, against my daughter, calling her a little whore. It is not enough that the monks have been executed. They are pawns in the game of dissension. Fisher and More must die, and after them Katherine and Mary, if there is ever to be peace, male heirs to the throne, salvation on earth.

I told Henry, though I lied about having consulted a psychic. I referred to a higher source. That God revealed himself to me in a dream, though it was hardly a dream, for his words were exact and authoritative, possessing a clarity more palpable than any waking state could ever produce. I relayed these words to Henry: Tell the king, God said, if he cares about his realm and wishes to see healthy sons born to his wife, Queen Anne, he must first dispatch all those who stand in the way of this happening, for they are the cause of every evil plaguing the kingdom. Bishop Fisher, Thomas More, Katherine and Mary. Queen Anne is barren because of them. For her to be fruitful, they must be extinct.

He looked at me with such loathing. You do not understand my situation, he said. What of mine? I asked. I care not about yours, he replied. You must care about it, I demanded. You are bound to me. I delivered you from sin, from an unlawful marriage, from Rome, the church and all its corruption, to your own great profit. His face reddened, his voice rising in pitch. What you ask will take away all that profit. The emperor will not stand by idly to see his aunt and cousin dispatched. His Imperialist army will invade and devour this great island like an unstoppable flame, turning all of us to ash. Consider that before you make unreasonable demands upon me.

I matched his temper. You lay down your life and those of your people so easily. Have you forgotten how to fight? What shall happen otherwise? An alliance exists. You know it does, and it will stop at nothing to turn back the clock, restore the old religion of Rome and its corrupt traditions and see to it that Mary becomes the successor to the throne. Consider your daughter Elizabeth. And if not her, what of me? Yes, what of you? He responded. It is a question I ask myself daily. And what is your answer? I asked. He turned away, as if he found the sight of me revolting. I reached for his arm, which he moved from me violently. And if it were Lady Shelton, my cousin, who asked, What of me? Would you have a quicker answer? He grumbled something indecipherable and left.

I chose not to follow and instead saw myself in the looking glass: gaunt, thin, my eyes large and haunted, my black hair hidden beneath a jeweled cap which revealed the hollows of my heart-shaped face. Questions flooded my brain: Where am I? Who am I? How did I get here? Where am I going? I spoke aloud finally, though no one was near. You can dismiss me, if you so desire, but you cannot dismiss God. If you harm me, He will be watching, and his wrath toward you will be great.

121

Henry

He, Cranmer, tried to stop me, saying that executions of popular figures, such as Fisher and More, could be counter-productive. Perhaps we can have them subscribe to a modified form of the oath, he suggested. Am I a modified king? I asked. Are my duties modified? There is no such thing as modification, archbishop. There is for and against. That is all. A modified form of the oath? What does that mean? Nothing, if they don't actually believe in it. My argument should have sufficed for most men, but not Cranmer, a Cambridge man, a theologian, a scholar, who believes reason the lord over emotion. Do the rest of the English who swore believe? Or do they swear out of fear? Fear or not, it matters not to me, archbishop, as long as they swear. Do you not want their love as well? He asked. I want their obedience, I yelled, as I want yours. I want peace in my realm, however I can get it, and as I see it the best way to get it is by laying down the hammer, or should I say the blade? Let them know what they're up against. You compromise once, they will expect it next time as well, and before you know it the whole country expects it.

The archbishop showed not the slightest trace of sweat on his brow. He sat, as if on the lap of God, as serene as could be. Do you believe the arrests and executions will rid the realm of dissent? Yes, I do, I fumed, for logic tells me if I dispatch the dissenters, I eradicate dissent as well. Do you know of another way, my esteemed scholar? Perhaps change, he answered. Change? I moved around him in circles. Do I look like a man who is amenable to change? Besides, what kind of change? Do you mean I should dispatch the queen and take back Katherine and Mary, go riding and have dinner and mass with them each day and forget all thoughts of having a male heir? Is that the change to which you refer? You really should get out into the world more, archbishop. Be more like Cromwell. He knows what I am saying, for he is like me, a gambler, believing the next throw of the dice will wipe out all previous losses.

So, I gambled, played my cards the only way I know how, uncompromisingly, authoritatively, ordered first Fisher's execution, which can be blamed as easily on the pope, for he was the one who enraged me, making Fisher, while imprisoned in the Tower, a cardinal. Not on my watch, I said to the pope, though I never actually talked or communicated with him. I conveyed it through my actions. I wasn't there that morning, but I heard Fisher wore his finest clothes to the scaffold, that he called it his wedding day, that he died to preserve the honor of God. I am happy to report he no longer has a head with which to talk such rubbish. Last I heard his head is on a pike on London's bridge, black and rotting, hardly suitable for a wedding day. His only solace is that his friend's head, Thomas More's, is next to his, though it is unlikely they are aware of each other's presence. No one can say from now on that they are men of conscience, for they are no longer conscious, having suffered for their arrogance, believing their principles greater than my will. I offered them the oath, upholding my supremacy in the church. They couldn't see sense, especially More, stubborn as any Spaniard.

The oath is a test of loyalty More was told, more than once or twice. Not many things in life are simple, but this is simple. If you do not swear to it, you indict yourself by implication, traitor, rebel. Still, he wouldn't swear. I waited. For what, though? I knew, he knew, everyone knew, he would never change his mind. Meanwhile, Anne harassed me. Do not make an exception, for anyone. If you excuse one person, everyone will expect to be excused. Be ruthless, establish your authority. Otherwise everyone will abuse your mercy. Thomas More is not above the law, and he has shown continued loyalty to Rome. Consider his sins, she said. As chancellor, he persecuted good men and women, he burned them, he stood in the way of reform, he defied our marriage, my position as queen. By not taking the oath, he is in essence disrespecting me, validating what he said of me, or do you not remember? These dances of hers will prove such dances that she will spurn our heads off like footballs, but it will not be long ere her head will dance the like dance. That is treasonous. I demand his head! Yes, of course. His head. I gave her that. Now, she should leave me be, in peace.

He died on the scaffold, in a torrent of rain that never stopped, splashing about, soaked to his knees, saying he died my good servant, but God's first. He has no one but himself to blame, for he failed to heed the simplicity of life in my realm.

122

Katherine

I know now that any evil is possible. How else should I feel, my heart pained, my mind in a state of limitless consternation, having learned of the executions of Bishop Fisher and Thomas More?

I know also that Henry has lost all sense and reason, and I am culpable. Each day and especially at night when I close my eyes, when I try to sleep and cannot, I think on it: What have I done? What haven't I done? Will God forgive me my sins, if they are indeed sins, though He must know I never intended them to be sins? I wanted only to remain my husband's wife and with it retain the title of Queen of England, a right granted me by Pope Julius and by God. I wanted only to survive and live by principle, though I was a fool to believe that principle alone ensured a person's survival. It, in fact, made it more likely to ensure a person's death, evident by the passing of my good friends, the most noble men to have lived in this country.

My last communication with Thomas More is testament to this truth. I am the king's true subject, he wrote, and pray for his highness and all of his people and all the realm. I do nobody harm, I say no harm, I think no harm, but wish everybody good. And if this be not enough to keep a man alive in good faith, I have not long to live. The offer of the oath is like a sword with two edges. One edge, refusal, will kill my body. The other, to swear, will slay my soul. I prefer the former, for what is my body but something temporal, proving we live for only a minute under the king's rule? My soul counts for much more in the end, wherein we live forever with God. Do not grieve when I am gone. Celebrate knowing I am among the fortunate to see paradise.

Old wounds do not always heal. They often lay the foundation for newer ones to fester. The Earl of Warwick's ghost still speaks to me, having never quieted, since 1499 when he was beheaded, clearing the way for my marriage to Arthur. Why? The ghost asks. Now, the newer ghosts—the Carthusian monks, Bishop Fisher, Thomas More—ask the same: Why? How should I answer? If I had known the outcomes of my defiance toward the king would result in Henry splitting from Rome and declaring himself supreme head of the church of England, in his ransacking the monasteries, dispossessing the monks and taking their wealth and property, in his mistreating Mary, forcing her to live under the jurisdiction of Lady Shelton, Anne Boleyn's aunt, kept prisoner, made miserable and ill, faced with the danger of death, in his arresting and executing many of the saintliest men in England, would I have done anything differently?

I am ashamed—or bold enough in my honesty—to say to those who have predeceased me: No, I would have followed the same course, fighting what I believed (and still believe) was an unjustness to me, to the laws of man, and to God. For this honesty, I hope they will forgive me, for whether or not I have sinned (I leave that to God), I must acknowledge having been the source of so much violence. I must live with this acknowledgement. Even more so, I must die with it. I appease myself, saying the men who have died are martyrs in heaven. I tell them, in their ongoing visitation to me, I wish to join them, in martyrdom especially, if it were only possible. Many times I have cried out in the dark: Bring me to the scaffold, Henry, let me wear my royal best, let the people see what you have done to me. I pray for its outcome, though I have seen the specter of death, and it tells me my end is otherwise. That I shall pass like a sick animal in the wild, rotting away among these damp, dense stones here at Kimbolton, far from London, where it's possible no one will even know I have died.

123

Henry

When I read the letter Cromwell found in Fisher's Tower cell, written in Katherine's hand, I slammed my hand on the table, a joyous, I-knew-it reaction. It turns out that after all these years she *despaired of the mercy of God*. Other innocuous scribblings were included, about noble causes and martyrdom and paradise and similar rubbish, but it was this one line that stirred my interest, especially now, given the political fallout from the recent executions. The more I asked myself, Why did she doubt God's mercy toward her? The more it got me thinking. To start with, had she committed perjury in court by claiming she never consummated her marriage with Arthur? And if that was true — that she lied — what other guilty responsibilities has she kept hidden in the darkness of her heart? It's not hard to guess at the answer. Wolsey's fall from grace and his subsequent death, her own exile and supposed mistreatment, her daughter's repeated illnesses, the break from the pope and Rome, the closing of the monasteries, the nuns and monks being left homeless, the Act of Succession, the many executions. I can go on, but I believe the point is made. All the problems in England have their source in her lying and obstinacy, and she knows it. Otherwise, she wouldn't have written that she *despaired of the mercy of God*.

I should publish this letter to the world to shift the blame from me to her for what has taken place here and abroad. Perhaps then Pope Paul wouldn't declare a holy war against me, inviting the European sovereigns to fight under his banner, which is laughable, considering that those same sovereigns (see, Francis, Charles) execute far more people in their own countries than I do in mine. I hear the pope wants the emperor to force me to forfeit my kingdom and to punish me for refusing to bow to the divorce sentence. I can't believe that man still thinks of my divorce. Doesn't he have better things to do, such as shine the gold that surrounds him?

I can't remain cut off as I am. Cromwell.has been trying to convince me to form an alliance with the German princes, to join the Schmalkaldic League, though I have told him repeatedly I cannot make a treaty with Lutherans. I cannot surrender the way I practice my faith. I will never stand for forms of the mass being varied. I should prefer to be alone in the world, without allies, before I succumb to that. To which Cromwell, ever the pragmatist, says: If you do not protect your realm from foreign invasion, you will have no faith to practice and you may find yourself forced to speak Spanish. As long as Katherine and Mary live, the threat always exists that Imperial ships could land at the mouth of the Thames, that Charles' mercenaries could land in Scotland or at the northern border.

I can understand now why Cromwell said what he did, purportedly to Chapuys, though everything finds a way to me at some point, especially one like this: What harm or danger could there be in the Dowager Princess dying just now? Would the emperor have reason to regret her death? Things would be much easier for everyone, including him, though especially us, since Charles will not keep up a quarrel for a dead woman. That is a far better scenario than aligning with Lutherans, to have peace with Charles, he who practices the same faith, without any variation to the mass.

124

Anne

If only Katherine should die, I said to Cromwell. There would be no need for an alliance with the German princes. We would all be safe then, would we not? He stared at me, which I hate more than anything, that blank expression with its hidden motives. Why do you not speak? Do you know something I do not? We shall all be safe, you are correct, he said. Why didn't you say that without pause? I like to think before I speak, madam. You should think before you act, as well, I said. For I do not favor your alliances, you know that, and I do not favor your plans to destroy the monasteries rather than fix them. Your motives are sometimes suspicious to me, Cromwell. You should be careful if you mean to keep your head on your shoulders. His eyebrows arched. Am I in danger of losing it? I smiled, forcibly. Aren't we all in danger of losing our heads, Cromwell? This is England, after all. Yes, I shall keep that in mind, he said, flatly.

Funny, isn't it, I continued, that the German princes should not like me when I have done more for the Lutherans here and abroad, those being persecuted, than you or anyone else at court, and unless I am mistaken, in England as well. Do you wish to comment on that or just stare? I am agreeing with you, silently, to myself, he replied. I shall like you to agree with words, for I do not understand silence, especially yours, masking as it does much intrigue. The Gospel of Christ was never so truly preached as it is now under your encouragement, he responded. The lay people know the scriptures better than many of us. I laughed. If only Lord Norfolk, my uncle, read the Bible, which he boasts never to have done. Cromwell responded quickly, making me believe he is not beyond being trained. He still believes, madam, it is the job of priests and no one else, to convey scripture to the rest of us. What we call the old religion, and what I, as Vicar

General, am trying to abolish in the monasteries. I applaud your efforts, Cromwell, especially if it means the eradication of foolish relics. You have no idea, madam, the extent of the corruption.

Why should you say I have no idea? I am well informed, Mr. Secretary. More informed than you know, for only yesterday I received a report that the blood at Hailes Abbey, for which the monks receive money from curious visitors, is not really the blood of Christ, but only the blood of ducks. Be assured, madam, he said, they shall be properly punished for their abuses. The work I have set out to do is only just begun. Good, Cromwell, though I should like to think your motives are in keeping with Christian morals. My motives, madam, are in keeping with the King's morals. That is not the same thing as Christian morals, I said. He nearly smiled, though he caught himself in time, as he arranged his face more to his liking. Do you not believe my devotion sincere? Your face wears an expression of doubt, no matter how hard you try to conceal it. I shall like to tell you what I have conveyed to my chaplains.

I have carefully chosen you to be the lanterns and light of my court, I told them, to watch over its morals and, above all things, to teach its young ladies and gentlemen to embrace the wholesome doctrine and infallible knowledge of Christ's gospel. Beseech God to grant understanding of the glad tidings of our salvation, this great while oppressed with the tyranny of thy adversary of Rome. Does not my saying that to them prove I am honest in my devotion to my faith? I assure you, madam, he said, I have no doubt concerning your defending of Christ's gospel. All in this realm owe much to you. The bishops, whom you have appointed to their seats and titles; the scholars, especially the poor ones, whom you have aided with money for their education; the persecuted heretics here and in France, whom you have sheltered. No one has done for them, any of them, what you have. And yet I am looked down upon, I said. How do you explain that, Cromwell? Speak, do not give me a pause. Bestow upon me your wisdom. How should I be seen in more favor, so that I am queen not only in appearance but more so in the people's esteem, so that they recognize me for who I see myself to be, a patron of new learning, a godly matron?

His face turned a shade of pink, his eyes smaller and more unreadable. Clearly, he did not want to answer or, in fact, had no answer in which to satisfy me. Finally, he stepped back and bowed, offering only two words: Patience, madam. You offend, me, I said, with your ill-timed reticence, you who are never reticent in the giving of words and advice. Leave my sight at once! As he stepped outside, I followed him, my temper rising. I shall not forget this, Cromwell, that you have failed me again, due to your growing disrespect of me. If it one day means your undoing, you have only yourself to blame.

125

Henry

I scolded Cromwell, saying, I came on progress, and especially here at Wolf Hall to the fine hospitality of Sir John Seymour, to get away from bad news, not have it brought to me. Can't you stop the world from moving when I wish to stop and relax? It is a skill I haven't yet mastered, Your Majesty, he said. Well, it should be atop your priority list, I deadpanned. I will make a note of your recommendation, he replied. You're a funny fellow, Cromwell, in the most unfunniest of ways. Why shouldn't you laugh at my jokes when everyone else does? Shall I place the practice of laughing on my priority list as well? He asked. I laughed, loud enough for both of us, then stopped properly to yell at him. What am I to do with this news just now? You need not do anything, he answered. Just receive it. Otherwise, relax, as you have requested. I snorted. You interrupted me to tell me you received news that Charles defeated the Turks, meaning he now has no excuse or other preoccupation. He is free to invade England. Yet I should relax, as you say? I have already sent messages that all our ports, north and south, should be well guarded in case of an invasion.

Will he do it this time? I asked. He is not an impulsive man, he answered. That is not what I asked. I asked, Will he do it this time? No, I do not believe he will, he said, for he is waiting. For what is he waiting? I shouted. What we are all waiting for, Your Majesty. For Katherine to die, an event even her own nephew wishes for, considering the peace it will bring. Yes, the peace, I said, though she is not one to just lie down and die, Cromwell. She will fight death as she has fought me, with all her strength and determination, using prayers and God as her shield. She will live just to spite me. Perhaps, he responded, but I hear she has developed a chronic cough and a pain in her chest and does not eat or drink and sleeps little. Who is your source? I begged to know. The ambassador and I are friends, he was quick to answer. Is it a personal or political friendship? I asked. It's personally political, he quipped. And what do you hope to gain from this friendship? I inquired with eagerness. He responded with a question of his own. What should any friendship offer other than advantage, Your Majesty? Yes, of course, I said. Is that how you look at our friendship, if it is to be called that? No, he said, I would not call it that, for you are my king, and I am your subject.

Wrong, Cromwell. If you were my subject, you would laugh at my jokes. I am a serious subject, Your Majesty. Well, I suppose it shouldn't matter, as long as you are loyal to me. And honest as well, as I hope you are about her failing health. Just think, Cromwell, what it would mean. Not only to my relations with the emperor. What it would mean for me. I could, how should I say this, take another wife, could I not, without the village idiots and drunken farmers saying, if you leave Anne you must take back Katherine. Your abandonment of her is the reason it rains, they say, without end and will do so until she is restored. They should all learn to swim, I say, for the world will flood before I return to her. Let us hope—as you give me hope—she will soon die, wherein I will be free.

How free, Your Majesty? He asked. With your help, I mean, I answered. He seemed genuinely surprised, though I could not confidently say anything about him was genuine. My help? He asked. Yes, what if Anne wasn't my legal wife? What if she had had a pre-contract with Henry Percy? We've been down that road, Your Majesty, he said. I went to see him, do you not remember? He swore they never had a pre-contract. You saw him swear, his hand on the Bible. It is what you wanted then. Yes, then. But what if it's not what I want now or when Katherine dies, if she ever does? You will talk to him again and do whatever it is you do to convey your persuasiveness and make him recant his earlier swear, making him say he lied and swore under duress, and that he now wished to tell the actual truth, which is that he and Anne were contracted to marry. He no longer looked genuinely surprised. He appeared to get what I was saying, evident by the steady glare of his eyes and how they drank my words with a swelling effect, increasing their size and color.

How is it that I married her, Cromwell, other than what I now believe, that she bewitched me? Why else should I do it, she with her sharp tongue, always upbraiding me for my dalliances, always laughing at my poetry and ill-fitting clothes, behaving with such arrogance and hauteur that, frankly, it is embarrassing to me, and that is not even the worst of it. She has made enemies with people. You know she has, affecting my standing here and in the world, resulting in England's isolation, our fearing an invasion any moment, and as if none of this is sufficient enough to damn her, she has not produced a son, making me believe God has forgotten me entirely, that I have been cursed like so many of my ancestors before me. Think about it, Cromwell. What if I could marry again to a woman on the right side of the fence, religiously and politically speaking? Would that not lead to a friendship with the emperor and an advantage?

Any particular one in mind, Your Majesty? He inquired. Yes, I answered gladly. Have you noticed Sir John's youngest daughter, Jane? I do not study women the way you do, he said. It's a worthy scholarship, let me tell you, I declared, and this one pleases me indeed. The way she lowers her eyes and blushes when I look at her, appearing helpless, and I like women who are helpless. They are much more appealing than those, like Anne, who spread their wings and make noise. But Jane, she is a citadel, a shrine, a place where I can see myself kneeling and worshipping. She is Chaucer's Griselda, is she not? The patient, suffering woman. So silent, so submissive, so ideal.

126

Anne

It unnerves me to stay here, knowing as I do the family's history, that Sir John took his son Edward's wife, Katherine, into his own bed, that he begot two boys with her, improperly naming them Edward and John, that the elder Edward banished his wife, sent her to a convent, where she died, and put the children aside, cutting them out of any inheritance. Henry is not bothered by such a background. He, in fact, thinks little of it, evident by his behavior, his laughing, eating and drinking, his joking loudly with Sir John and his meek wife, Margaret, who bore the old man many sons and daughters, one of whom is Jane, one of my ladies in wait, whom the king tries to engage with his eyes and humor, though she offers little response other than blushing and keeping her head down, her mirth suppressed by her tight-lipped mouth.

She scurries in and out of the room, making herself small as a mouse, seemingly innocent, though I am not fooled. I notice her interplay with the king, her darting, furtive eyes, pretending the chaste virgin, giving him what he wants, to play the chivalrous knight, saving his damsel in distress. I know her game, for that is what it is, though Henry, I'm certain, sees no subterfuge in her, only maidenly honesty and feminine helplessness. I should like to say to him: You know nothing of women, you never have, for if you see what I do and sense what I sense you would not like nor trust her. I have my reasons, knowing she served in Katherine's household before mine, knowing she still holds allegiance to Katherine and Mary and the pope, knowing she is unable to read, relying on priests to tell her how to be a Christian, knowing she would love to watch me fall, wherein she would promptly walk over me or stand atop me.

She is likely glad that Charles has defeated the Turks. I

imagine her saying, It is a victory for Christendom, maybe now Charles will send his ships to the coast of England, maybe now the Catholic faith can be restored, that we can return to Rome, that Lady Mary can find her rightful place in the succession or perhaps replace her father on the throne. She shall be disappointed, though, for I shall not fall.

It is said the continuous rains have ruined this year's harvest. That is not true, for on this progress, the king has visited my bed. The harvest is coming, and I shall bear fruit, and the king will cater to me as he once did, rubbing my feet, allowing me to put them in his lap, giving me his undivided attention, as is my right, having married not for dynastic purposes, but for love.

127

Katherine

My dearest nephew, I write, I am filled with joy to hear of your victory in Tunis, realizing what it means to you, the emperor, and to all of Christendom. With this victory behind you, I am hoping you will now have more time and attention to address the concerns here in England, where I, your aunt, and Mary, your cousin, are virtual prisoners. I wrote to Pope Paul and have received his return communication, much of it pertaining to what you already know, the plan to unite Spain, France and the Papacy, with the aim to restore Mary to the succession and renew the Catholic faith in England, which is sorely needed, though it is only one of a long list of problems that face us. People are discontented, more than ever. The weather is so dangerously bad across the whole country that people have not reaped half the cereals they need, and their religion is being ruined in front of their eyes, not just in Henry anointing himself head of the church and having the pope's name erased from prayer books. Monasteries are being closed and destroyed and pillaged for their gold, relics and property, while nuns and monks are being displaced, they who have always devoted themselves to God and to the poor people whom they have served and who depend upon them for their livelihood. All are exasperated by the queen, who as you know is not the queen, saying terrible things about her which they express in thousands of terrible, damning words, believing she is responsible for the recent executions of men who followed, as we do, the faith of our forefathers and the only faith recognizable to God.

The people of England have reached a collective breaking point. If there is a war, people will rebel. Pope Paul promises to excommunicate Henry, not merely make threats as his predecessor, Pope Clement, had done, to which he is answering to God, rest his soul. You, together with the pope, must devise a cure and in doing so bring Henry to heel. Now is the time to act, for as an excommunicate, in the words of Pope Paul, Henry has no right or title to the crown. If your action is delayed, they—the heretics who govern England—will do with me and my daughter what they have done with many holy martyrs. I do not say so out of fear, for as I have written before, I am comforted to think that I would follow in the same kind of death those who, sadly for me, I could not imitate in life, as their lives were religious and mine worldly. I will tell you what I told the pope: If you do not apply a remedy to these matters with all speed, there will be no end to the damnation of souls or the making of martyrs.

You have written to Ambassador Chapuys, saying it was not possible at present to remedy the mischief by force, as you yourself admitted you had just cause to do. Here are the words you wrote: *We think it best to temporize, entertaining the said personages and others in hope and waiting to see whether God will inspire the said King of England to bow.* You must know that Henry will never bow to God, that is not until he dies and is forced to reckon with his soul. Until then, he feels it is his divine right to roar like the lion he has become. Only another lion with more might and bite can defeat him. Here's what you wrote in that same letter, a line later: *Some good opportunity may arise to compel me by force.* Nephew, are not the executions of good Christian men examples of what you call good opportunity? Is not my captivity, moving from one damp house to another, with reduced households and income, with the inability to visit or receive guests or to write freely, example as well? Is not Mary's mistreatment, her many illnesses? Is not the destruction of Christendom?

Death is everywhere, nephew, and it beckons, especially to me. I am old and ill. I'm sure you have heard of my failing health, the result of having lived the past three years in cold, drafty castles, living without love, without my daughter's presence, without my dearest friends. You must know it has been purgatory for me, or even worse. You must know my suffering and yet your actions do not suggest that you do. You have done little to show your love, always making excuses not to do anything. If my condemnation is false, please show otherwise. If not for me, then for Mary or for God, whom you say you worship. Please, I beg you, as your aunt and one who reveres you.

128

Henry

The threat of war has turned my mind fanciful at night when I wish for nothing but sleep. I wake to see the faces of Charles and Francis, sometimes conjoined by one neck. I see them lick their chops and say in one garbled, synchronized voice.

If he is indeed an excommunicate, with no right or title to the crown, a usurper like his father, with no leverage with God or the pope, is it not an invitation for us to come across the channel with fleets of ships, come to the Scottish shores, and into England to pillage what we can and distribute it accordingly among our Roman-Imperial alliances?

Envious bastards, I yell, making my servants jump to attention. No, no, I say to them, it is just a fit, a dream, a nightmare, fever or pain induced from my aching legs and throbbing head, leave me be. Still, the threat of excommunication and invasion lingers long as darkness gives way to light, when I say to myself, I care not a fig about excommunications. Lesser people, such as Luther, were excommunicated, though he got on well enough, married to a nun last I heard. I shall not be deterred, nor thwarted, nor threatened by those who are motivated by envy.

That's right. It's clear as day, is it not, that their actions against me are motivated by what I possess that neither of them does, the physique, the stature, the fine features of a true prince, with skin the color of gold and eyes blue and vast, able to encompass the world in a glance, wherein they are not worthy to stand aside me in a looking glass, for Francis has the beak of a Toucan bird, and Charles carries on his face a chin the size of Spain. And it's not just my appearance they envy. Whatever they have, I have more. If they are learned, I am twice as learned. If they are gifted with music and language, I am their tutor and teacher in compare. If they are merciful, I am the exemplar of mercy. If they are soldiers, I am their captain, modeling how to wear a suit of armor. If they are gallant with women, I am the standard for knighthood, chivalrous and fair, unstoppable in the bedroom.

I attribute these nighttime ruminations about Charles and Francis to Katherine, for she is up to something, which does not favor my position or standing with them. I don't care what Cromwell says about her failing health, on death's doorstep. If she doesn't die soon, and I fear she won't due to her determined will to make me miserable, I have no recourse but to provide my own means. I shall tell my Privy Council that in the next Parliament session proceedings should be taken against both she and Mary. It is an action long overdue. If it causes dismay to some of my councilors, who should wear sad, wry faces, those who pine for the return of the old days, bowing to Katherine, or for the new with Mary sitting on the throne, so be it, and if I should lose my crown for eradicating their presence, I will do what I have set out to do.

129

Anne

This child I carry is my savior. How else should I say it but truthfully? I watch the rain, I study the shifting winds, I listen to the call of the wild, in darkness, alone, wherein its voice speaks without censure or deception: Henry wishes to be rid of you. I appreciate this truth. It alerts me to myself, to the world surrounding me, to the shuffle and signing of papers, to the sailing of ships to and from, to the silence in the halls, absent of music and mirth, to the snakes in the garden, of which there are many, begging me to take the bait, to eat the forbidden fruit, to move wrongly, to misstep, to fall, to never again stand or return to Eden. Ambassador Chapuys is the largest of the snakes, he who has never bowed to me, never acknowledged me as queen, and who now has become Henry's chum. I see them, from my window, walking outside on the Greenwich grass, resplendently green and wet, Henry's arm draped over the ambassador's shoulder, not caring that he will catch a chill in the late November cold, caring only for agreements and alliances and what could be gained if this or that were to happen, such as Katherine's expected death and Charles' sudden reversal of feelings for our English king, once his trusted ally, when both called Rome home and the occupying pope holy father, when Katherine was a beloved aunt and Mary an adorable cousin, one he wished to marry, though twenty years her senior, long before I entered the stage to play my part.

My womb tightens. Yesterday, Henry greeted me, among his courtiers, with cordiality, even politeness, though soon after in the privacy of a room he shrank from me. Shouldn't you cherish me at this time? I asked. I shall cherish you, he said, when the child you carry is born healthy and male. And if it is not? You ask what you already know, he answered, starting his departure from the room and, in particular, from me. I held to his arm. What you see in her I can't imagine, I said. I know not what you mean, he replied, not facing me. Jane, I said. He stood his ground, head down. She does not read, nor talk. She passes as a breeze through the hall, invisible, silent. You find that appealing?

He lifted his head and faced me, fussing with his mouth, aligning his lips and tongue, swallowing with great effort. I searched for something recognizable in his eyes, something that would tell me he might still be the man I married. You are a man of learning and theology, of language and music, of medicine and astronomy. You possess a vast mind, and yet you choose to share it with someone who has inside her head little more than stuffing one would use on a cushion. He turned away, though I continued, more loudly. She is, in fact, a doll, one finds atop a mantel. He turned sharply. His face turned red, his eyes bitter blue. What's wrong? I asked. Have you as well grown silent? Are those traits of hers rubbing off on you? Or is it that you find silence charming, as you once found my conversation, my mind to match yours, charming? His small mouth formed words he had hoped not to speak, to hold from me any form of civility and communication. What is charm but pretense? He said, spitting the words. It is a lie, false behavior performed for a prize.

Are you saying I used charm to trick you? I asked. I could easily say that about you, could I not? Did you not woo me with poetry and adoring letters of your affection and wish to marry me not for dynastic purposes as kings are wont to do but for love. Well, didn't you? You owe me that much, to admit you once loved me. He hoisted the girth of his chest above me and raised himself, looking down at me with burning flesh. If anyone should be owed, it is me, for having suffered much to see you made my wife and crowned queen, without any reward. Such as a son, you mean, I responded quickly. Yes, such as a son, he said, seemingly satisfied with himself for having made a punctuation to his words.

I took his hand and pressed it against my womb, hoping to cool his fire, make him see a future he may have forgotten. I may yet make you the happiest of kings. Can you at least tell me that is possible? If I deliver you what you want and need? He wanted to smile. It took great effort for him to suppress it. Yes, I will be the happiest of kings, he said quietly, as if to himself more than to me. And I shall be the happiest of queens to not only give you the son you desire, but to be the only woman you seek in the mornings and at night, the woman you hold in your arms and speak to, as you once did, lovingly. Can you promise me that? I wiped at the tears on my face. He raised his arm, as if to hold me, before placing it against his side. Give me the male heir I desire, and I shall give you that and so much more. Until then, much is to be done.

Yes, much is to be done. I can only imagine what that is as Henry and Ambassador Chapuys vanish from my sight, around a bend, Henry still holding the Spaniard close to him. I am left to wonder if I am part of what needs to be done and whether it is something in my favor or, as I suspect, something for which I need to worry.

130

Katherine

I shall not die a martyr, as I had hoped. I shall die as one should not, in isolation, far from my husband and daughter, deprived of their love, withered, weathered, wondering: Should I have relented to his demands, accepted being called his sister, knowing I could live in more comfort and peace, my daughter by my side, Henry as my friend and brother? Am I to blame for his enmity and the destruction of so much good? I ask God, though He remains mute on the subject. He will not involve Himself in the trifling matters of men and women, occupied as He is, managing Heaven and the souls He either receives or rejects. Such are my thoughts, confined to bed, as I have been more than two days, though I am only guessing at time for after so many hours, so many blistering fevers, sleeps and dreams, the continuous vacillation of light to dark and dark to light, I cannot be certain that it has not been two years. It was the Welsh beer, I hear Dr. de la Saa say. Since she drank it, her illness is worse. He talks to men I do not recognize, nor wish to, for fear they are licensed traitors like most who surround me here in this dreaded castle?

Have I been poisoned? I want to say, yet I am too weak to speak, too weak to hold open my eyes long enough to see the faces near me. If I hear the voice of someone I love, such as my daughter and, yes, even Henry, I shall open my eyes. Until then, I keep them shut and mumble prayers. To whom, I am no longer sure. I know only that I am disappointed in the manner of my dying, if this is indeed my final stage. I should like one more chance at sitting up in my chair, to knit, to stitch, to embroider for the poor, one more opportunity to stand near the open window, my most sustaining joy, and look at the sky, no matter that it is rainy gray and frosty cold, for I have trained myself to see far beyond the desolate landscape that is England, to stretch my sight, deep into my memory, where I am again a young woman, barely thirteen, running in the sunshine of the Alhambra, my bare feet warmed by the marble pavements, living complete in my senses, the sound of crystal water running into basins, the drag of a white peacock's tail, the scent of lemons, apples and pears. How much more preferred it would be to die at home, where my death would be a public spectacle, to see a procession of men, women and children, followed by donkeys and dogs, arrive to celebrate my life and honor my death, wherein they cook meats and slice fruits and later sing and dance, laugh and cry, speaking the Spanish language of my birth well into the night, till the morning birds herald the new day and life is born yet again.

131

Anne

Well, is she dying or not? I asked Cromwell. Her death seemed certain I was told, until a report came that she got out of bed and sat in her chair and later stood near the window, smiling to herself, singing in Spanish. I am in no condition to have such contrary information come to me, wherein one day I am filled with joy and the next worried that I am being mocked by those who wish to see me become ill-tempered and lose yet another child. I promise, Cromwell, that if anything bad should happen to me, I will hold you accountable for providing me with false information. He tilted his head in a half bow. Do you wish to warn me again that I might lose my head? This is not a laughing matter, Cromwell. I am serious. As my question was serious, he said. Believe me, madam, I take the placement of my head on my shoulders very seriously. You are mocking me, Cromwell. How should I mock you, madam, knowing if I do, I may not remain intact? You are attempting to use wit, though you are failing, as you have failed in so many other matters of late. Still, I offer you another opportunity to redeem yourself. If it concerns France, madam, you must know by now that negotiation with Francis will never happen. No, not that. I mean to know whether Katherine is on death's door or whether she plans on living for years to come. Go to Kimbolton, report to me whether she is feigning sickness or not.

My going to Kimbolton is unnecessary, madam, he said. Those who live there in her household report to me on a daily basis. If there is a change in her health, and if and when she is dying or has died, you will be the first to learn of it. You know, Cromwell, it may surprise you to hear this. Though I want her to die, it does not mean I don't understand her and in some way find a common ground with her. If Henry cast me off, I, too, would be unforgiving and intrigued with foreign powers, seeking vengeance through invasion and war. He curled his mouth into a near smile. I'm sure she would be comforted to know you sympathize with her. Perhaps you should make the visit yourself, the two of you sitting around a fire, chatting like school chums, the subject of your conversation: how to live with Henry. There you go again with your failed wit, I said. I am bound to succeed one day, he said, if I am able to keep my head on my shoulders. Which is beginning to look less likely with each passing day, I snapped, before modifying my earlier comment.

Do not misunderstand my sympathy for her. The truth is if she plans on living much longer, then it is time for Henry to dispose of her, as he has promised to encourage Parliament to do. Be assured, madam, he intervened, her illness is real. The king will not need to expedite her end. You better be right, I said, for I can have no rest until I am freed from these poor ladies, I mean Mary as well as her mother. I understood the reference the first time, madam. Don't be smart with me, Cromwell. I am not being smart, madam, just efficient. Don't be efficient either. Just do your job, absent of word play. You may have power, but you're not the king, nor the queen. My gender hardly qualifies me to be queen, madam. Enough of your sorry wit, I said. Can't be helped, madam. It is natural to my constitution. Then change your constitution, I stammered. That will take some work, he replied. It will be worth the effort, I said. He performed another of those half bows, indicative of his insincerity.

Is there anything else, madam, before I take my leave? Yes, Jane Seymour, I answered, Henry's newest paramour. I shall like to know if you favor her, as does the king and, by all indications, Ambassador Chapuys? Favor her as a paramour? Let's not pretend, Cromwell. Favor her as a replacement. In your condition, madam, you should not think such thoughts. But I do, Cromwell. How can I not? I see Henry with her outside, inside, and in my dreams. I have to practice not getting upset when she, with her pasty face and little, compressed eyes, walks near me, for fear of disturbing myself and injuring the prince. I find myself pulling my skirts aside when she passes, huddling into myself, my shoulders narrowing and shrinking. Afterwards, I force myself to believe he will never abandon me, that he waited for me too long, that I have made his wait worth the while, that if he turns his back on me, he will dismiss the great and marvelous work I've done for the gospel and the reformed religion. I convince myself to feel better, saying Jane is no different from all the others, flowers that quickly droop and wilt, losing their petals, at which times he loses interest. I have told Henry this, also that I am in comparison a tree, with deep roots and branches that do not bend. He laughed and said, trees get old and are sometimes cut down to make way for new seedlings. Can you believe he said that to me, the woman who carries his heir? Why do you not speak when I reveal the secrets of my heart to you?

He took what appeared to be an exasperated breath. You should look the other way and not trouble your mind about the king's affairs. Is that the best you can do, mimic the king's words? I shouted. Have I failed you again? He asked, cold as stone, mockingly. I felt tears forming in my eyes. I held them at bay and told him I needed his presence no longer.

132

Henry

Lord Bedingfield assures me that her doctors believe she is not long for this life. Yes, she had recovered briefly for a few days, wherein she walked and sat up and stood and even ate small morsels of food and drank some wine, chatting ceaselessly in Spanish with her ladies, but her illness has taken a turn for the worse. She can no longer hold down food or drink. She lies all day and night in bed, coughing blood into a small basin, complaining of great pains, which she claims emanate from her heart. It is like her to say that, to torment me till the very end, wanting to blame me for her demise. I will have none of it, though. I offered her, several years ago, a different life and ending. She chose wrongly, so if it is her heart that has killed her, she has pierced it with arrows from her own shaft.

I imagine her thoughts. She will want to forgive me and will want to ask God to do likewise, declaring I have lost all reason in pursuit of dynastic power. If I could answer her thoughts, I would say, It is you, Kate, who needs forgiveness, for your blighted womb, for poisoning my children before they were born. Those are not the words I would want for our parting, though, for they are full of contention, and I am tired of contention, as she surely must be. I would instead offer her my mercy: Isn't this best, Kate, that you should join the saints and holy martyrs, as you have always desired? I will leave it at that, in a state of peace, for now that her long-wished for death is about to occur, I am relieved and want to shout to heaven: Thank you, God, for not having forsaken me. Let us make an alliance now that this matter is behind us.

Ambassador Chapuys enters my room. I receive him warmly, for now more than ever I need him. He, it turns out, needs me as well, for he asks for permission to visit Katherine before she dies.

She is alone and has no one, he says. It will buoy her spirits to see a friend. I see Cromwell's face before me, saying he will send his man, Stephen Vaughan, to keep an eye on Chapuys and his entourage, for even on her deathbed Katherine cannot be trusted in the company of Spaniards. Yes, I say to the ambassador, what harm could it do now? Go to her, and when you return, let us speak further about our earlier conversation, for with Katherine's death I should like to think the emperor can again be our ally.

Yes, of course, he says. One more matter, though. Lady Katherine's dying wish is to see her daughter one last time, and Mary cries for nothing else in her life. I feel the smile on my face wane. You wish to exploit my goodwill, Ambassador Chapuys. No, he says, with your mercy and with the blessing of God, I wish only to unite for a final time two women, bound by blood, who love each other dearly. I am afraid I cannot allow that, I say, watching the blush of his face turn pale. It is not so much political as you might think, though that is a consideration. It is personal, Chapuys. You do not know what I have suffered due to their collective defiance and disobedience of me. As a result, they do not deserve the right to see each other, regardless of the circumstance. They shall have to wait for a time in the future, when God accepts them both into his heavenly kingdom, where they shall have eternity in which to unite with one another. Until then, you shall have to accept the conditions I set. You may go, as I have said, but do not defy me or do anything sneaky. I am not a sneaky person, Your Majesty, he says. I look at him and feel the smile returning to my face. You're Spanish, are you not?

He bows. Before leaving, he asks: Would you like me to deliver a message to her from you, Your Majesty? No, I say, I have already made my peace with her. I shall take my leave, then, he says, for it shall take three days to travel, and I hope to see her alive. Yes, of course, I say, and wish him a safe journey.

The moment he leaves, a surprising image, a memory, enters my head. Twenty-five years ago, our son, Henry, was born on

New Year's Day. I wanted to give Katherine flowers, but it was winter and none could be found, so I had some made. I gave her six dozen roses made of white silk. Where are they now? I wonder. Does she still have them? If so, I should like them back, for she will have no use for them anymore. I should like to give them to Jane, for she is as delicate as any rose and nearly as white.

133

Katherine

I do not want sleep, I told the ambassador, kissing his hand, thanking him for coming, telling him even if I wanted sleep the pain in my stomach was too great to allow it, informing him I had slept no more than two hours in the past six days. You need rest, he insisted, squeezing my hand with both of his, rubbing the cold from it. A dying person does not need rest, I assured him. She shall receive plenty of it later. I wish to relish this moment, in the presence of an ally who shares my origin of birth and its language and who respects my title, having fought for its retention. I am relieved to know I may die in the arms of a friend instead of left alone like a beast in a field. He urged me to cling to life. I looked into his eyes, rich and deep, their color the soil of our homeland. It is not life I leave, I said, only torment. Better to pass on and live eternally with Christ and the Blessed Virgin, whom I have tried to emulate. The peace of Christendom depends on your survival, he persisted. No, I said, Christendom is left in the hands of God, for only He can save it. I am too old, too weary and weak, to make any further effort, knowing that in fighting Henry I am to blame for the heresies, scandals and problems of England.

You did what a queen must do, he said, as your mother, Isabella, would have wanted you to do, acting as a lioness, not a lamb. And yet if I had submitted like a lamb, how different this country might be, I said. At which he became adamant, his voice rising to a pitch. No one should lay down her life at the price of her conscience. Even for the general good? I asked. Not even then if it means a betrayal to your nature, he said, still fervent and impassioned. My nature, for which I am punished by God, I said, tears forming in my eyes, having inherited the sins of my father. I should have been born a man, to feel glory in place of guilt. Be assured, Your Grace, you have been good to your adopted country, a great deal more than this country and its king have been to you. You could have done nothing else. And, yet, are not my recent letters to my nephew and pope gone unanswered, proof that I have failed to make a necessary change? No, he said. Both men are so enraged by the executions that they are determined to act against Henry. You stretch the truth to calm my worries, I said. The actions of which you speak shall never happen, and you know it. I do not ask for lies or illusions. I ask only that you guide and protect my daughter, to see she lives to take her seat in the succession, and guard my legacy, that when people refer to me, they say the name Queen Katherine. Anything I can do, I will, he said, for my days are nothing if I am not living them in honor of you and Mary.

I wish something else, my friend. Anything, Your Grace, he responded, bowing. Inform the king that I always loved him and will continue to love him from the other side, where I await him and all our unborn children. Tell him I never desired war. I am a soldier of Christ, holding in my hand a spiritual sword, and I shall die as such, without venom or vengeance in my heart. He will be joyed to know that, he said, for in his heart the king wants only peace.

Three days he visited, waiting for my final breath, as I myself did, yet instead of dying I gained strength, both in morale and health, which I attributed to his touch and the song of his Spanish voice. Finally, believing I was better, he decided to return to London, not wanting to abuse the license the king had given him to visit me, receiving assurance from the doctors that they would notify him if my condition changed. On the morning of his departure, he asked me if I had a final request of him. I told him I did. Bring me your fool, I said, the one in your entourage who entertained my ladies on the previous visit, splashing about in the castle's moat.

He brought the little man before me. Make me laugh, I said to the fool. He drew for me a picture of an angel. He then posed like this angel and soon flapped about the room, moving his arms as if they were wings, saying in his sing-song Spanish language: *By the grace of God, bless this holy woman, our queen, here and ever after.* He repeated this line many times, until he soared from the room, wherein I still heard his voice in the distant corridor. I laughed, though it pained my chest to do so, and I continue to laugh silently to myself as I look at the picture which I keep under my folded hands, waiting as I do for the blessing promised me.

134

Anne

Katherine's death by natural means is not enough. What about Mary? She shall not die any time soon from old age, though she may already look the part of an old woman and act it as well with her daily illnesses and complaints. The Parliamentary judicial process is necessary I tell you, and you know it is, to remove her once and for all, so why do you delay? Henry, his back to me, looking out onto the Greenwich landscape, said he was not in the mood to discuss this subject. What subject would you like to discuss, then? Is it more fitting for you to discuss the status of your mistress, Jane, whom you shower with gifts and favors in front of my eyes, while I, your wife, carry your child, the heir to the throne?

You are mad, woman, he said, still facing away. Mad, how so? I am more sane than any of the advisers who surround you, for my obsession with your daughter is founded in what's real and pending, not in what is said to appease your changing moods. Is not Mary the one being courted by the French and the emperor? Is she not the one, with the sanction of Rome and Charles, conspiring to flee England, to revolt, to marry a foreign prince, to come with an army to see that I am well buried in the ground and that you are replaced on the throne? Is she not the bane of my existence, as she should be yours? The answer to all of these questions is the same: Yes, resoundingly so. If I have a son, as I hope shortly, I know what will become of her, and that is not an idle threat. If you have more significant interests, such as standing near the window and dreaming of how you shall court Jane and the Catholic alliance that comes with her, I shall take matters into my own hands.

Not so, if your hands are tied, he said, turning and thrusting his size and girth at me, his eyes small, though blue and piercing against the red of his face. Why should they be tied? I asked. If I say they should be, his voice screeched. I am king, after all, though sometimes you forget that, as you forget that you are a woman. Meaning what? I said, moving forward to meet him. That I have only one task, to deliver birth? No, there you are wrong, he said, for you have another, just as important task, and that is to keep your mouth shut. At that, he walked away, though I followed after him. As Jane keeps her mouth shut? I shouted. As does a stone or a block of wood? Is that how you wish I behaved? Think where you would be if I had behaved that way since you courted me? He stopped and again turned to me, matching my temper with his own. I know where I would be. Living in peace, that's where. Again, he moved away.

At what price that peace? I lunged for him. At a price to your mind and to the development of the reformed religion and the church of which you are supreme head, wherein you receive tributes, thanks to me, such as this Bible that sits on the table? I lifted Miles Cloverdale's English translation, recently sent. Do you see what it says here on the inside page? *Dedicated to Henry and His Dearest Wife and Most Virtuous Princess, Queen Anne.* I do not see a dedication to Jane, do you? Look closely at the image on the frontispiece, done by Holbein, and tell me what you see, and I'll tell you what I have done for you. I do not need to look, he said, covering his face with a hand.

Then I shall tell you. It is an image of an Old Testament king, though, in fact, it is you, enthroned above the lords spiritual and temporal, holding a sword and a Bible, which he is handing down to three kneeling bishops. Before you met me and allowed me to influence you, it would have been an image of three bishops conferring spiritual authority on the king. It is my doing, all this, the dedication, the frontispiece, the glory, the honor, the title of supreme head, placing you above the pope and all the bishops in your own realm, and it was done by voicing what I have believed, not by being a stone or a block of wood or shutting my mouth as you so desire me to do. Go to Jane if you want silence and peace. Come to me, though, if you want a son and if you want to be reminded of your greatness and the woman who has had much to do with that greatness. He refused to face me as he advanced to the door, thrusting it open, hoping I would not hear the intermittent sounds of weeping that he tried his best to conceal.

135

Katherine

Rain falls and wind rattles the windows and floorboards and makes of the walls a shrill whistle. I fall back, whereas earlier I had sat up. I begin to fidget, loosening my long hair, and ask the time. I want badly to see the light of day but fear I shall not. Where is my Spanish bishop, my confessor, Jorge de Athequa? He must administer me communion, in case I never again see the dawn, gray though it be. I cry out to no one in particular: I wish to be buried in the chapel belonging to the Observant Friars, to have five hundred masses said for my soul, to have someone go to the Shrine of Our Lady of Walsingham on my behalf, to leave Mary the collar of gold which I brought out of Spain, to have church garments made from my gowns. Bring me paper, I say and see a familiar face come toward me, my oldest, dearest friend, who came to England with me thirty-five years ago, Maria de Salinas, before she became Lady Willoughby. She stands over me. How she came from London and was allowed to see me when her presence for years has been to me forbidden, I do not know. Speak, and I shall write for you, she says.

My most dear Lord, King, and Husband, I say, the hour of my death now approaching, I cannot choose but, out of the love I bear you, to advise you of your soul's health, which you ought to prefer before all considerations of the world or flesh whatsoever. For which yet you have cast me into many calamities, and yourself into many troubles. But I forgive you all, and pray God to do so likewise. For the rest, I commend unto you Mary, our daughter, beseeching you to be a good father to her. I must entreat you also to look after my maids, and give them in marriage, which is not much, they being but three, and to all my other servants, a year's pay besides their due, lest otherwise they should not be provided for until they find new employment. Lastly, I want only one true thing, to make this vow: that, in my life, mine eyes desire you alone. May God, protect you. Queen Katherine.

The bishop arrives. The holy sacrament, please, I say, a crucifix folded in my palm. It is not the canonical hour, he replies, though in case of urgency it may be advanced. Yes, I say, it is urgent, for my soul. You must, I beg. We must wait still, he says, till the light of day and then I can advance it, according to the saintly fathers who govern us. I cannot break law. Under any circumstance, I cannot. In the meantime, pray, he says, and make your final confession. God forgive me, if I am to blame, I say. That is all? He asks. Yes, father, that is all.

I feel the slowing of my breath and the weight of a lifetime, fifty years, leave my body. I shut my eyes and expect to die, without the partaking of the host, seeing my worst fear manifest, falling from the heights of heaven to the crowded corridors of purgatory. Haven't I already been to purgatory these past three years, God, alone, abandoned, without the touch of my husband or the smile of my daughter, just my prayers, which You exclusively have received? Must I suffer more penance among those not of my pedigree? I give myself to your mercy. Though time has tricks for me still, for next I know it is light, gray to be expected, with steady rain and wind, the frost and cold of January chilling my bones as the bishop anoints me, touching holy oil to my eyelids and lips, my hands and feet. Recite with me, he says. *Domine, in manus tuas commendo spiritum meum.* I do as he says, with great effort opening my lips to form the words.

Maria stands closer. She takes my hand. It is the hand of my mother, and her face is the face of Spain. The dusty terrain, the burnt brown soil, the mountainous shadows of the horizon, the oxen carrying stones from the shimmering surface of the sea, where the ship waits, where we leave for England, Maria and I and many others, where the bird long buried beneath the sand and waves emerges, taking flight, finally, after all this time, all these years, wherein my life has been lived and now is passing.

I follow the bird, deep into the sky, further with each remaining breath, until there is only one, which I allow to linger for a final affirmation. Am I home, mother? Yes, comes the voice. You are home, Caterina.

136

Henry

Yes, I really did wear yellow from head to foot, with the exception of a white feather in my cap. I did it for her, the Dowager Princess of Wales, Katherine, whom I had known from the age of ten, when she came to England and married my brother, for yellow is the color of mourning in Spain, and I wanted to show my respect, which will be more manifest once her state funeral is undertaken, wherein I plan to have a monument erected at Peterborough Abbey, above her tomb, where her body will be interred. She had hoped to rest in the chapel of the Observant Friars, a wish she had long made clear to me. I didn't have the heart to tell her that the chapel had been burned to the ground, after its jewels and gold had been removed, the result of its occupants believing they were above the law. Enough of their sorry history, though. Their ordeal is over and done with. This is not a time to look back on dissident behavior. It is a time to celebrate.

I will not attend the funeral, but I will make sure others, close to her, Lady Courtenay and Lady Carew and such, are there to speak on her behalf. It's the least I can do for our dearest sister, who by dying has shown me a great act of loyalty, one she could not have shown while she lived, and for that I am most appreciative. When I heard the news of her passing, Sunday past, I took little Elizabeth in my arms and ran around the court, shouting, *Praised be God who has freed us from all suspicion of war!* Cromwell said I looked like an Olympian god, dressed in yellow as I was, Apollo perhaps, the emblem of the sun. I responded that even Apollo shining bright in the sky couldn't emanate with such warmth and jubilation as I did.

Consider what this means I said to him and others of my council. I am no longer reliant on the French king's good offices.

I shall now play the emperor against him, as I am used to doing, rival against rival, and as for the German Protestant princes, they can find another suitor more in keeping with their heretical practices, for the real cause of our concern no longer exists, that what the pope has said, that I have no right to the throne, that whoever took it from me would be carrying out a papal mandate, no longer sticks to the eyes and ears of his listeners. Charles will not be sending his armies, and I can admit now, I am not ashamed, that it is a good thing for all of us, for we would have been doomed to defeat, for no one would have come to our aid, the reason being Anne. That's right, let's not fool ourselves.

All the more reason to celebrate Katherine's death, for it gives me life and hope and a chance at new opportunity in which to change my political fortunes, redeeming myself in the eyes of my subjects and all of Christendom. Who should argue against such reason? Not while much mirth lays ahead, starting with jousts and banquets, the likes of which haven't been seen in a long time. I shall, my excitement rising, dress myself in armor, like the young man I remember being and show off my horsemanship, which no man in my realm can match. I shall recall my past glories by entering the lists, jousting and winning, as it is expected I shall, for I do hate losing. Kate, may her soul rest in peace, knows that all too well.

137

Anne

I wore yellow as well, though I did not understand why I should wear the Spanish color of mourning for a woman I did not mourn. Henry did not mourn either. I had never seen him so happy. He twirled Elizabeth in his arms, dancing with her, shouting gleefully that we were free of invasion. I hoped his gesture toward her was not just a moment, but would become commonplace as she grew older, as we grew older, together, that it was a beginning, for which we had Katherine to thank, mercifully dying in order to save us, our marriage, Elizabeth's succession, Henry's standing in the world, my finally being able to say, after the long wait, I am sole Queen of England, wherein my life would become forever more secure.

It *was* a moment, though, nothing more, replaced by another moment, a realization that Katherine, while she lived, was my protector, that now that she was dead, I was more vulnerable than ever, that she had buffered me from the changing winds, which Henry at any time, on a whim, could blow at me, hurtling me into the unknown or the banished or the dead. For the truth is this, and I strive to have only truth speak as my guide: To those who have never acknowledged me as his true wife and queen, Katherine's death means he is a widower, free to marry. Why shouldn't he? Divorcing me would be easier than divorcing Katherine, for I don't have a nephew who is emperor. I have only the child in my womb, and I will have to wait until July, to see his healthy birth, to stake a claim in the foundation of Henry's heart. In the meantime, he visits Jane's apartments, formerly Cromwell's, in Greenwich, conveniently close to his own, encouraged by those who whisper in his ears—though to me they may as well be shouts—that she is a more suitable wife to give him an heir, for it would be more celebrated by the emperor and Catholic Europe and those who pray for the salvation of the realm, wherein I am excluded.

Men such as my uncle Norfolk, who enters my room and tells me Henry has had an accident, that he was unhorsed during a joust and fell heavily to the ground, his horse atop him, that he was at that moment, as he has been the previous hour, lying unconscious in a tent. Will he survive? I ask. Who knows, is all he says, in his cold, distant way, though not without motive, for my uncle does not say or do anything without motive. He is thinking of himself and what the king's accident means to him, not in the least considering what I think or feel.

He must live, I say to myself, and the baby I carry must live, and it must be a boy and healthy. All that must happen, in that order. I feel the weight under my feet leave me. I collapse on the bed, overwrought, and see with my eyes closed the alternative to his recovery: Henry's councilors, especially my uncle, fighting to the death for control, while Charles and Francis, the vultures they are, come from across the sea with armies, in alliance about one thing, seating Mary on the throne and seeing that I am dragged from my rooms and brought to the Tower, where I await my beheading. It matters not that I am with child. He will die with me, and we will fade like dust after it is kicked by those who trample on it.

I open my eyes. My uncle is gone. Perhaps it has already started.

138

Henry

The first face I saw was Norfolk's. His mouth parted, like a dumb cow's. Good morning, Thomas, I said. Good afternoon, Your Majesty, he replied. Did I win the match? I asked. One of my councilors said, excitedly, The King is alive! Yes, of course, I'm alive, I said. Why shouldn't I be? You fell from your horse, you were unconscious, your breathing had slowed, came the responses. I sat up and laughed. I have lived through a long, protracted divorce, I have survived the infectious disease of Luther's ideas, I have endured being excommunicated, and I have withstood the threat of invasion. How should falling from a horse kill me? My councilors, with bristled beards and slack jaws, gasped and sighed. I shouted, Long live the King! They repeated, Long live the King! I tried to stand, but Dr. Butts, ever cautious and annoyingly rational, stopped me. The old wound on your leg has reopened and an abscess has formed, he said. Yes, yes, I said. Dress it and bind it, as you would, but make it quick. I have business which needs my attention. Your Majesty should not ride or hunt or dance until the wound heals, he insisted. Fine, doctor, I said, but speak no more, I implore you. Bring me to my room at Greenwich, where I can have some peace and comfort, and inform Jane that I am well.

I did not walk for several days, and on the day of Katherine's funeral, I stayed home, showing my respect by wearing black and attending a solemn mass, with Jane at my side. Why is it you weep? I asked her. It is for the passing of the queen, she said. Queen Katherine, whom, as you know, treated me with love and affection, as she did to all those who served her. A more saintly woman there cannot be. I took her hand and did not bother to correct her and say, Do you mean the Dowager Princess? for fear that she might break if she frowned. She spoke with such a fair innocence that I could say nothing but, Yes, the queen was well loved.

The serenity of the day disappeared in a flash when later that afternoon Anne came unannounced into my room while Jane and I sat holding each other. Take your hands off that wench, she yelled. Jane stood up and tried to leave. Anne caught her arm, slapped her and tore the locket—a picture of me I had given her—from around her neck. Jane, her head bowed, quickly left, at which time Anne rushed at me, her eyes dark as the devil's. Peace, I said, standing. All shall go well if you calm yourself. She threw herself at me, hitting at my chest with her fists, yelling, Why do you do this to me? Why? I am your wife, and I am carrying your child.

I took her hands and threw her down. I meant not to harm her or the baby. I meant only to disengage her from me, to settle her down. She lay there on the floor, weeping, sobbing and screaming, I hate you. You are the most unkind man the world has ever known. Fine, I said, but do not come crawling to me when you need my mercy. She grabbed at my ankle. Why should I need your mercy when I am soon to be the mother of your heir? God be willing, I said, shaking my foot free of her hand, leaving the room and escaping her hysterics.

139

Anne

I have miscarried my savior, and I am not to blame, yet no one shall believe me or exonerate me from responsibility. How far from God this world is, where to be a woman means living in the skin of Eve, condemned, bearing dead babies and the hatred of men. If there is a reason why I should continue to live, I do not, at this moment, know what it is, for I am loathed and shall be loathed more, my womb defective and empty, wherein I am nothing, not a woman, not a wife, not a queen. Who then, or what, am I? Lost and desperate, wondering whether my struggle to rise and stay risen, to be revered and honored, to live in harmony with myself and the world, is worth the price I have paid.

Still, in my sorrow, through my tears, I am angry and wish to lay the blame of my fate on others. Henry for being unkind to me, loving others in full view of my eyes, Jane for being a wench, taking Henry's affection and attention from me, making me fear he wishes to leave me, my uncle for giving me fright the day of Henry's accident, doing it purposely to upset the baby in my womb, Katherine for being alive when I conceived when it was told I shall not conceive while she lived, Mary for existing, calling herself princess and challenging my daughter's legitimacy to the succession, Francis for invalidating Elizabeth, withdrawing his son from a potential union, Cromwell for turning his back on me when I have done so much to make him rise, my father for having educated me in France, only to learn afterwards that I was not French enough for the French and too French for the English, and especially Wolsey for having broken my engagement with Henry Percy, whom I loved, knowing that if I had married him instead of the king I would not be lying in bed, weeping for the loss of yet another potential heir. I would be living far from court, up north, in comfort, surrounded by children, both boys and girls, born in peace, in love, free of desperation and fear of failure.

I know now the day Henry snared me in his net, like an unsuspecting bird, I was cursed, for though I have lived with all the wealth and trappings of a queen, I am miserable, and can now understand, finally, the misery of my predecessor, mistreated as she was for failing as I have failed to give the king an heir. I do not want him to come to my room, to see the disappointment on his face, to hear his harsh words. I shall cry further, and he will not care. He will walk out, and this time he may not return.

140

Henry

I hear the news and soon after God's voice. He will not give me male children, and it can mean only one thing. My marriage to Anne is not legal. I tell this to Cromwell. He asks, How so? I believe she seduced me by sorcery. Is that not a proper ground to make the marriage null and void? He curls his brows. It is a proper ground to do much more than that. I lean toward him. Such as? Witchcraft is a capital crime, Your Majesty, punishable by death. The proof must be clear and evident, though, not based primarily on supposition. Though his face is hard to read and his tone never varies, I sense his unease with what I propose. I modify accordingly. Perhaps it is not that, then, after all, though I remember the feelings, uncontrollable and unmanageable, that possessed me when I courted her, quite alien to human experience I would call them, when the passion I felt consumed me the way a fire consumes a stick of wood. Does that sound normal to you, Cromwell?

He clasped his hands together as a chaplain would. I possess insufficient knowledge to speak about the emotions associated with love, Your Majesty. Well, I am very knowledgeable, I said, for I have had much schooling, and the feelings I had for her were hardly normal. I must have been bewitched. I know of no other way to explain it. In comparison, the feelings I have for Jane have none of the fire and intoxication that took hold of me ten years ago. I should like to call it fondness rather than passion, more pragmatic and sensible for a man of my position and age. Would you agree, Cromwell? What you describe is reasonable, he answers. Yes, of course it is reasonable, though what I have to do now is hardly reasonable. But you must, Your Majesty. Yes, yes, I know, though I cannot bear it, Cromwell, to go to her room and in doing so face much sorrow and disappointment. You have my sympathy, he says. I don't need your sympathy, I say, but I suspect sometime soon I will need your judicious mind to help me with the matter I have presented to you. He nods and bows.

When I enter, she sits up and sobs. It was a boy, I say. It is not my fault, she responds through her tears. I look past her. I have lost yet another son. Do not be angry with me, she cries. If this has happened, it is only because of the love I bear you. I turn to face her. Only her sobs prevent me from yelling. Do not speak such nonsense. If it were love, you would bear me a healthy boy. I stop myself from saying that Jane's mother has borne nine living children, many of whom are sons. She sobs louder. My love for you is so great that I cannot bear to see you loving another woman. It broke my heart to see you with Jane yesterday, and a woman with a broken heart cannot conceive a normal, healthy child. If anyone is to blame, it is you for your unkindness toward me. Do not speak thus, I say, sensing the rise of my voice and the blood in my body boil. I have been nothing but kind and patient with you. I have not come here to hear your excuses and have you explain your feelings to me. It should be me who deserves consideration, for I am the one who has suffered most, having lived through ten conceptions with two women, and for what? I have just two daughters and no sons. Therefore, do not accuse me of unkindness. It is you who has been unkind to me. She thrusts her head from side to side, sobbing, hitting her fists on the bed, saying she wishes for nothing in the world except to deliver me a son, to make me love her as she loves me. She promises to recover soon, to conceive again, to deliver me an heir. I say nothing, think only to myself: I will have no more boys with her.

I look at her one last time and see her as she is, a thin, old woman, barren, expendable. I walk out swiftly, boldly, into the future, hearing only the voice of God. Or is it my own? Do what you must and what you can, for no one but yourself can stop you.

141

Anne

I summoned my chaplain, Matthew Parker. He, like Archbishop Cranmer, a Cambridge reformist, more Lutheran than Luther himself, if his critics, the serpent Catholic alliance, are to be believed. I implore you, good reverend, to be Elizabeth's caretaker if anything should happen to me. What should happen to you? He asked, wishing to be evasive to the truth, aware, as my confidant, that Henry hadn't visited me since my miscarriage and my having been churched, wherein I am again ready to conceive. It shall not happen, though. I know that. He does as well, having heard the same whispers I have, though he does his best to pretend his innocence, evident in what he said next. You are Queen of England. Yes, I responded. Today, I am, yet who knows of tomorrow. What if my marriage is annulled and I am sent, following Katherine's precedent, to a remote, country house, forbidden to see my daughter? I wish to be prepared as a woman, and more so as a mother to one who is still the legal heir to the throne. Oversee her education, as one befitting a princess, ensuring she receives the best scholars and becomes a defender of the reformist cause, despising as we do religious intolerance. He assured me he would remain devoted to her for as long as he lived, as he would for me.

Now, at Greenwich, I walk with Elizabeth in the garden, holding her hand, seeing the first growth of flowers after the long winter. She has her father's color and—if one holds valid the views of the court—nearly every feature of his as well. That is false, though, for her eyes are mine, and it is into those eyes where I look, for in them I can see what she, at two years of age, cannot, her life to come, which I lay out for her rapidly developing mind. My dear, Elizabeth, I say, an age of reform is sweeping through Europe. It will not stop anytime soon, and England will soon be swept up in it, completely. It is only a matter of time. The educated men and women—and there are more each day, both here and abroad, even of our sex—will move forward the world, wherein you, much more so than me, will be respected for your intelligence and voice and live to fulfill your destiny. I know not how or under what condition you will advance yourself, but I am certain that someday you shall rule and witness all the people of your realm, from the most common to the exalted, reading the gospel in English, saying in unison the words my chaplain has spoken with eloquence. Christ's sheep hear no man's voice but Christ's.

So, live well, Elizabeth, in steadfast resolve, and forget not from whose womb you came, she who desired to be Queen Esther to her people, she who, due to the dissembling of men who crave power more than God and hate more than love, find myself as if on a ship at sea, the wind and waves rocking the hull, the rain pelting the stern, upon which I stand unsteady, watching the downward trajectory of the bow, bracing myself for the inevitable sinking to the bottom of an eternal water, where, after much initial suffering, I shall rest forever in peace.

Acknowledgements

I have read and studied Henry VIII's reign for many years, going back to my college days and throughout my long teaching career. It is a subject that has been inexhaustibly of interest to me. I would have never discovered that interest if it weren't for the many writers and historians whose biographies and histories engaged my mind and stimulated my imagination, making me want to recreate for myself what historical people thought and felt beyond what they did. I am indebted to these writers, who spent years researching comprehensively, allowing me to drink liberally from the fountain of their knowledge. Any misrepresentation of historical detail is due to my negligence, not theirs. With that said, I, of course, do not pretend to be a historian. My work belongs in the realm of fiction, not fact.

Among the writers (and their books) who influenced my book many stand out. Giles Tremlett's *Catherine of Aragon*; Linda Porter's *Katherine the Queen: The Remarkable Life of Katherine Parr* and *The Myth of Bloody Mary: A Biography of Queen Mary I of England*; Diarmaid MacCulloch's definitive, scholarly work, *Thomas Cranmer: A Life*; Carolly Erickson's *Mistress Anne* and *Great Harry*; Derek Wilson's psychoanalytical book, *A Brief History of Henry VIII: Reformer and Tyrant*; Allison Weir many books: *The Six Wives of Henry VIII, The Children of Henry VIII, The Lady in the Tower, Henry VIII: The King and His Court*; Jasper Ridley's *Henry VIII: The Politics of Tyranny*; Joanna Denny's *Anne Boleyn*, and Eric Ives's *The Life and Death of Anne Boleyn*.

These writers have allowed me to travel back, to open doors, to listen to the dead, who have much to tell the living. Thus, I listen. I would, in fact, not be a writer if I didn't invite the visitation of ghosts, for their stories give birth to life.

About the Author

A native of New York City, Thomas Crockett worked as a writing teacher and theater director for 30 years. His current passion is researching sixteenth-century English history, evident in this book and in his prior one, *Thorns in a Realm of Roses*. His other books include *The Florentine Trinity*, *The Hitchhiking Journals*, *Hope Beyond All Hope: New York Stories*, and *Teaching Drama: Fundamentals and Beyond*. In addition to his books, he has written numerous short and long plays, including the *Burrow People* and *A Tyrant for all Seasons*.

Author's Note

Thank you for purchasing *The Great Matter Monologues*. I hope you enjoyed reading about this compelling episode in English history as much as I enjoyed researching it and re-imagining it in the words of the characters. If you have a few moments to add a short review on Amazon, GoodReads or another online site, I would be grateful. Reviews are important feedback for authors, and I appreciate every one. If you would like to connect with other books I have written or learn about my next work, coming out in the near future, follow me on my Facebook page or at my website, www.thomascrockett. Thank you.

**TOP HAT
BOOKS**

Historical fiction that lives

We publish fiction that captures the contrasts, the achievements, the optimism and the radicalism of ordinary and extraordinary times across the world.

We're open to all time periods and we strive to go beyond the narrow, foggy slums of Victorian London. Where are the tales of the people of fifteenth century Australasia? The stories of eighth century India? The voices from Africa, Arabia, cities and forests, deserts and towns? Our books thrill, excite, delight and inspire.

The genres will be broad but clear. Whether we're publishing romance, thrillers, crime, or something else entirely, the unifying themes are timescale and enthusiasm. These books will be a celebration of the chaotic power of the human spirit in difficult times. The reader, when they finish, will snap the book closed with a satisfied smile.
If you have enjoyed this book, why not tell other readers by posting a review on your preferred book site.

Recent bestsellers from Tops Hat Books are:

Grendel's Mother
The Saga of the Wyrd-Wife
Susan Signe Morrison
Grendel's mother, a queen from Beowulf, threatens the fragile
political stability on this windswept land.
Paperback: 978-1-78535-009-2 ebook: 978-1-78535-010-8

Queen of Sparta
A Novel of Ancient Greece
T.S. Chaudhry
History has relegated her to the role of bystander, what if Gorgo,
Queen of Sparta, had played a central role in the Greek resistance
to the Persian invasion?
Paperback: 978-1-78279-750-0 ebook: 978-1-78279-749-4

Mercenary
R.J. Connor
Richard Longsword is a mercenary, but this time it's not for
money, this time it's for revenge…
Paperback: 978-1-78279-236-9 ebook: 978-1-78279-198-0

Black Tom
Terror on the Hudson
Ron Semple
A tale of sabotage, subterfuge and political shenanigans
in Jersey City in 1916; America is on the cusp of war and the fate of
the nation hinges on the decision of one young policeman.
Paperback: 978-1-78535-110-5 ebook: 978-1-78535-111-2

Destiny Between Two Worlds

A Novel about Okinawa

Jacques L. Fuqua, Jr.

A fateful October 1944 morning offered no inkling that the lives of thousands of Okinawans would be profoundly changed—forever.

Paperback: 978-1-78279-892-7 ebook: 978-1-78279-893-4

Cowards

Trent Portigal

A family's life falls into turmoil when the parents' timid political dissidence is discovered by their far more enterprising children.

Paperback: 978-1-78535-070-2 ebook: 978-1-78535-071-9

Godwine Kingmaker

Part One of The Last Great Saxon Earls

Mercedes Rochelle

The life of Earl Godwine is one of the enduring enigmas of English history. Who was this Godwine, first Earl of Wessex; unscrupulous schemer or protector of the English? The answer depends on whom you ask…

Paperback: 978-1-78279-801-9 ebook: 978-1-78279-800-2

The Last Stork Summer

Mary Brigid Surber

Eva, a young Polish child, battles to survive the designation of "racially worthless" under Hitler's Germanization Program.

Paperback: 978-1-78279-934-4 ebook: 978-1-78279-935-1 $4.99 £2.99

Messiah Love

Music and Malice at a Time of Handel

Sheena Vernon

The tale of Harry Walsh's faltering steps on his journey to success and happiness, performing in the playhouses of Georgian London.

Paperback: 978-1-78279-768-5 ebook: 978-1-78279-761-6

A Terrible Unrest

Philip Duke

A young immigrant family must confront the horrors of the Colorado Coalfield War to live the American Dream.

Paperback: 978-1-78279-437-0 ebook: 978-1-78279-436-3